# LIKE A
# MOTH
## TO A
# FLAME

# LIKE A MOTH TO A FLAME

### CARMEN ROSALES

Carmen Rosales

Copyright © 2023 by Carmen Rosales

Cover Design © 2023 by Jay Aheer

All rights reserved. No part of this book may be reproduced in any form or by any electronic or mechanical means, including information storage and retrieval systems, without written permission from the author, except for the use of brief quotations in a book review.

This book is a work of fiction. All character are fictional. Names, characters, places, and indigents are of the authors imagination. Any resemblance to any of the elements of events, locales, persons, living or dead, is coincidental.

Erotic Quill Publishing, LLC
3020 NE 41st Terrace STE 9 #243
Homestead, Fl. 33033
www.carmenrosales.com


Manufactured in the United States of America
First Edition November 2023

If I am the phantom, it is because man's hatred has
made me so. If I am to be saved it is because your love
redeems me.

— GASTON LEROUX

*To my daughters,*
*A queen has no need for a mask.*

# ACKNOWLEDGEMENT

Like a Moth To A Flame is the first novel I have written that blends Dystopian, Romance, and Gothic genres. I wanted to write something different. It is different because it is a world created in the future. Something I have never done. I hope you enjoy it.

I want to thank my editors, Jenny and Cate. Thank you for your time and patience. To my readers, thank you for supporting me and loving my books.

# PREFACE

*She set my darkness on fire—unleashing the beast within.*

**Killian Cross**

My wife will serve a single purpose — to bear me a child. After
that, she is nothing to me. *But even I am a fool for beauty.*
As soon as I see her, I know nothing could have prepared me
for the powerful attraction that overwhelms me. Like a flame
in the darkness, a spark of light in a city consumed by evil, I
can not resist the pull of her beauty and grace. Choosing her is
a risk, but it can't stop me from being engulfed by the unholy
fire she's lit within me.

**Lillith Sinclair**

My fate was sealed the day my father sold me to a man I'd
never met. My beauty is a bargaining chip, an ornamental toy
for the wealthy.
The man who owns me is feared and reviled — some say he's
disfigured, a beast beneath a mask that hides his ruined face.
All I know as I step into the depths of his dark estate, is that a
burning desire draws me closer to his dangerous allure.

But with each passing moment, the shadows of his enemies loom, threatening to consume us both in a fiery cataclysm of lust and destruction.

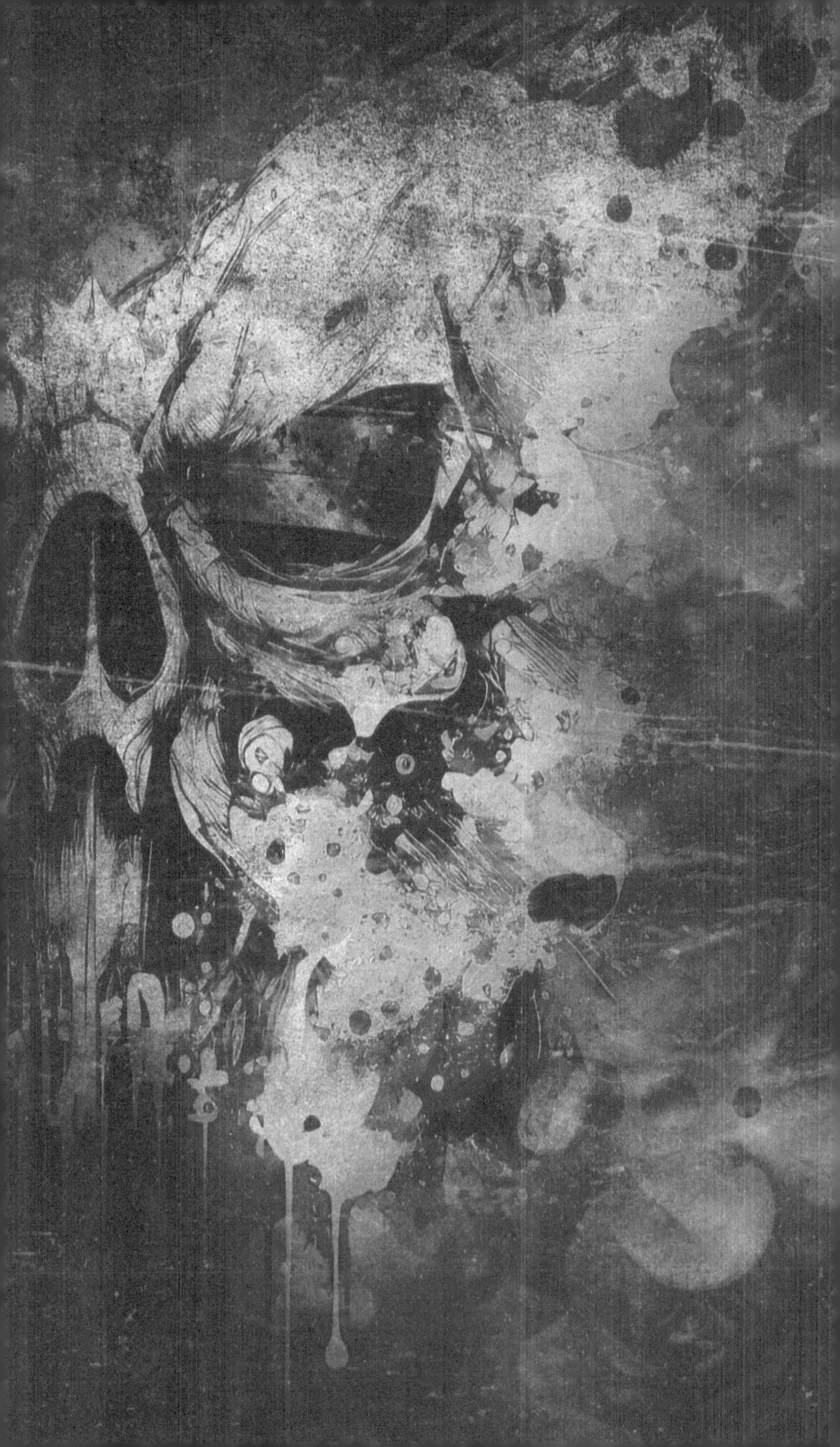

# PART ONE

## The Moth

# I

## LILLITH

I angle my head, admiring a painting of a woman with her hands out looking down below. It looks like she's asking for help, but what is crazy about the painting is that there is nothing else. She's completely naked with a look of anguish. It kind of reminds me of myself at this very moment in a room full of people wearing modern designer outfits. Women wearing futuristic designs made of fabric that could feed the poor for a month. The scent of different perfumes suffocates me for every second I'm standing here among the cold and unfeeling. I want nothing more than to not end up being one of them. Since I walked in with my father, I can feel their eyes burning my skin, trying to undress me with their eyes. My father introduces me to high society like a prized horse, hoping to pass me around like a fine cigar.

Like the man currently watching me across the room, his gaze never once leaving the tops of my breast as he raises his glass in a mock toast. My chest begins to tighten, and suddenly, I need air. I tear my eyes away from the man relieved that I'm near an exit.

The French door clicks softly as I lean against it and close my eyes. Exhausted. I felt like I was hyperventilating, and I was only inside for about twenty minutes at most.

A normal father would be offended or maybe outraged by a man looking at his only daughter suggestively. A normal father would expect other men around him to respect his sixteen-year-old daughter, but those were different times, and now, that sort of thing was expected when you're unmarried. Because your father knows it's customary for you to marry and produce an heir for another member of high society when you turn eighteen.

I push off the door and walk toward the immaculate garden of topiary shrubs. The oversized animals loom above me, glaring down in disapproval. I'm not meant to be out here, in the dark, unchaperoned. I'd be safer inside, surrounded by black suits and lingering touches. But I might scream if I have to spend another second in that room.

"Do you always sneak away?"

Pausing, I turn around and must look like an idiot walking in a circle to find the source of the voice. I turn to the left, noticing a screen with faux plants meant to offer privacy from the other side of the makeshift garden.

I didn't notice another exit when I was inside. I step to the side to get a better look at the man standing behind the screen, but all I can make out is that he is tall, and based on the timbre of his voice, he isn't old.

"Do you always follow people you don't know?" I ask sarcastically, annoyed I can't see the man's face.

I can hear the smile in his voice when he says, "No. I'm not a follower, but I like to take a good look at things that interest me."

My heart pounds inside my chest, but if he came from the room I just escaped from, he's one of them. Part of the 1 percent of the assholes in this world who help build this place. Faux plants not needing sun; water too precious in a world trying to rebuild from a war caused by man because they valued technology instead of humanity.

"I'm sure you took a good look when I was inside, just like everyone else."

Other beautiful women are inside the room. All you had to do was ask another rich asshole willing to share his wife or available whore. What makes me so special?

I've seen some of those women leave my father's side of the house. It's all the same if you're a woman on this island; you are young, beautiful, and passed between men like fine wine.

"I'm not sure what you mean. I only heard about one good thing inside that room, and it was you. I also noticed you like fine art. It's rare to see a beautiful woman in a room full of powerful people only be interested in an evocative painting."

I snort. "Is that what you tell all the women you're interested in screwing when you go to these things? Business first, and then you try to find the first willing woman by following a young woman alone in the garden."

"You are quick to assume, Miss Sinclair. I thought maybe you were different."

He knows my last name, but I'm not surprised. Everyone in that room knows who I am and that my father brought me here to show me off. I know I'm being a bitch, but it's hard to trust anyone.

I can hear him walk on the stone steps behind the screen, and I wait in anticipation to see what his face looks like when he comes around, but he pauses and turns to head back inside.

Wanting to have the last word since I'm pissed off that he didn't let me see what he looked like and was quick to dismiss me, I blurt, "Judgment is for the blind. Are you going to tell me your name or properly introduce yourself?"

"There's no need, Miss Sinclair. Like you said, there is nothing out here that I can't find inside."

I hastened my stride in my pointed sock-styled boots, attempting to reach him before he disappeared with a retort on the tip of my tongue, but I was too late. He was quick, and all that stared back at me was a dark wood French door with a tinted window.

When I went back inside, I spent the next two hours trying to find the voice that belonged to the infuriating man outside, but all I heard were different voices and eyes giving me suggestive looks. It was like he didn't exist, and I imagined the whole conversation.

# 2



Three Years Later

Year 2035

"**Y**our father is in his study, Miss Sinclair. He would like to speak to you. He says it's urgent."

I glance up at Gretel, my father's assistant, standing at the threshold to my yoga room from my pose, noticing that she looks like a freak upside down with her upturned nose and raised eyebrows. From this angle, she looks like she's smiling.

"What does he want?" I ask, raising my voice over Nostalgia's "Plastic Heart" playing from the speakers.

"I don't know. He wouldn't say." She's annoyed, probably because I don't lower the music. "It's obvious...it's important, or he wouldn't need you otherwise."

I straighten, watching her face change to the pathetic one she always sports as I right myself. Gretel doesn't like me very much, but the feeling is mutual.

I pin her with a stare, letting her know the message was received and that she could fuck off somewhere doing the next thing my father instructed her to do besides belittling me and pointing out my father couldn't care less about me.

I wait a few seconds until she leaves to bend down to retrieve my phone and cut off the music, wondering what my father wants.

As the only daughter of John Sinclair, I have one job: take care of my looks and body, and all is well. I have done what he wants. Until I marry. Then I have to do what my husband wants— which is whatever the hell that is because there is no room for divorce.

Before heading out, I turn on the air purifier by pressing the button on the screen to the appropriate setting. According to scientists, germs are spread by sweating, and it can alter the atmosphere by airborne pathogens. Another thing that has changed since the pandemic. The need to purify every room after exercise. Even sex.

With a towel draped around my neck, I walk into my father's study without bothering to knock. "You wanted to see me?"

He looks up, scrolling through the trackpad connected to the holographic screen. He's probably looking at his financials like he usually does on Sunday afternoons.

"Have a seat," he says curtly.

My father still looks handsome in his forties. He hardly has a wrinkle on his face. Probably from all the rich food he consumes and lack of sun. The food is organically grown, of course, and free of preservatives. Heaven forbid he eats the occasional piece of cake loaded with carbs.

I look at the modern transparent chair made from resin before his desk and meet his gaze. "I think I'll stand. I wouldn't want to contaminate the chair with my sweat."

"Very well, Lillith. I don't have time for your theatrics, so I'll get to the point." I swallow audibly because even though my father and I don't get along very well due to our disagreements about how he raised me, the look in his eyes is different. Unfeeling. "I've been having problems."

Problems? What kind of problems? You have an assistant you fuck whenever you want and choose to bring other women into our home when you're bored. You never asked how I felt about it. You have more money than most people I know, except a handful who live on this island.

I want to tell him that, but I ask instead, "What kind of problems?"

He sighs, rubbing his eyes with his thumb and index finger, and leans back in his office chair. "The money kind."

That has my attention. The money kind means you lose things, then you have to move off the island. If you don't have enough digital currency, you're fucked. It's how you are allowed here in the first place. *But how? What did he do?*

"What happened?"

"I made a mistake, but I corrected it," he rushes out. I sigh in relief, holding the ends of the white towel around my neck for dear life.

I'd like to know what mistake he could have made and what he needed to do to correct it. But what does this have to do with me? Why is he telling me this now? He never tells me anything he does. He does whatever he wants and only includes me when it has something to do with me. *Wait?*

I see him tap his finger on the transparent desk, his face stoic. "I made a deal to clear the debt. The deal is that you have to marry the man who got me out of that debt and give him an heir."

My chest tightens, and my vision blurs. *He's marrying me off?* He used me as payment for his fuckups. Why?

"Why?" I ask, my voice vibrating with anger.

"Because that's what needed to be done, and... it's about time you do something with your life. Every time I have taken you to one of my business gatherings or a fundraiser, you look down that pretty nose at everyone. You won't go out with any man who so much as looks your way. You refuse to partake in any fundraiser. You just fuck that kid who comes here on the island to work in our house!" He yells the last part, his face flushed red and the veins on his neck bulging like he struggles for air.

Bastard.

I don't think I'm better. He had nannies raise me until I was old enough to take a bath without assistance. But he still has them pick my clothes, tell me what products are safe, what to eat, and what I can and can't do.

I look up, fighting back the tears. I can't believe he could be that cruel.

"Oh, you didn't think I knew about your little sexcapades with the hired help? He looks at you like you're his next meal ticket while he sneaks into your room to fuck you when I look the other way. Well, guess what, Lillith? I know all about it. I know you lost your virginity to him and all the bullshit love notes he likes to write because he is so pathetic and can't afford to call you. You have such a blatant disregard for yourself that you don't know if he's fucking someone else behind your back. He can give you a disease. Did you know that?"

*That is why he had the doctor visit me every month.* I thought it was because he cared if I got sick like my mother had when she was pregnant with me.

Then, a thought crosses my mind. It's not the best one to hide the fact that Ethan does sneak in my room behind his back. The hired help allowed on the island is screened for health purposes.

My gaze meets his, and I fold my arms over my chest. "But the hired help allowed on the island is screened, so that isn't possible."

"They don't check his cock every day, Lillith," he says harshly, his face changing colors like a mood ring.

It feels like I'm breathing fire with how angry I am with him. He sold me. He fucking sold me as payment for whatever mess he got himself into, and now he wants to throw Ethan in my face. What about him?

"So I can't grow up my way, but you can screw your assistant and whoever you bring here? It's okay for you, but I have to marry some dirty man who sees me like a piece of meat?" I shake my head. "Some asshole deemed acceptable by society's standards because his pockets are thick, and I'm pretty enough to be here."

"I'm sorry I don't agree with your romantic ideals, Lillith, but this is the real world. The crap you read in those pathetic excuses you call books is nothing more than an illusion, and it doesn't exist."

"It's all about how you look, your health, and money, right?" I retort. Tears are now falling down my cheeks, and I lean over the desk, placing my hands on the edge, hoping I smear it with my sweaty hands. "How much am I worth, Father? I know what my mother was worth. How. Much. Am. I. Worth?" I seethe.

His eyes harden. "Six hundred and sixty-six million. And for the record, it's health and money for the men and health and looks for the women. Be grateful you have both."

I push off the desk, and a sick chill runs up my spine when I hear those three numbers followed by zeros. Evil.

My father's face twists in anger, and he continues to lay down the details of the arrangement I have no choice but to accept. "It was his number. It's what he wanted to pay me to settle my debts as long as I gave him... you. He requested I provide him with your last medical records to ensure you can provide him with an heir. One heir. That's all he wants from you."

I blink, trying to clear my eyes from the tears that don't want to stop falling and sniff. "Why me?"

He shakes his head in disbelief. "Lillith, do you know how many men ask me if I can convince you to go out with them? Colleagues, business associates, and sons of my closest friends all want a chance. But I've had to turn them all down and tell them I can't convince my only daughter to go out with her own social class."

He means the super-rich. If he only knew their cocks are the contaminated ones.

"Who did you sell me to?"

He dodges the question, trying to convince me he did it because he cares. "You just have to give him what you would've eventually given any other man on this island. I made a choice for you, and given the type of life I have provided for you, based on your lineage and birth, it was in your best interest."

"No, you mean in the best interest of you and that bitch Gretel," I shot back.

The little muscle in his jaw clenches because I hit the truth square on the head. "Look here, you ungrateful little bitch! I did what was necessary!" I rear back at his loud tone. My father has never called me a little bitch before, but he does prefer Gretel over me. That much is clear, and it has always been that way since I was old enough to understand how important her role with my father was. "Go pack your personal shit and leave your clothes. He said those won't be necessary. Everything else will be provided for you." I turn to leave. "Oh"—I pause with bated breath—"and for the record, his name is Killian Cross." My stomach drops, forming a knot, and

I suck in a breath when I hear that name. I've heard about the masked man who lives near the coast. It is hard not to when he's the richest man on the island. The recluse. Some say he was involved in a bad accident and lives like a moth in a dark mansion. He doesn't venture out, and no one has seen him in years. There are no photos of him anywhere. They said his parents died in a horrific accident, and he was the only survivor. The few who have seen him said his face is badly scarred, and that's why he wears a mask.

I walk out of my father's office, hating him more than anyone right now. I now have two choices—run away without a dime until they find and kill me, making it look like an accident, or marry the man my father sold me to. *"It's the way things are, Lillith. What did you think would happen?"*

Closing my eyes, I hear his words playing in my head. I knew I had to marry someone eventually, but I hoped my father had an ounce of respect for his only daughter to at least let me choose when I was ready. When I open my eyes, I wipe my tears, knowing this is the last time I will be in this house and probably one of the last times I'll talk to my father privately.

"I hope you and Gretel are happy now. You have me out of the way. My mother would be proud of you," I say, looking at the ceiling when I plop down on my bed. I hope the next chapter of mine isn't worse, but I know deep down it will be. How could it not? I was bought like a piece of furniture because of how I look. There is no other reason.

# 3

LILLITH

"What do you mean you have to leave and get married? To whom, Lillith?"

I zip up my carry-on. The only thing I'm taking with me along with my favorite books.

I glance at Ethan, hating myself for lying to him, but I have no choice. If I don't evade his questions, he'll track me down, and I can't let anything happen to him. What if he gets hurt?

"The son of one of my father's business associates," I reply, watching his face fall. "I'm sorry, Ethan, but I don't have a choice. You know that is the way things are, and I don't have a say."

He looks up with a frown. "But... I love you."

My stomach drops because as much as I like Ethan, I don't love him. I loved our time together when my father was too busy to pay attention to me. I loved his company and the fact that I could explore my sexuality and experience the touch of a man without any obligation or commitment. But I knew it would all end one day.

There is no love story. I was raised in a world where none of that exists. Carnal desires exist. Greed exists. But love? The love of money is what matters most. My father is proof of that.

"The car is waiting, Miss Sinclair."

I turn to look at Mrs. Whitt, the housekeeper my father hired three years ago. The one before Mrs. Whitt smiled and spent time with me, but then she was fired because that wasn't allowed.

"I'll be right there."

I wait until she walks away to approach Ethan. He's looking at me solemnly while I hold his face in my hands. The look of anguish that crosses his features makes my insides cave.

"I have to go, Ethan. I've loved the time we spent together. The nights and the days. I'll never forget them, but you know this had to end."

"It doesn't have to, Lillith. You can talk to your father. Reason with him."

I shake my head. "You don't understand, Ethan. It was never a forever between us." My hands slide down his face, feeling the loss but knowing I don't have a choice.

I turn, hearing his last words as I exit my bedroom. "It was forever for me, Lillith."

*I'm sorry. He doesn't understand. If I don't, I'm as good as dead.*

I don't respond as I leave him standing in my bedroom alone because the truth is, I knew deep down what my forever is, and it has nothing to do with love. Even if I want it to be.

I'm practically running to get outside the house's front door to the awaiting vehicle. The trunk pops open, and I place my carry-on inside. The door opens automatically, and I realize the electric car is a Rolls-Royce Spectre.

When I slide inside, I notice the automation. The luxury of the vehicle tells me what I already know. The man who owns it is beyond wealthy. He's also an asshole for having me picked up like something to be delivered to his doorstep.

The vehicle glides forward quietly through the dark streets. Looking out the window at the shining lights and tall skyscrapers, one may think it's a city of opulence and glamour. Clean and functional. Pure. All I see is the filth it hides and the evil it masks.

The City of God. That is what they call it—what everyone calls it—but I know the truth. It's the city of fallen angels.

"Fifteen minutes until you have reached your destination," the female voice from the navigation system says. The glow of the screen highlights the points on the map.

Fear and anticipation claw my insides as I wonder what I'll walk into when I arrive to meet the mystery man who bought me.

When I pull the visor down, the light flicks on, and I stare at my light eyes in the mirror's reflection like a curse. Some people wish for beauty. To me, it's a death sentence. A curse bestowed upon me, born to be used and looked upon like a prized possession.

*What if he hides from me, and I can't see his face?* I open the long lace shawl where there is a hidden pocket and pull out the soft mask I kept if there was ever an outbreak.

If I can't see his appearance, neither can he. Once he marries me, I don't have a choice, but for now, when in Rome and all that.

# 4

LILLITH

The car circles the massive entrance of the property. Once you passed the electric gate, a sense of wonder and eeriness gripped me. The structure stood proudly, like a relic from a forgotten era, yet it bore subtle signs of adaptation to the present surrounded by the echoes of history and the shadows of decay.

The imposing exterior of the house had walls constructed of ancient, weathered stone that had witnessed centuries of changing seasons and passing generations. Moss and ivy clung to its surface, weaving intricate patterns as if nature herself sought to reclaim the edifice. The windows were tall and narrow, adorned with wrought-iron bars that evoked a sense of imprisonment, a reminder of bygone days when security was paramount.

The roof, a labyrinth of turrets and spires, reached for the sky, the once-bright pennants that may have fluttered in the wind now mere tatters, a contrast to the somber gray backdrop. Chimneys spiraled upward like sentinels, symbols of the life that had once thrived within these walls. Yet amid the antiquity, hints of modernity emerged. Solar panels were discreetly integrated into the roof, their gleaming surfaces juxtaposed against the medieval architecture, a testament to survival in an altered world. It looks ancient, but I know it isn't. It wouldn't be here if it was.

Under the moon's light behind gray clouds like a backdrop, birds fly across the sky as soon as I step out of the car. It looks like no one is home. There are no cars and only two white LED lights illuminate the entrance, but I know better. The man who owns this home loves technology because it allows him to remain hidden. Everything is automated. When I step closer, the pathway lights up, sensing every step I take.

I adjust the mask to ensure it covers my entire face. I hold my carry-on in front of me like it's my lifeline. I grip the straps, causing it to squeeze my skin and burn my palm. I'm glad I chose to wear a long shawl that looks like a dress wrapped around my pantsuit with my pointed knife boots. My power outfit gives me confidence.

I take a deep breath and walk the last steps toward the door. I notice the square screen mounted to the wall to the left. I'm about to press the button on the blue-lit screen, but the door makes a whirring noise as it unlocks. A voice like the one inside the automated vehicle greets me. "Welcome."

Walking into the foyer, I step on the large black tile. Lights line the floors against the wall, reminding me of the movie *Tron*.

Looking up, I notice a shiny black chandelier. *Odd.* No one uses chandeliers in their homes anymore. It didn't take away the thickness of the air when I walked farther inside. The entrance was an awe-inspiring portal, a shimmering archway that seemed to materialize from thin air. Its surface rippled with a liquid sheen, casting iridescent reflections that played across the walls in a mesmerizing dance. As I moved deeper into the house, the walls themselves transformed, displaying ever-shifting holographic artworks that told stories of distant galaxies, celestial phenomena, and the mysteries of the cosmos.

The main chamber sprawled out before me, a symphony of light and form. Furniture seemed to emerge from the very floor, curvaceous and ergonomic, inviting me to experience a comfort beyond imagination. Luminescent panels lined the walls, their colors shifting in response to my presence, creating an ambiance that adapted to my emotions, from tranquil blues to vibrant purples.

The ceiling was a virtual reality masterpiece, a dynamic canopy that projected scenes of lush landscapes, starlit skies, or even breathtaking views of alien worlds. It was as though I could reach out and touch the stars, their brilliance intensified by the juxtaposition with sleek, metallic accents that adorned the architectural features.

I take two steps forward but pause when I notice an older woman with a serious demeanor approaching me from the left. She stops in front of me, wearing a white pantsuit with a black stripe down the middle with black boots.

"You must be Miss Sinclair. Right this way."

I smile to introduce myself, but she turns around, dismissing me without a smile, an introduction, or a soft welcome. I guess *the house did that already.* I'm not surprised. Normal human interaction is lost these days.

I follow her since I'm already used to the cold treatment from back home. I've been treated this way all my life by my father and his staff, but I was hoping that would all change.

She turns the corner down a hallway leading up to a set of stairs lit up the same way as the entrance. When we reach the landing, I notice a hallway on each side. The place must be enormous with a left and right wing.

From the landing, you can see the living room down below. There is a digital screen displaying a faux fireplace casting a glow reflecting from the chrome legs of the furniture with white leather seats.

Not giving me much time to study my surroundings, she takes the left hallway and stops in front of two doors leading to what must be my room, then stands impatiently as she waits for me to catch up. I could tell she isn't too thrilled about me being here. But if I want any information from her, I read somewhere that it's best to get what you want with a dose of honey.

"My name is Lillith, by the way. I don't expect you to call me Miss Sinclair. It seems—"

"That doesn't matter, does it, Miss Sinclair? I will soon have to address you by another surname. What I call you is what Mr. Cross would like for me to address you as. It is what he wants. So you see, there is no point in your request. However, I do not think Mr. Cross would appreciate the way you are mocking him right now."

She means the black mask covering my face. In her eyes, it might look disrespectful, but how he treats me isn't fair. She hasn't so much as greeted me warmly, considering the circumstances, but then again, I guess I could understand why. She is loyal to him.

Even if she isn't privy to the details and doesn't know me, I stand to my full five-foot-two-inch height and angle my head. "So he can wear one, and I can't?" I scoff. "That's right... I'm here because of how I look, what I can give him, and nothing else. I have no feelings or say as to what I can be called or wear. For the record, I'm not here because I want to be here. I was forced to be here..." I shake my head, knowing this is pointless. "You know what, never mind. Call me whatever you want, and if you don't want to tell me your name, that is fine too. Now show me to my prison cell. It won't be the first."

I glance at the door, my jaw set tight, wondering why I bother to be civil. I hope it will lead to some semblance of respect between two people living in the same world who don't have control. I've always respected the working class. I believe it is an art to serve others day in and day out.

She opens the door, and I walk inside, expecting a single bed and a dresser, but I'm shocked at the room's opulence.

I expected modern simplicity like the rest of the house, not rich opulence. The king-sized bed is framed with redwood that matches the floors. I wonder if it is recycled wood because there is no way they would allow it to be cut from trees and brought onto the island. It goes against the rules of preserving the planet. Square screens are mounted on each wall by the nightstands, not hiding the modern conveniences. The bed is already turned down, like in the Regency novels I've read. The room feels warm and inviting, not cold and simplistic.

"Mrs. Cross designed this room. It was her favorite room in the entire house. It is only natural that this will be your room from now on."

I nod, not wanting to ruin the moment by responding. I also want to bask in it a bit longer. The room is perfect.

"I will come get you for breakfast at eight o'clock in the morning." When I turn to say thank you, she is gone, closing the door with a resounding click.

After placing my books neatly inside the wood nightstand, I remove the shawl that made me look like I was wearing a long dress. I remain dressed in the black top with plain boots and pants made of neoprene that fit like a second skin.

Checking the time on the screen, I see it's already ten o'clock. I decide to check all the drawers and look around the room for any clues about Mrs. Cross. She must have left something behind if she designed the space.

After another hour of checking all the drawers, behind the bed, under the bed, and in the modern bathroom, I give up. There is nothing. The room is empty except for the furniture.

In the morning, I hear a knock on the door. I check the time and notice I overslept. It's quarter past eleven. *Shit.* When I open the door, I notice a tray of fruit and yogurt on the floor with a glass of water and granola.

I peer down the hallway left and right, but it's empty. Not a soul. Like the person who dropped off the tray disappeared into thin air. I can't even thank them. I take the tray and shut the door behind me.

After finishing my breakfast and freshening up, I decide to wear another neoprene suit in black to go exploring, hoping the rest of the staff is friendlier. There is also the fact that I haven't seen the man of the house. In a way, I'm glad he hasn't shown up. It gives me time to get used to my surroundings and accept the reality. I have to marry the masked man.

Taking the tray, I open the door, hoping I can find the kitchen. I don't expect to be waited on. Back home, I wasn't the type to leave my clothes on the floor and wait for someone to pick them up like they were slaves.

I return to the landing where both hallways meet and figure the kitchen will be on the first floor. I find the kitchen after crossing the dining area, noticing someone sat at the head of the table because dirty plates are left to be picked up. It must have been him.

He didn't bother summoning me like I expected, but I have to remember that this isn't a love match. I'm here for a purpose—his purpose—but you can learn a lot about a person's surroundings. The way they live in their personal space.

I turn once the automated kitchen door slides shut, looking around at the ultra-modern white kitchen and black floors. Every room seems different in this house. It feels like a time warp—the past and then the present.

"Can I help you?"

I turn to my left, and an older woman with a white jacket and black pants looks at me like I'm lost.

"I was looking for the sink to wash the plates?" I ask, holding the tray stacked with dirty dishes.

She steps forward with a confused expression marring her face, causing the corner of her eyes to crinkle. I'm sure no one has ever come to the kitchen to ask that question unless they work here.

"You must be..."

"Yes, I am," I rush out. "These need to be washed, and I was looking for the sink."

She rushes forward to take the tray. "I'll take those."

I step back. "That's alright. I can wash them."

She stares at me or rather at my mask. "You're not—"

"Where I come from, the cook doesn't wash the dishes," I lie.

I read that in a book. Everyone knows rich people don't wash their own dishes, but I do. Back home, I would help the staff around the house. I wanted to know what it felt like to cook, clean, and wash your own things. In some of the novels I read, the wives would cook and clean for their husbands and take care of the children. Things used to be that way in the past before the tech war, where civilization changed and people adopted technology to do all their work, not realizing it was a way for the government to control them.

She walks over to a counter and presses a button. The counter opens, and a sink is below. "You can place them there, and the machine will do the rest."

I lean in, placing the tray on the smooth surface of the white counter. "Fancy," I mutter.

My father didn't have anything like this. You still had to wash the dishes, then place them in a sanitizing machine.

"This cuts the work in half. It's unnecessary to have to wash the food off first. Cross designed it."

I'm stunned. Impressed. So he is smart. Interesting.

"It's...brilliant," I say with a smile, placing the dishes inside with food and all.

"He is"—I look up, waiting to hear more—"brilliant."

For the next two weeks, I read, eat alone at the dining table, and stay in my room most of the day. I always clean my own dishes and made sure to learn my way around the kitchen in case I got hungry. I don't want the staff to think I'm a snob. I was hoping to talk to someone and make a friend, but everyone is curt with me. And he never shows. Not at the dining table when I make a point to sit at it, hoping he would make an appearance. Not when I hear a knock on my door and it's just my dinner tray. Two weeks of being alone in a big mysterious house and I've never felt so at war with myself. My father never called me. It was like I never existed.

To anyone.

It's funny when you look around and notice everything, but when no one cares you exist, it's the worst pain of all.

# 5

LILLITH

The following Monday, I decided to explore the common areas of the house. I stayed out of the west wing, making sure I wore my mask and only took it off in the privacy of my room.

Moving through the house, I find corridors illuminated by pathways of light that seemed to guide my way, responding to my footsteps with a gentle brightness. Smart windows show-cased panoramic views of both the futuristic cityscape outside and the distant ocean, blending the urban in a harmonious embrace.

The heart of the house was like a nexus room—an interac-tive area where technology and imagination merged. Holo-graphic displays floated in midair, allowing me to explore virtual realms. It allowed you to communicate, but I had no access. Even if I did, there was no one to call. I've accepted that my father was done with me.

I spent my time looking through immersive holograms and even conjured up lifelike simulations for entertainment. Furni-ture in the room morphed at a thought, adapting to my needs in real time by appearing from the wall. As I settled into a chair, it seemed to mold itself to the contours of my body, creating an experience of comfort and connectivity unparalleled by anything from the past. It was surreal.

The fusion of technology and nature was perhaps most evident in the Biosphere Garden. It felt like a sanctuary, transporting me to a bioluminescent wonderland, where plant life intertwined with luminescent fibers, casting a soothing, ethereal glow. The air was crisp and purified, thanks to a network of advanced filtration systems seamlessly integrated into the futuristic architecture. It was gorgeous. It was peaceful. But I was alone.

By the third week, I can't take being in my room anymore. It's Thursday evening, and I'm bored and want to see the other parts of the house. I quietly pull the door open and adjust the mask over my face, glad it's made of a breathable fabric.

I step into the dark hallway with concrete-colored walls. White strips of light illuminate each side of the hallway, so it takes a minute for my eyes to adjust to the lighting. Heading on the opposite side of the west wing, I want to see what's on the east side of the house. I draw a mental picture like the nexus room and figure it's probably where Killian Cross sleeps. My stomach clenches in anticipation, wondering if he's there. What he might look like. Maybe he isn't wearing his mask, or maybe he doesn't take it off. Spending so much time in his house, I know he designed it all. From what I have seen so far, there is no way he wasn't a genius.

In a way, I'm glad he doesn't expect me to share his room. What if he's violent? A shudder rips through me, thinking of being married to a man like that. All the what-ifs.

Passing the landing and walking farther into the hallway on the west side, I hear a faint tapping noise from one of the rooms. I can see that a door is slightly open, letting a glow of light reach the hallway.

When I reach a safe distance to look inside the room, I hear a woman's moan. My eyes widen; a man fucks her with her legs wrapped around his waist, and he's holding her suspended in the air. The glow of the light illuminates her perfect skin and breasts. The man's face is hidden in the dark shadows as he moves inside her.

"You feel so good, Kill. Right there."

I blink twice, trying to figure out why I'm simultaneously bothered and aroused. I've never had sex like that. Ethan has never held me that way, and I've never felt the need to moan because it felt good. The times I did have sex, there was a lot of rubbing, but it was nothing like I read about. No butterflies. No moans escaping my lips. Just sweating and when I expected the fireworks to start, nothing. It was over. For Ethan, it was perfect. He always said I was when we were done. I wasn't sure if he was just being nice or maybe something was wrong with me and I couldn't feel what he was feeling.

"Yes. Harder, Kill," she begs.

With a growl, he begins to savagely fuck her. His strong, inked hands grip the sides of her torso as he thrusts harder, and I notice she lies flat on a table. Her small breast bounce with every thrust.

I can hear how their bodies come together, and then it hits me. Kill is short for Killian. It's Killian Cross, and he's fucking someone while his paid soon-to-be wife is in another room on the other side of the hallway. Jealousy pricks my insides, running through me like a poison with no cure. Her body is voluptuous, and the way she calls him Kill means she isn't some random woman. Killian could have any woman because of his wealth alone, yet her familiarity grates on my nerves, causing them to tighten. From the lighting in the room, I can tell she isn't gorgeous or what they would consider pretty, but he's having sex with *her*.

I tear my eyes away and practically run toward my room, hating myself for feeling this way. I should be relieved he doesn't want to have sex with me. I also shouldn't be surprised that the man who bought me for a crazy amount of money is no different from the other men who live on this island. Evil men who live together serve each other like demons and use women for their guilty pleasure.

I try to bake a cake, but an annoying siren goes off, then a whooshing sound. I wince when the light of the oven turns off and dings. I couldn't sleep last night. My mind kept going back to Killian and the woman. At six o'clock, I gave up and went straight to the kitchen to bake a cake. I found all the organic ingredients, but I guess the oven cooks a little faster than what I'm used to.

"Are you okay, miss?" Kiera asks, rushing to open the oven door, followed by a cloud of smoke.

"Smoke detected. Purifying now," the automated voice says from a speaker in the ceiling.

"I'm fine," I say, a flush creeping up my cheeks. "I'm sorry—"

She presses a button, and the burnt clump of cake is tossed out.

A tall, dark figure looms in the doorway. My heart begins to beat hard inside my chest, but then the figure is gone. I blink twice. Maybe I'm seeing things from lack of sleep.

Kiera moves around the kitchen, preparing trays. "That was Mr. Cross. He doesn't like to be kept waiting for his breakfast. You should join him," she says softly.

I chew on my bottom lip nervously. I almost burned his house down. I'm the last person he wants to see, but seeing how nervous the older woman is rushing to do her job, I ask," Do you need help? I could help you—"

"I've got it. It's okay. Go have a seat at the dining table."

"WHAT'S WITH THE MASK?"

My eyes lift from the other side of the white Italian table for ten with clear resin legs to the man sitting across from me dressed all in black with a mask. An upside-down cross that reads No God sketched on the front.

"What's with yours?" I retort.

His faint chuckle vibrates between my legs, and I squeeze them tight under the shawl I chose to wear, hiding my body from his view. His voice calls to me in the back of my mind like I've heard it before, but I can't remember where.

"Oh, I'm sure you've heard. The beast. The freak. The recluse living in a dark mansion like a moth."

I pause with my fork full of strawberries midair to the opening of my mask. I lower it and lean back in my chair. "I'm not sure what you mean because I don't gossip and couldn't care less what you look like underneath your mask."

"And why is that?"

"Because...nothing about you interests me."

"Is that why you were watching me fuck? Does that interest you?"

I stiffened slightly. I didn't think he saw me. Did the woman he was with see me? My mouth is suddenly thick and dry as I think about what I saw.

Nervous, I take a sip and place the glass of water back, feeling the edge of the fabric of my mask with the tip of my tongue cool against my lips, deciding how best to answer.

My eyes focus on the words on the black matte of his mask, reminding me of who he is and what he represents.

"I couldn't concentrate on what I was reading," I lie. "I could hear pathetic moans from outside the bedroom, so I decided to see where it was coming from."

"And?" he challenges, his head angled to the side like a masked murderer from a slasher flick.

"And...I wasn't impressed. More annoyed, actually, but it was nothing I hadn't seen or heard before. Now that we've met, it's to be expected."

"What did you expect?" he asks in a tight voice.

I can tell I'm getting under his skin, and it makes me feel good that I can.

"Exactly what I saw and what I imagined when my father broke the news to me yesterday. Nothing special. We both should get tested before you make me spread my legs for you. Safety and all."

I see his fist clench on the table, and I smile inwardly, watching the ink of his tattoos flex. It's the only skin I can see besides the tattoos on his neck and jet-black hair.

"Now, why would you need to do that?" he asks, but I don't miss the way his knuckles clench tight.

"Because you wouldn't be the first man to touch me. I'm not a scared little virgin, Mr. Cross. I'm just not as filthy as you."

I slide my chair back and stand, not wanting to remain in his presence. I know I pissed him off and offended him, but I couldn't care less.

As I walk away, his hard voice has me slowing down when I reach the bottom steps of the stairs. "The doctor will be in later today."

AFTER I GAVE in to my pathetic crying, feeling sorry for myself, I hear a soft knock on the wooden door to my room.

I rush to the nightstand and pull the mask over my face. When I open the door, I'm greeted by an older gentleman and a young woman wearing a pair of white scrubs.

"Good afternoon, Miss Sinclair. Mr. Cross said you are expecting me."

"Yes, he mentioned it."

"My name is Dr. Archer, and this is Emily, a nurse who works with me. Do you mind if we come inside?"

After he injects me with a known medication so I can ovulate, he draws my blood, collecting the necessary samples to test for other diseases as a precaution or, rather, for Killian Cross. The nurse gives me a wan smile as she places all the items inside the tubes and begins testing.

Before, doctors needed to send blood to be tested and samples collected to a lab. Now they can get the results instantaneously. If you have money of course. Fewer privileged people who live on the mainland don't have that luxury. I heard from Ethan that even when they pay, they wait for days, sometimes weeks, for a test because of how many people need them.

It's a fucked-up system.

"She's clean," the nurse says to the doctor like I'm not here.

He looks at the results, then glances at me. "After I've conducted the exam, Miss Sinclair, I want to let you know that you are fertile. Nothing I see will prevent you from falling pregnant." He hands me a tablet. "Could you please fill this out?"

I scan the screen, and my face falls when I read the questions.

"What about him?" I blurt. "Is he clean? Do I have to be careful?"

The nurse gives the doctor a worried look, but his expression remains neutral when he responds, "You have nothing to worry about, Miss Sinclair. Mr. Cross is a cautious man."

He means he wears protection when he fucks his whores. Good to know.

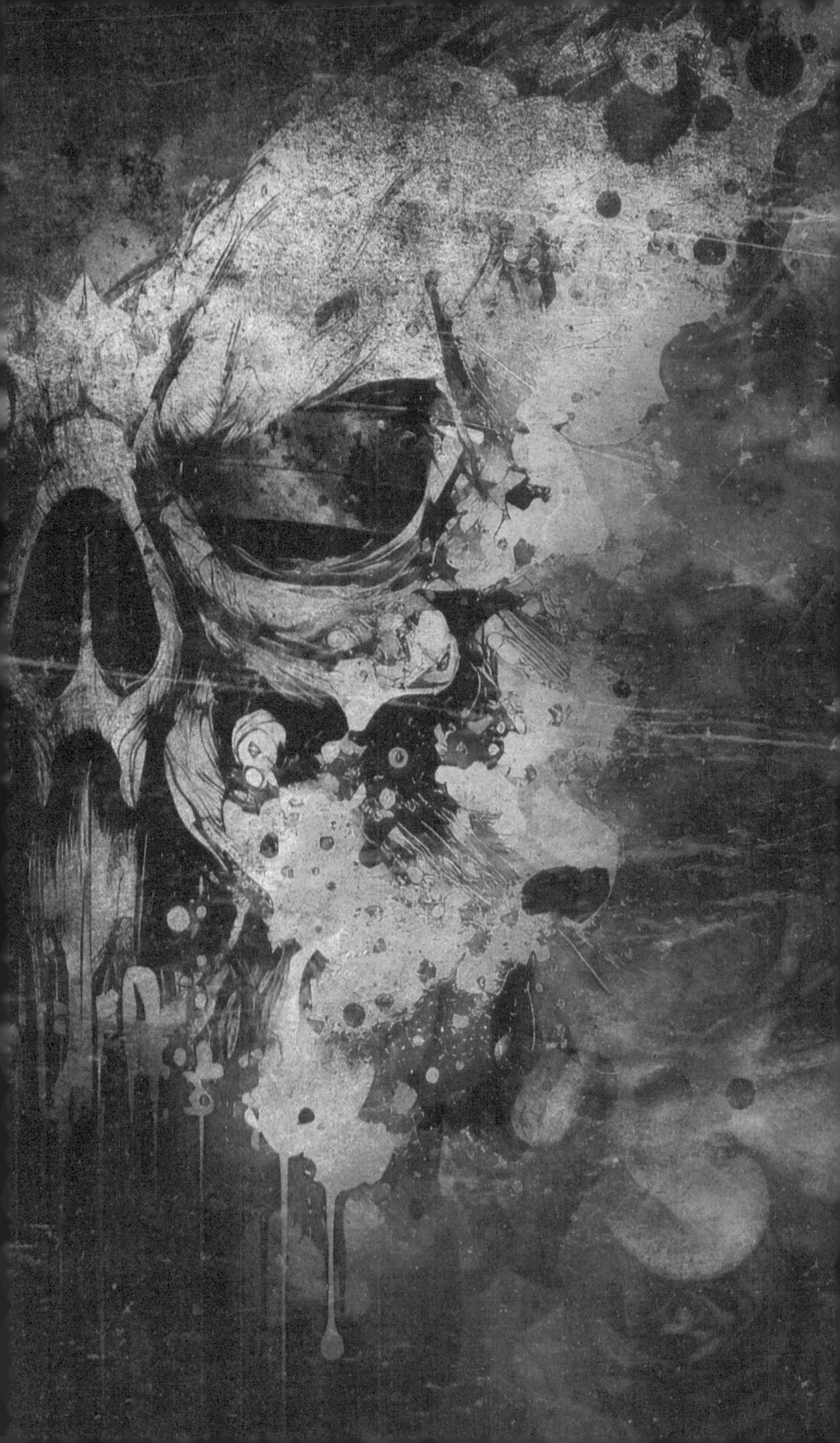

# 6

KILLIAN

"You are a very lucky man, Mr. Cross."

Seated at my desk in my office, I tear my eyes from the augmented reality screen under the glass of my desk, sliding my fingers to shrink the view. Dr. Archer approaches my desk with a pleasant smile, and I curse myself for not putting a camera inside her room—my mother's favorite room. I'm still trying to figure out why I placed her there.

My lip curls in irritation under my mask. He either saw her face, or he means because he was able to see firsthand what I bought. What belongs to me. "How so?"

"She is *all* woman."

Her pussy, then. He's talking about my future wife's pussy. A pussy I have yet to see for myself, let alone her face. I expected some form of respect, but sometimes I forget who I'm dealing with on this island. I'll deal with him in a bit, but first, I need the information I paid him to get. He is a well-rounded doctor and also a robotic surgeon, and I need him.

"I bet she is, Dr. Archer. Now give me the information I'm paying you for."

"Very well." He hands me the tablet with all her results. "I will give you access right away, but she's clean. No STDs or issues to worry about. She's fertile, and you will have no issues with her conceiving. She also indicated that she is not a virgin." I grip the tablet, wondering why I care or thought maybe she was bluffing and was untouched. My mind turns like a hamster on a wheel, trying to picture the piece of shit who touched her, but I can't. "But she is...fragile." He finishes.

I drop the tablet on the glass of my desk. "Fragile?" *What the fuck does he mean she's fragile?* He glances at the tablet nervously, and the fact that my knuckles have turned white from gripping the edge of the glass. He clears his throat and continues. "Based on her answers."

"Meaning?" I drawl, making a forward motion with my hand for him to get to the point.

"It means you should be careful with her. She's had one sexual partner and intercourse a few times compared to *your* experience based on the questionnaire she filled out."

I pick up the tablet like I'm reading a juicy tabloid on the web, scrolling down to the question that asks how many partners and times you have had sexual intercourse.

I look up at him. "It says she has felt discomfort during sex."

"It's not uncommon, but I thought it was important, and you should be aware. Maybe it's not her. She hasn't experienced any discomfort any other time herself."

Whoever she was fucking is a lame piece of shit who doesn't know how to pleasure a woman. My lips lift into a grin, glad for the mask covering my face.

*She lied.*

I won't lie to myself and say her mouth doesn't make me

want to grab her and bend her over the nearest table and slide my cock inside her to shut her the fuck up.

It's crazy that I haven't seen her face, and she already drives me insane, but none of that matters. I need to stick to the plan. Her pleasure is of no importance to me. My thought of fucking up Dr. Archer evaporates like smoke for making a comment about her pussy.

I hand him the tablet, switching on the holographic screen to more important business matters. Dismissing him, I say, "Thank you but that is not my problem. Have a nice day, Dr. Archer."

She's here for one thing, and that is to give me a child from her womb and nothing else.

"Do I send you the results?" he asks with the tablet in his hand.

"That won't be necessary."

I turn up the music, and In This Moment's "Sick Like Me" drowns out anything else he has to say.

# 7

## LILLITH

Checking the doors down a hallway leading to the garden, I'm looking for a workout room or a gym. It's been a month since I've gotten a good workout in. I'm sure Killian Cross works out. Both times I have seen him, he seems fit underneath the long black shirt he fills out.

I walk past each room on the first floor, noticing how clean and open this part of the house is. An occasional table and chair attempt to fill the space, but no pictures. Usually, there is at least a screen with one, but not in this house. Some rooms feel sterile, but I know there is not much I can do about it to make it feel welcoming. Killian seems like a man who isn't used to a woman's touch when it comes to his house, only a certain woman who calls him Kill. Every time I think about them together, my stomach burns. I can't even read a spicy scene in one of my books and not think about them together.

"Are you going to walk around like an intruder looking in every room?"

I turn around, and my stomach flops, feeling like it turned

upside down when I see Killian leaning on the wall looking down at me from a distance—watching me through his mask.

"It's better than looking like a creep following me while I look in every room," I shoot back.

"How is that?"

"If I *was* an intruder, at least I'm looking for something I want instead of being a creepy stalker," I retort.

He pushes off the wall and steps closer. "How does that make *you* better?"

I try to see if I can glimpse what he looks like underneath, but the word on the mask covering his face is distracting. It reads EVOL.

I tilt my head, noticing he is a lot taller than me this up close. "Well, my mask doesn't have EVOL written on the front of it, and I'm not following anyone."

He steps closer, his chest almost touching my chin. He's wearing a tight long-sleeved shirt outlining what I was wondering about a minute ago, if he worked out. Nothing prepared me for the muscles rippling underneath his shirt.

My eyes travel over the outline of his muscles, wondering what his skin must feel like. Is it smooth? Does he have tattoos on his chest like the tops of his hands and neck?

"Are you done?"

My head lifts. "What was that?"

"Admiring."

His head dips lower, and my stomach flips sideways. The smell of his clean ocean-scented cologne has my head spinning. My eyes home in on a tattoo that says I AM THE MASTER OF MY FATE. I don't move. I fist my hands to keep them from shaking. "All you have to do is ask," he says softly.

I lean my head back, taking a step away from him. "I..."

"Of course, you weren't," he whispers.

I look away toward the wall and ask, "Do you have a gym or a workout room?"

He turns and walks down the hallway. Then he pauses and angles his head so I can only see the side of the mask. "Do you want to know where the gym is or not?"

I step forward and follow him down the hall toward the west wing of the house until we reach a door at the end. He steps aside, punching in a code on the screen by the wall. The door opens.

"The code is 42135."

My eyes dart around the room, and it's a gym with the latest equipment. Mats and dumbbells of all kinds line the right side of the wall with mirrors. To the left, modern workout machines, including treadmills, are placed in front of mirrors framed with white lights, giving the space a functional feel.

"Thank you," I say, giving him my back.

I feel his presence behind me, and right when I think he's going to leave, not realizing he is still standing behind me, he leans in and whispers, "Now, who is following who?"

I whip around with a retort on the tip of my tongue, but his next words melt it away. "Meet me for dinner at seven. We have much to discuss."

*Yeah, like when does the sacrifice take place.*

My eyes trace the letters of the word written on his mask, and I know he can probably see the color of my eyes through mine, but I don't care. I'm curious as to why he would wear a mask with the words EVOL, which I noticed is love spelled backward. He's a mystery, but I have much more to learn from the man behind the mask. *Like the fact he makes me wet.*

He remains still, and I can feel his eyes on me even though I can't see them. I can feel the pull of energy mixed with the danger he gives off. It reminds me of lightning when it flashes, and you're waiting for the sound of thunder.

"I'll see you at seven," he finally says, breaking the silence. He walks away, disappearing out of the room.

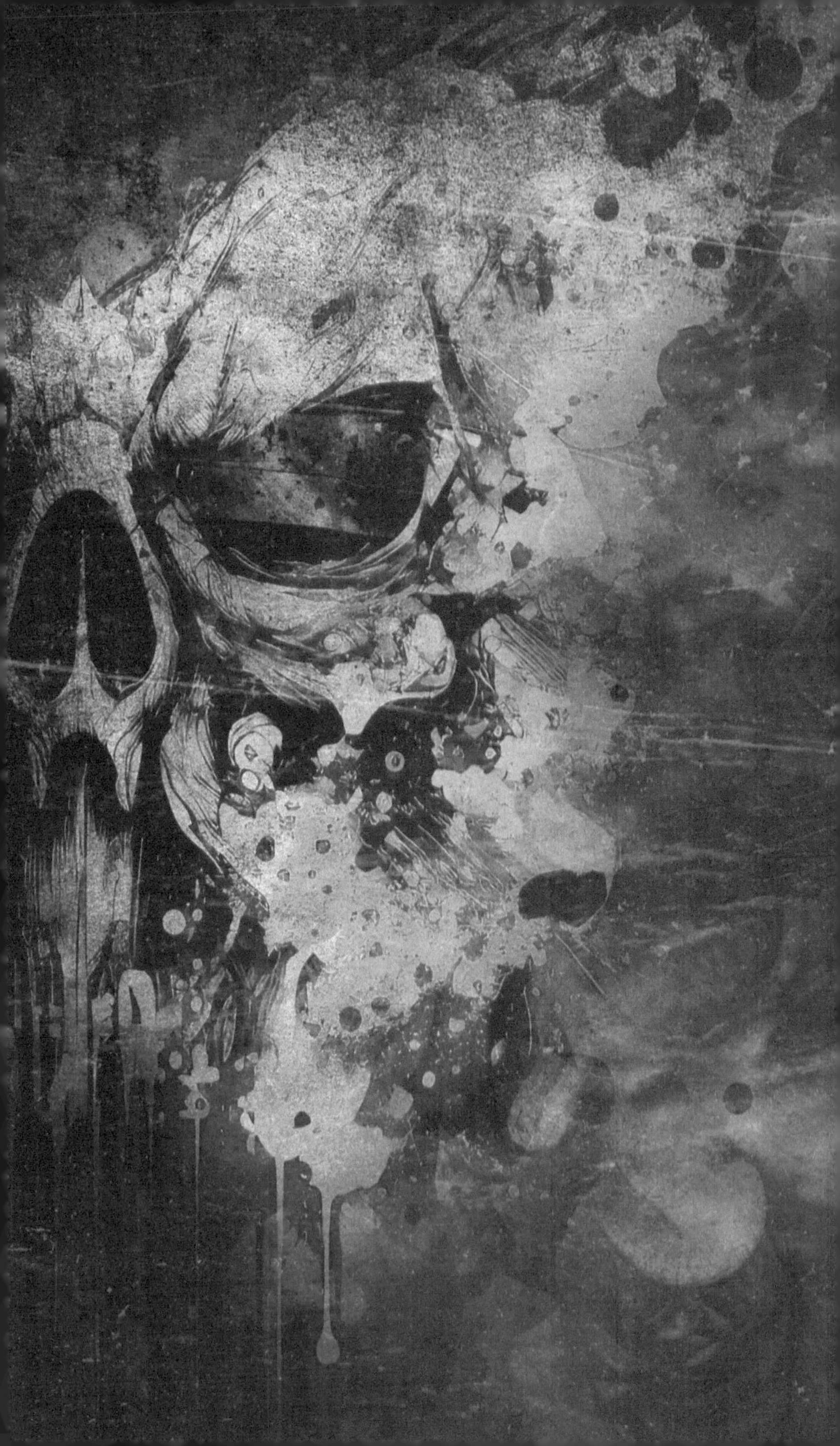

# 8

KILLIAN

I keep looking at the image under the glass of my desk. Seated in my office chair, I'm watching her place a mat on the floor. No way will she work out with so much clothing on, so I wait patiently, wanting to see what her body looks like when she removes the hoodie and sweatpants.

When I asked her to meet me for dinner at seven, I stood there like an idiot staring at her eyes. From what I have heard, I know she's beautiful. She doesn't post pictures of her on the internet; there are only pictures of John Sinclair's daughter from when she was a lot younger. The color of her eyes reminds me of a hidden oasis in a vast desert. The hue is a delicate fusion of cerulean and emerald. Fucking breathtaking.

I was so close, within arm's reach, and I itched to rip off the mask from her face. But I know I have to be patient. The last thing I need is to be married to an unwilling woman. If she wants to be difficult and wear the mask for now, then so be it.

I continue to watch her like the creep she accused me of being when she finally slides the sweatpants the rest of the way down her legs. *Jesus.* She's wearing a full black bodysuit molded to her perfect body.

I shift in my chair, adjusting my hard cock as I watch her move into a headstand, curving her body with her legs in the air.

"Kill."

I look up at the sound of Ciro's voice. My best friend since I decided to conduct business off the island and into the city of the mainland. I met him when I decided I needed answers as to why my parents died and what they were into. He was on the streets dealing, trying to make money, saving as many people as possible from hunger and disease.

"What's up?"

I brought him and a group of his friends to help me build a network off the grid where people can buy what they need to feed their families. A network hidden from the assholes who run the world or live in the City of God.

Everything will be accessible like the old days through the black market—drugs, medication, gas, banned items, and food—real food. Not the synthetic healthy shit they make seem is better.

He walks closer and looks down at the screen. "Damn, Kill. Is that her?"

I close the window on the screen from inside the gym and meet his gaze. "Yeah."

He rubs his hand through his straight blond hair and gives me a smirk. "Why is she wearing a mask?"

I shrug. " She's trying to get under my skin, I guess."

He laughs. "I guess with a body like that, it doesn't matter what her face looks like. Does it?"

For whatever reason, Ciro mentioning her body bothers me. It's the second time it's happened. First with the doctor and now with him.

"You know why she is here... for me."

He raises his eyebrows. "How does Blair feel about it? Does she know?"

"My personal business doesn't involve Blair. She knows the score."

"Are you sure about that? I don't think she sees things that way between you two."

"You let me handle Blair. What is going on with the next shipment?"

Blair knows that we can never be more than what we are. We fuck when the moment arises, and that's it. There is no room for her in my life other than that. I have a legacy to fulfill and need an heir to continue what I have built. It's high society rules. I need to play both sides to stay viable, and I can't complicate my life with a woman who doesn't understand the bigger picture.

"The shipment is fine. Payment should arrive at midnight, and it will be sent as scheduled. By the way, the race is at the end of the month. Are you showing up?"

"You know I don't miss a race. It's still on."

"Now, that's what I'm talking about. It's going to be epic. Huge party, motorcycles racing, and of course, you on the track." He points at the black screen. "When is the big day?"

"Sooner than anyone thinks."

"Are you going to tell her?"

I sigh. "Tell her what?"

"What you do? Who you are underneath." He grins. "The beast everyone loves."

Ciro loves to gas me up. He doesn't know my plan for my dear wife after she gives me what I need, but some things are better left unsaid.

"I don't think it matters to her who I really am off this island."

"But why the mask?"

I tap my finger on the handmade plastic one I'm wearing. He means why is *she* wearing a mask. "I don't know. Like I said, she's probably mocking me or some shit."

He snorts. "I doubt it. Pissing you off wouldn't help her cause."

Trust me, she does a good job pissing me off. But I don't tell him that. What I do or say with Lillith is my business and no one else's.

He takes a seat in front of my desk. Ciro is honestly the only friend I can trust and count on. The rest only care for what I can provide or give them. I decide to give a little.

"I don't know, Ciro. She keeps to herself most of the day and wears the mask when she's out of her room."

"Those eyes, dude. I wonder what she looks like underneath. Everything else is...perfect."

I tighten my jaw because as innocent as his comment about Lillith is, I can't help the feeling that creeps up every time someone mentions how attractive she is, and she's wearing a fucking mask.

"Please don't talk about her. I'm not interested in the bitches this island produces. I'm only interested in what she can give me so I can keep up my image."

"You want a kid. That's...crazy, but I get it. You need to make sure they think you are one of them. Are you going to show her what you look like?" he teases.

I throw an empty jump drive at him, and he dodges it, laughing.

Every muscle in my face tightens when I think about the injury I sustained on the right side of my face. Injuries that people from the City of God look down upon and find hideous.

"Eventually."

I hear a tap on the door, and I watch Ciro turn around to

see Blair and her friend Sarah standing at the threshold. He looks back at me and smiles, giving me a wink. "I guess I better get going. I have to take care of the shipments," he says, backing up toward the door. Blair and Sarah smile when he passes.

Blair brazenly walks inside my office and presses the button to the automatic door. She turns around and sashays toward the side of the desk while Sarah leans on the edge. Her skirt rides up, exposing her fishnet stockings.

I look up at the clock. 6:19 p.m.

"I have to get going. Blair, you can't just show up at my house whenever you want."

I give them access by way of a solar-powered boat docked on the edge of the island. It's why I chose to live here as my main home because I have direct access to and from the main-land. She takes a risk bringing Sarah with her on her own, but Blair likes to push the limit.

I care about Blair. Her parents were poor, and she was taking odd jobs in the city when I met her at one of the races. She needed to make money, so I brought her into my circle. She handles the requests for needed products, and I pay her so she can support her mother and father. She also doesn't mind the mask on or off.

I watch her lips form a pout. "Is it because of her that I can't?"

She's referring to Lillith. My team knows why Lillith is here and that I have to marry and produce an heir.

"That's part of it."

She inches closer and stands between my legs. Her dark hair falls like a curtain on my desk as she leans back, exposing her stomach with her belly piercing. Blair is not what they would call beautiful but exotic. She doesn't have classic features. Her top lip is smaller than the bottom. Her eyes are a deep brown, and her breasts are smaller than I normally like, but she is good in bed. It is also a plus that she likes to bring a friend once in a while, like Sarah.

I think it's her way to keep me entertained. Blair's somewhat of a close friend that I care about, and we have fun, but that's where it ends— where it has to end.

"Are you going to forget about me once you're married? You know that doesn't mean things have to change," she purrs.

I ground my teeth together because I don't want to discuss this now. I'm about to push her away, but I see the sadness in her eyes, and I feel like an asshole. My intention was never to hurt Blair; she has been there for me without judgment for my appearance. She never complains and is always available.

"I have things I need to deal with, Blair," I tell her, trying to make her understand that now is not a good time.

Sarah leans across my desk, her breasts spilling out of her black top. Her blond hair frames her average face, giving me a sultry smile. "You're not married right now, Kill." She isn't my type, but Blair knows that, and it's probably why she chose to bring her.

I look down and see Blair pulling my cock out from my pants and stroking it to life. I close my eyes. Blair whimpers while Sarah spreads her legs to give me a view of her pussy. "Fuck me," Sarah says on a moan. "Hard, Kill."

# 9

## LILLITH

I walk in the dining room promptly at seven like he requested. I don't know why I felt a surge of excitement getting ready to meet him after finishing my yoga work-out. The butterflies came and went for the first time.

I took care in selecting something nice to wear. I still opted to wear the mask, but I washed and straightened my hair. I was surprised to see various brushes, organic lotions, and a makeup collection in the bathroom.

Checking the time on my phone, I notice it's ten past seven, and his seat at the end of the table is empty with a cover over his plate of food. I sit at the table and watch Agnes pour a glass of water near my plate.

I heard someone call her name after leaving the gym when I was craving a shower, and I smiled to myself because I liked it. It's a strong name.

I want to ask her where Killian is, and if I should start eating without him. I don't know why I should care, but I was hoping we could talk so he could tell me what his plans are with me besides the obvious. Maybe we could come to some type of agreement.

Living with my father felt like I was in a prison. I ate, worked out, took care of my appearance, and only had Ethan as a friend. But this is different.

My head lifts when a man I have seen working around the house walks in, checking a light I noticed was flickering alongside the baseboard, and I muster the courage to ask, "Do you know where Mr. Cross is?" The man straightens, but he doesn't look at me directly. Maybe he is put off because of the mask I'm wearing, or he's nervous and doesn't know if he should answer me, but then I hear him murmur, "In his office." He straightens and clears his throat. "Down the hallway to the right, third door on your left." And he's gone. Waiting a few seconds, I look around the dining room and feel stupid sitting here by myself.

Getting up, I leave the food untouched and make my way to Killian's office. My heart pounds when I turn to the left and reach the third door. My finger pushes the screen slightly, and it slides open. I instantly look away, closing my eyes.

*Killian.* I blink the sting from my eyes. *Why?*

Looking down at my feet, I feel like my life just keeps crumbling. I shouldn't care because he is nothing to me. Just a man who bought me for selfish reasons.

I get the courage to look up, and the girl I saw him with the first night gasps, "Harder."

I suck in quick breaths but can't tear my eyes away because another girl is in the room. She is blonde compared to the other girl with long black hair.

The blonde whispers in his ear while he has the other girl bent over the desk on top of her with his pants below his ass, and judging from his position, he's thrusting inside her. The blonde sucks on his neck at the same time.

It hurts.

I have a ball lodged in my throat. He left me waiting for him while he was in here having sex with two women. Needles prick the inside of my nose, trying to seize my throat. I look down and notice my hands are shaking. A tear slides down my cheek, and I press the fabric of my mask over my cheek.

He's fully dressed, wearing his mask, but to those two girls, he is God. It doesn't matter to them what he looks like underneath, and judging from their moans as he picks up speed, he's probably not bad to look at without it.

I notice the way he walks around the house all confident and arrogant. He doesn't care that he had to hide his face from anyone. Including me.

Holding himself with one arm on the edge of the desk, he wraps his arm around the girl's neck while thrusting inside her, and she smiles at something he said to her.

I've never had sex like that. Ethan never took me that way or whispered in my ear.

The blonde slides her hands under his tight-fitted shirt, and he grinds his hips into the other girl in slow, measured thrusts, causing her to moan. "Killian, I'm coming."

His other arm snakes behind him after releasing her, and the blonde moans while he plays with her clit. He doesn't waste any time making them both come, and he doesn't let up. He increases his speed, growling under his mask, fucking one while fingering the other. I could tell his skin was smooth from how his ass muscles flexed while thrusting inside her in swift movements. The contrast of his inked hands touching the dark-haired girl's breast while he loses himself in her.

I wipe my neck from the tears falling under the mask, causing it to stick. When he growls, probably close to his release, I smack my hand on the screen hard and watch the door close.

"What the fuck!" he bellows before it closes completely.

I run, making sure I don't stop or look back. I saw enough. I scramble down the hallway, mentally picturing the turns in my head back to my room.

"Lillith! Lilith!" His yells echo down the hallway. I keep running, cursing my favorite pointed boots, wishing I'd put on a pair of sneakers and a sweater instead.

Fuck Killian Cross. Fuck him.

I make it inside my room in record time and flick the lock to the door, backing away like I made it safe from the gateway to hell.

"Lillith, open the door," he demands in a gruff tone.

"Go away," I yell at him through the closed door in a shaky voice, my chest rising and falling from running so fast. My lungs burn from the cold air.

"Shit, Lillith. Please, let me explain."

"There is nothing to explain. Now please. Just... leave me alone." My voice cracks at the last part. Rushing into the bathroom, I close and lock the door so I can remove my mask and no one will see or hear me cry.

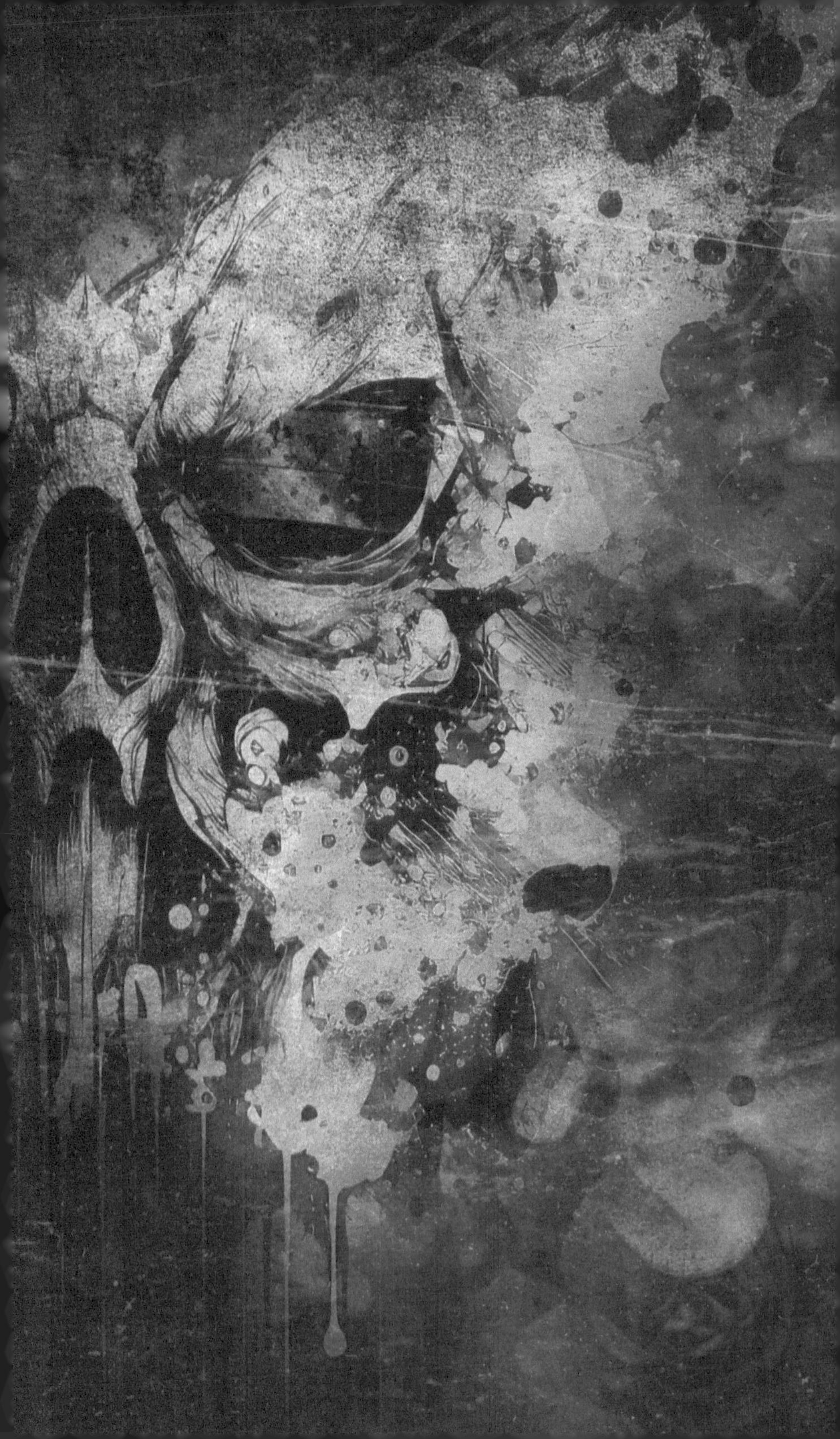

# IO

## KILLIAN

'm so fucking stupid. *I fucked up.* I look down at my unbuttoned pants and feel disgusted with myself. She saw me with them, and I don't know what to do. I fix myself and walk into the dining room, looking at my smart watch to see the time, 7:45 p.m., and look at the plate of food placed on each end of the dining table.

"She waited for you." I turn to see Agnes walk in and give me a pointed look.

"I see that," I respond in a clipped voice.

"She didn't eat, waiting until you showed up, and then went looking for you."

Agnes has been here since my parents were alive and they brought her to live here from the mainland after I was born. She stayed on when her husband died of an illness they couldn't cure because they didn't make enough money for treatment. When my parents found out and offered to help, it was too late. He passed away from complications.

"She found me."

She nods, picking up Lillith's untouched plate and making me feel like a total ass. She didn't eat, and I don't think she will ever sit here and eat with me again. Why would she?

"You know, I thought she was mocking you by wearing that mask, but I figured out why she wears it. I understand now."

I bow my head, listening because Agnes has guided me after my parents' accident. She has been a mother figure and has always had my best interest at heart. She sees things I don't, and when I start to derail and lose my head, she talks some sense into me. I don't feel like being scolded right now because I'm a grown-ass man at twenty-three, but I respect her.

"Miss Sinclair doesn't strike me as shallow compared to the people who inhabit this side of the world. I think she has lived in solidarity all her life with no one to count on or talk to. It seems like, in her mind, her face is a curse. Something she doesn't think is important because no one cares about *her*. I'm not sure about her father or mother. But if her father sold her to a man she didn't choose, just so she could bear a man a child without caring how she felt about it. It's obvious she wears the mask to see how she would be treated without anyone seeing what she looks like, and you just proved to her the truth."

I don't understand what she means. Mask or no mask, what is the difference? Everyone knows that the offspring of the rich on this island are gifted with natural beauty from two parents with similar traits. I don't have to see that to know that she must be nice to look at. She gets a pass no matter what.

"I don't understand."

"Of course you don't, Killian. Because you haven't taken the time to get to know her without seeing what is on the surface. The same way you want people to overlook how you look on the surface. She understands now that it doesn't matter. Mask or no mask, she will get treated the same way everyone has always treated her."

"Like what?"

"Like she's nothing." She straightens her hair, making sure her neat bun is still in place.

"What do I do, Agnes?"

How do I even get her to look at me now? I won't force her to sleep with me. I'm not that kind of man to force a woman to have sex with me. I may look like a monster, but I'm not that kind of monster.

"There is nothing you can do, Killian. You got what you wanted. You will soon have a wife that you won't feel bad about when she looks at you with indifference. You can continue to live happy with your friends like Blair and the other one—I can't quite remember her name." She waves her other hand, balancing the plates. "Either way, she knows what type of company you prefer rather than having to sit with her at dinner after you requested her to attend."

"Agnes?"

Is she mad at me on behalf of Lillith?

"Yes, Killian?"

"Are you mad at me?"

Agnes's eyes soften and give me a sad expression. "I'm not mad at you, Killian. I'm disappointed in how you treat a lady you plan on having a child with. I'm sure your mother would have to agree."

She just made me feel more like a piece of shit. I have treated her like crap since she arrived. I didn't even greet her or offer her anything. I let Agnes deal with her because I don't want her to be repulsed that she's marrying a man with half a face who wears a mask everywhere he goes.

I shouldn't feel bad because, in the end, beautiful or not, I have to continue the plan. I need to finish setting up the grid. Information that could save lives and provide ways to make it easier for people struggling on the mainland. The freedom to access information without it being controlled.

# II

## LILLITH

After crying for several hours, I sit in my room for the next three days, preferring to be served three meals a day like I'm locked in a cell.

I have no interest in seeing Killian.

He is no different from the men I have seen all my life except Ethan. I wish I could speak to him. He always treated me nice and with respect. He didn't give me butterflies in my stomach or an orgasm, but he tried. At times, I had to finish myself in the shower after he left. I didn't know why. I was coming into adulthood and felt like something was missing, but now I know what it was. Passion.

There is a knock on the door, and I make sure my mask is on before I pull it open. Agnes stands with a woman who is supposed to fit me for a dress so I can attend my dreadful wedding.

"Come in," I chirp.

"Miss Susan has taken the measurements already from your other clothes and would like you to pick a dress for tomorrow. Mr. Cross expects to see you downstairs in the living room, where he and the officiate can complete the ceremony."

"Thank you, Agnes."

*Bastard doesn't have the balls to tell me himself. Coward.*

I look down at the red and black lace gown of my wedding dress. He requested a light color, but I did the opposite. I wanted something dark just like the feeling in my chest. No veil. He can take off my mask if he wants to seal the deal.

The City of God has no room for religion, so there are no churches or religious practices, just a piece of paper you sign off like a piece of property. And that is what I am to him, a piece of property bought and kept in a room like an animal.

What I look like is of no consequence. It only means my genes get passed on to breed acceptable offspring so rich society can control the population. Perfect in looks and free from impurities.

I place the mask over my carefully applied makeup and straightened hair ending in a mass of chocolate waves.

*Knock. Knock.*

When I open the door, Agnes's gaze sweeps me from head to toe.

"He won't be pleased. He said a light color."

"Come now, Agnes, we don't believe in that stuff anymore. It's illegal. I'm not getting married under the eyes of the church like the old times, and we both know I'm not a virgin."

The poor woman coughs like she is choking on a piece of food. "Miss Sinclair, I'm aware, but Mr. Cross will not be pleased. He hates to be undermined." *He better get used to it.* "His request was a cream or light color for the dress. This is... black and red."

A smile tugs at my lips. "It's modern Gothic. A fave on the mainland I've heard. Isn't it spectacular? It's perfect. It goes with his mask," I explain. "He should be happy, and it shouldn't matter what I get married in anyway."

"Why do you say that?"

I close the door to my bedroom behind me and turn to face her. "Because I don't mean shit to a man like Killian Cross. I'm just here to breed like sheep."

I see her eyes lower, and I think for a second Agnes feels sorry for me, but the last thing I need is her pity.

When we reach the bottom step, I'm careful so I don't face-plant on the hard black tile. A man waits by the fireplace, followed by what appears to be a friend or someone close to Killian who I haven't met before. He doesn't look much older than Killian. When I looked up Killian Cross, trying to figure out how old he might be, it wasn't clear. They said his parents died in a car accident when he was twenty, so that would make him twenty-three to my nineteen years of age.

My heels are the only sound I hear when I cross the room. I can feel everyone's eyes on me, but the silence has me on edge. Especially Killian's eyes behind the mask. My skin grows hot, and I feel like I can't breathe in my dress. My breasts are pushed up from the bodice, and I mentally kick myself for not choosing the high-necked one. The last thing I need is for him to think I'm trying to look good for him. I tried that the other night, and it blew up in my face. I ended up crying, trying to convince myself he wasn't worth it.

All I knew was that he would never be that person for me. He hurt me, and I felt the sting. I realized that night that Killian Cross was a man who could destroy me.

Putting a wall up is my best defense, and I'll ignore any kindness he bestows upon me as a threat. I will burn before letting it touch me.

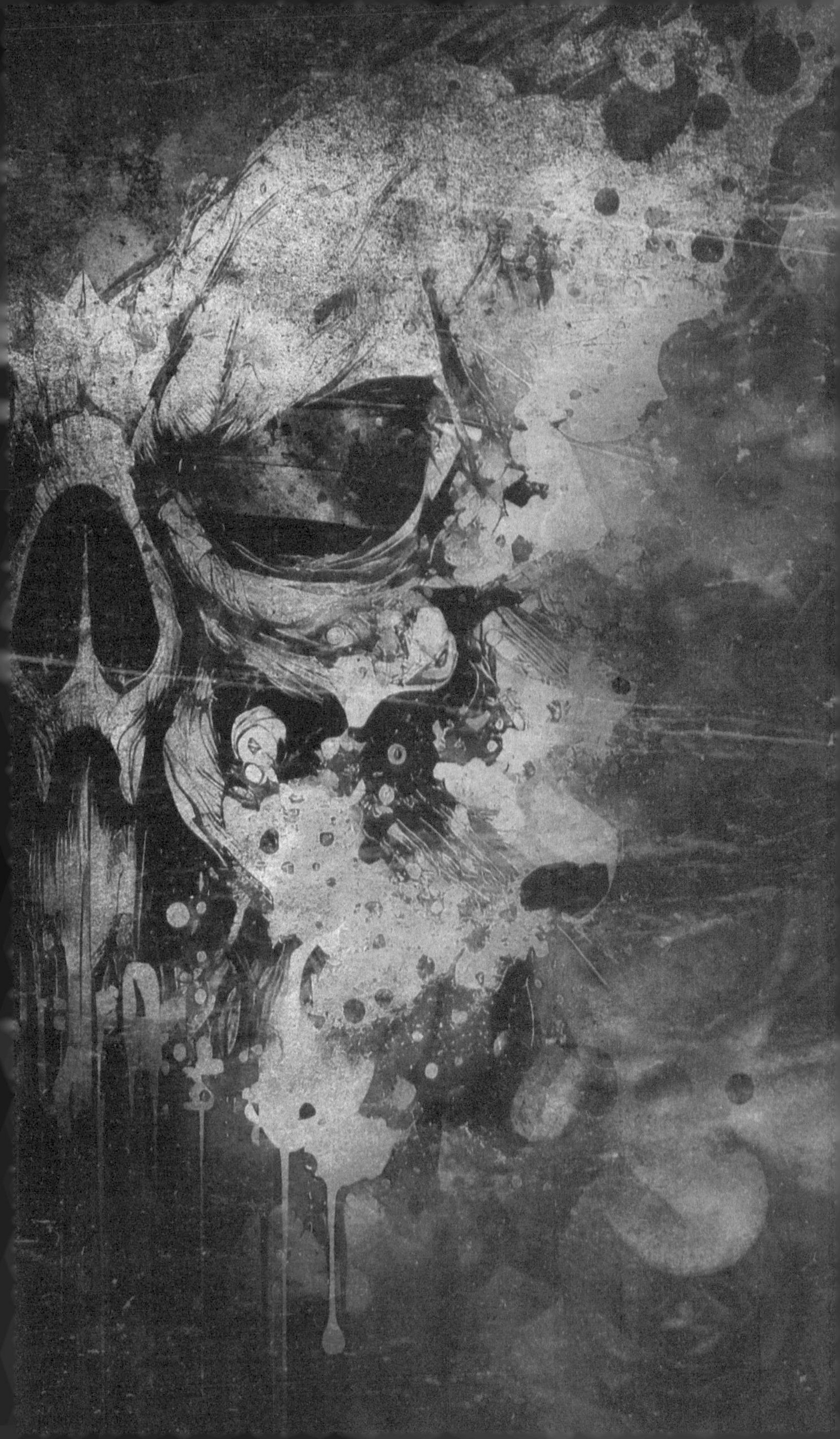

# 12

## KILLIAN

She went against my request to wear a light color, but I expected it. My mother always talked about wearing a light color when you're to be married, and I wanted to continue her wish after she passed.

There is no point in getting upset or disappointed about it. There is no way Lillith would view me with respect. I deserve it, considering how I've treated her, and I don't expect her to forgive me.

It was hurtful and cruel. I chose to be with Blair and Sarah that night over her, and she witnessed it. I knew this was a doomed marriage to begin with. I convinced myself that Blair has been through a lot and is a friend I care about. I also have known her longer. It doesn't excuse what I did, but I wasn't married. I don't even know Lillith.

"Are you ready to begin?"

I look at the priest I smuggled in from the mainland to officiate the ceremony in secret. One for the island and one for the eyes of God. One thing Lillith can be assured of is that this is the only time I'll get married. She will be the only woman who would carry my name. She also doesn't know that Father Jennings is both a secret priest and an officiate from the house of judges.

"Do you agree, Killian Cross, to take Lillith Sinclair as your wedded wife under the law of the house of judges in health?"

I look into the depths of her turquoise-blue eyes, getting lost in them. Her chocolate hair falls in waves around her shoulders. I say, "I do."

Father Jennings turns to Lillith. "Do you, Lillith Sinclair, take Killian Cross as your wedded husband under the house of judges in health?"

Those ocean-blue eyes look at my mask, pausing for a second, and I swear my heart bangs inside my chest as I wait for the two words to pass her lips. "I do," she says softly, but her eyes tell me something her lips don't.

But she said it. She's mine now. Lillith Cross is mine.

"Very well. You may seal this with a kiss to serve as a testament to your oath."

Fuck. I'm going to see her face. I feel like a kid opening a present that he has been waiting all year to see.

She tilts her head slightly so I can lean in with both hands and undo the fabric of her mask. The only thing I can hear is the pounding of my heart in my ears. The electricity runs through my veins as the tips of my fingers graze her skin as I continue to lift the fabric off her face.

The silence stretches thick. The room feels heavy. I think everyone in the room right now wants to see what Lillith's face looks like. I gently pull the black fabric off her face. Everyone holds their breath, hoping the flame from the fire doesn't blow out before it catches. When her aqua-colored eyes slide up to meet mine, I think my heart skips a few beats.

I'm frozen.

Her lips are light pink and plump. The skin is smooth and

fair with a touch of light makeup. Her hair is dark on top, transitioning to rich chocolate on the bottom in thick waves. Her dark and pronounced eyelashes contrast with eyes the color of the clearest sea.

She's the most stunning woman I have ever seen, and I'm lost in her beauty. I convinced myself that I wouldn't fall for the beautiful woman I had to marry, but nothing prepared me for...her.

I hear Ciro clear his throat. "Kill. The kiss and the ring," he whispers. I reach into my pocket, looking for the box. "The kiss, Kill," he reminds me.

*Shit.* I'm fumbling like an idiot in front of everyone. I grip the black velvet box in my hand and slide my thumbs under my mask.

Her eyes look away, and I hear her mutter, "It's okay. You don't have to take the mask off."

I pause, and she instantly grips my arms. Standing on the tips of her pointed heels, she places a soft kiss over the plastic lips of my mask.

The officiate thinks that was my intention, but it wasn't. I wanted her to see me, but she saved me from having to tear my mask off. I should be glad, but for some reason...I'm disappointed. I wanted to feel the softness of those plump lips, but I knew the reason. Deep down, I realize at that moment when her lips touched the plastic of my mask what *I do* really means. I'm married to her in name but not in her heart.

I'm pressing my teeth together, gripping the box to open it. The ring is a nine-carat flawless diamond mounted on a platinum band.

I hear her inhale when she looks at it, and I lean close, trying to make this moment special for some reason. "It was my mother's."

She nods, and I take her delicate hand, feeling the surge of electricity through our fingers. I slide the beautiful ring I used to see my mother wear all the time and smile to myself. It's perfect. It looks gorgeous on her.

I pluck my father's ring from the box and hand it to her, and she slides it on my ring finger.

"It is with great pleasure to announce Mr. and Mrs. Killian Cross."

Agnus claps with tears in her eyes, and my boy Ciro gives out a holler. "My boy is all grown up!"

All the staff are present as witnesses, and I turn to the priest. "Thank you."

"My pleasure, my son."

I can see the look of confusion in Lillith's eyes, but she doesn't say anything. Agnes hands me the bag I instructed her to pack.

Gently taking my wife's hand, I tug her closer and murmur, "Follow me." She resists for a moment, but I assure her. "I'm taking you somewhere alone, and we'll be back by morning."

I didn't have shit planned, but the last thing I wanted was to be away from her. I had to come up with something fast. There was no way I would be without her tonight.

On our wedding day, I realized it was only fair that my bride see me as the man she married. She can't possibly love me if she thinks I'm a monster. But the moment I made her mine and gazed into those azure pools, I've been unable to bear the thought of her being with anyone else.

# 13

LILLITH

I'm his in every sense of the word. Fear pools at the bottom of my heart for what my life will become. He can do whatever he wants, and no one would be able to do anything about it. Killian has my life in his hands. I'm numb.

I saved him from having to show me his face, hoping he would be relieved, but maybe I didn't want to see what he looked like. At first, I was curious, but it's for the best. The less I think about him, the better it is for my sanity. The rest of him is enigmatic.

Alluring.

He's all dark, encased in mystery. There was a moment when I wanted to see all of his perfects. He thinks that the scars on his face will turn me away, but he doesn't know that to me, it shows me his true self. Imperfection is the beauty that people judge because they are too blind to see that underneath that imperfection lies the greatest truth.

I follow him outside. The salty sea air whips my hair and dress, but he doesn't stop. He turns and pulls me gently by the hand down a lighted path toward the dock. The wind increases speed, assaulting my ears, and a heated chill slithers down my arms.

A sleek matte black boat is docked. It's long and looks like a powerful racing boat with four engines.

When we reach the end of the dock, he tosses the bag on the boat and steps in first. Turning around, he motions for me to approach.

He pulls and lifts me like I weigh nothing, setting me in front of him. I look around at the sleek vessel with the same lights as the interior of his home. The solar panels, carefully integrated into the boat's surface, absorb sunlight with precision, channeling it into the four engines that lie beneath. The interior is all sleek black with neon lights. Long screens with digital maps and GPS flicker on, sensing that someone is on the boat.

"Is this yours?"

"It is."

He slides open a dark-tinted door, and I'm greeted with warmth. Dark leather and more strips of neon lighting glow under the carpet of the interior of the boat. It has a small living and dining room, and below are steps that must lead to a private bedroom.

He places the large black bag on the table and turns to the touch screen. He presses a few buttons, and then I hear the hint of a whirl as the engines fire up.

"How are you allowed to have this? Aren't boats gas-powered? Or electrical? I don't see a way for it to be charged so far away from the house."

He leans in, concentrating on the screen, and presses another button. The boat pulls away from the dock and slowly increases speed without causing me to fall backward. "Not this one. It is both electrical and solar powered."

"I never thought a boat like this existed."

"It doesn't because I designed it. There are only two like this on the planet."

"Oh. T-that's amazing," I stammer.

"The judges on the island don't like it."

I frown, wondering why. It is safe for the planet and the ocean. Why would they not like this? It's amazing technology."

"Why?"

He turns and faces me while I zone in on the word written on the center part of the matte black mask. HATED. I wonder why he would write that when he is getting married.

"Hated can also spell death. Till death do us part," he explains like he could read my mind. "I thought it would be fitting under the circumstances. I'm almost sure I'm not your favorite person. I'm also positive that is how you feel about me—"

"You never gave me a chance."

He looks over at the screen and presses something that causes the boat to stop and anchor because I can hear a buzzing sound as it slowly lowers. "A chance?" he asks.

"To feel you," I blurt, realizing I said too much.

He straightens and turns to face me, and I take a few steps back until the back of my calves hit the edge of a chair.

His head tilts in that creepy way. "I'm right here, Lillith," he taunts, opening his arms out wide. "Come and feel me."

My knees begin to shake, not knowing how to respond. *Say something!* But my mind comes up blank for a few seconds. The silence stretches between us like a void. But then the only thing I have been wanting since I met him comes to mind.

"I-I want to see your face," I stammer nervously.

He drops his hands to his sides. "Is that all?"

I nod slowly. "Yes."

What else could I offer him right now but my body, and judging from his experience, I have nothing to offer him that would please him. It would happen eventually, but I'm in no rush.

I've read that it is customary to consummate your wedding vows on the night of your wedding, but we have none. There were no vows said. No promises of love to each other. Just a contract. Nothing special. We're nothing to each other.

"Follow me."

He walks toward the bedroom. My heart flutters, and my stomach hollows out.

*I'm not ready. No.*

When he sees that I'm not following him, he turns and sticks out his hand, motioning me to get up and go over to the bedroom. "Come on. I'm not going to bite." I get up, relieved, but his next word has a flutter of butterflies swarming between my legs. "Yet." He laughs.

I want to punch him.

"Very funny," I drawl sarcastically, "for a man who wears a mask with the word HATED scrolled across it to hide what he looks like to everyone. You have a lot of nerve to say you're going to bite me. You would have to take the thing off first."

He tilts his head back and laughs. "Patience." But then his laughter dies. "At least when you see what I look like, there is nowhere to run to unless I'm so ugly you prefer to jump off the boat into the icy waters of the ocean and freeze to death."

"That would defeat the whole purpose of me being here in the first place, wouldn't it? All that money gone to waste."

Silence.

I hit a nerve.

Good.

# I4



" **I** have plenty of money."

"Good to know," I shoot back. "As your wife, I can buy whatever I want, then."

"Do your worst, Lillith. Whatever you want, I can get. Whatever you need, I can provide."

I snort. "Cocky, too." I roll my eyes dramatically and tilt my head to the side. "Makes me wonder why?"

He inches closer to me, and I can feel the heat from his body on the swell of my breasts. He removes his jacket and tosses it toward the chair in the corner, undoing his bow tie, cuff links and dropping them on the floor.

I swallow thickly because I have to admit, he's hot, and I can't wrap my head around why. I haven't even seen his face yet. It's probably why he practically can fuck any woman he wants and probably has. *Except you.*

The heat between my legs feels suffocating. It feels like fire spreads across my thighs, and I need him to extinguish the flames.

He steps closer, his shirt feathering the skin on my chest.

The backs of his knuckles caress the skin right above the low neckline of my dress, causing my skin to prickle in awareness.

I can hear his breathing pick up behind the mask. A painful desire swirls in the pit of my stomach, wanting him to keep touching me. I don't move. I'm nervous and excited and turned on. My nipples pebble, screaming to be released from my dress, but it dies a slow death because he drops his hand and steps away.

Just like that.

I got sucked into his web, only to be spit back out like I tasted like shit.

"I think you should have a seat on the bed."

Walking away to compose myself, I take a seat and adjust the long skirt of the dress and wait.

He sits next to me on the bed and turns to face me.

Hearing him take a deep breath, he slowly lifts the mask off his face, and I swear I can hear my heartbeat slow down. The anticipation is thick in the air. The tension stretches like a band between us.

He removes the mask, our eyes meet, and my chest flutters, lost in the eyes of the most beautiful man I've ever seen. He has scars on the right side of his face and what appears to be a prosthetic eye, but it shifts color like a reptile.

His eyebrow has three permanent lines that slice right through it, reaching a big red scar on his right cheek. He's gorgeous. The scars just add to his appeal. His nose is straight, and his cheekbones are high. His lips are full and sculpted. His straight hair is the color of dark coal, and his left eye is the color of the darkest ocean.

Heartbreakingly beautiful.

His eyes caress my face, and I continue my gaze down his neck, where there is a barcode tattoo.

I whisper, "You're gorgeous."

"Don't," he chokes out.

He is, but he won't hear it because on this island, the City of God, he isn't. But to me and the female population who has a pulse, Killian Cross is fucking hot.

My cheeks heat, and his left brow rises in mock surprise. "Are you blushing?"

I look away, embarrassed about getting caught fangirling him with a playful smile.

He points at my face. "You are." I snag my bottom lip with my teeth to make myself stop, but I frown when I see that his face hardens. "Don't pity me or feel sorry for me. The last thing I want is for you to lie to me and tell me what I already know. I wanted to show you because the day is going to come when I fuck you." My eyes flick up to meet his eyes, my jaw set. His eyes search mine, but for what, I don't know. "I'm not going to be wearing it. I'm going to look you in the eyes, knowing I'm putting my child inside you."

Oh fuck.

"Then what?"

His jaw clenches. His right eye shifts like a predator, and his left eye darkens. "You bear me a kid."

"And then what?" I challenge.

He gets up from the bed. "I haven't decided."

I stand. "If you think I'm going to have a child and leave it with you so you can then get rid of me or whatever sick plan runs through that thick skull of yours, then I suggest you annul the marriage and find someone else to marry because I'm not the one."

His lip curls into a snarl. "I don't work well with threats."

"Like. I. Give. A. Fuck."

I grew up without a mother, and it seems to me he wants a child just to appease the judges by continuing his family's legacy and making me the sacrifice. A woman no one would care to look for if she goes missing. Money does things to people, like making them inhumane. Evil. My father taught me that.

I would rather die than bring a child into this world knowing he or she will not have a mother because its father is a cruel bastard on a sick power trip with an agenda.

He bares his straight teeth and dips his head. "Be careful, Lillith, you might wake up the beast. I guarantee you it will be a lot worse than what I look like," he warns. He looks at the bathroom and then back at me. "There is a change of clothes in the bag on the table. Get changed and meet me for dinner."

I raise my chin. "Why? So you can leave me there while you go in the bedroom and fuck." His eyes harden, and his nostrils flare, but I push. "I'm sure you have them holed up somewhere waiting for you. You could have saved yourself the money, you know— shack up with one of your skanks in secret and let her have your child. But that would go against the rules, wouldn't it?"

I flinch when he rushes me, closing my eyes and waiting for the blow. My father hit me a couple of times for running my mouth. I shouldn't expect anything less from him.

He lets out a breath. "You think I'm going to hit you?" My eyes pop open, and I realize I have my hands up, covering my face defensively, waiting for him to hit me. I lower them and look away. "Who hit you? And don't lie to me."

I remain quiet and move to go around him, but he grips my arm and stops me before I exit to retrieve the bag.

"I'm sorry. I run my mouth sometimes. It's none of my business who you take to your bed. You've made that clear." I rip my arm away from his grasp, refusing to answer him. I ignore the feeling in the pit of my stomach, clawing my insides, because he didn't say he was or wasn't taking anyone else to bed. He doesn't have to because he already showed me.

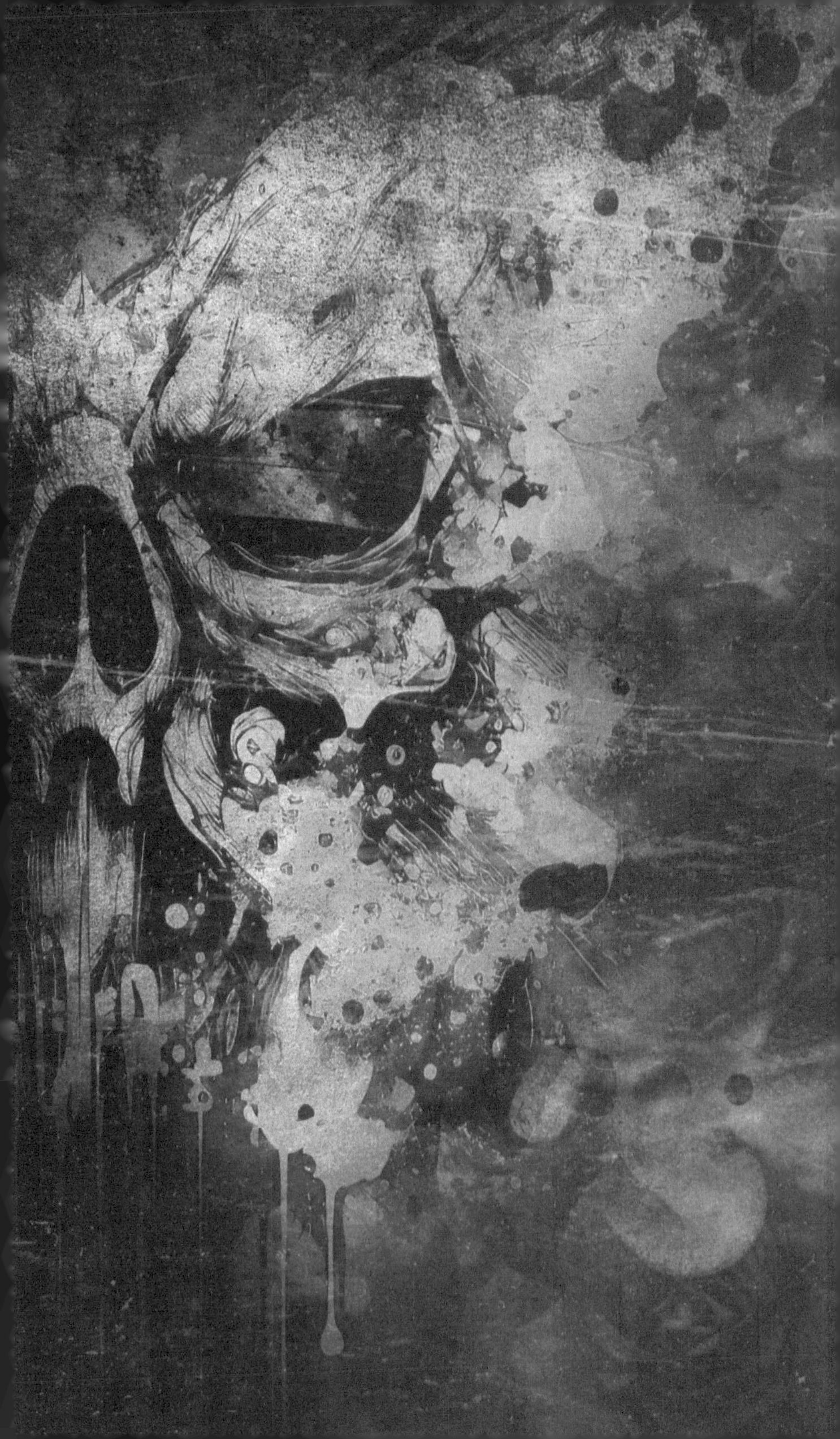

# 15

KILLIAN

"How was it?"

I look up from the screen working on the server while Ciro codes. "How was what?"

"Your honeymoon, dick," he deadpans. "I thought it would be more than a day with her, but I guess you didn't want to take it slow."

My fingers pause over the keys on the pad. "I took her on the boat alone for one day so that no one would think any different. Nothing happened except that I showed her what to expect."

"You mean you showed her your face. And?"

I steeled my jaw because it's a touchy subject for me. She is beautiful, and I'm a monster who had to pay to have a wife who looked like her.

I didn't ask her to marry me. I forced her to through her piece of shit father. It didn't take a genius to know that he hit her when she spoke her mind. I felt like an animal on the night of my own wedding. Lillith thought I would hit her.

Her reaction gutted me. Her words made me feel ashamed

of myself for the way she views me. It shouldn't matter, but for whatever reason, it does.

"And she saw the monster underneath."

He smiles. "Brother, you're too hard on yourself. The female population thinks otherwise. The only monster they think you are, is when you break their heart when they want more from you. Now that you're married, a lot of tears will be shed."

I don't want to admit that he's right. Even with my fucked-up face and eye from the car accident where I made it and my parents didn't, I have no problems finding a willing woman who would sleep with me. If anything, they like that they can't see my face, and the few who have, like Blair, think it's a turn-on.

But no one has ever told me I was gorgeous. Not after the accident.

No one but her.

I wasn't sure if she was pitying me or if it was genuine, but I couldn't take the chance. A woman raised under the rule of the judges on this island would never look at me twice. They would be disgusted and repulsed by my face.

I don't want to admit I like the way she made me feel that night on the boat. It's been a week, and I still don't understand what I feel when it comes to Lillith. I'm not ready to find out either.

"Who said there will be tears shed?"

I watch his mouth turn into a frown from the corner of my good eye and hear him suck his teeth. "Yeah, man. Why would they? You married her for a purpose. She means nothing. Killian Cross. The man and the legend on the mainland doesn't have time for love."

"In this world, love kills you. If I die, I would be no good to anyone. I wouldn't be able to save the people counting on me.

She'll get over it when the time comes. Lillith understands. She already caught me with Blair and Sarah three days before the wedding."

I hear the click of a buckle from his bag, and as soon as the words leave my mouth, I wish I could take them back. I shouldn't have said that. Hell, I wish that night never happened. It was fucked up she saw me with them, and I regret every moment of it.

He gets up, swinging the strap over his shoulder. "I gotta head back. You good here?"

I flatten my lips because I know he's disappointed in me. Ciro is a guy with feelings. A girl back on the mainland did a number and cheated on him. I didn't help the situation, but I didn't know. Ciro sleeps around but isn't serious with anyone, but neither am I. I had to marry, but marriage means something to Ciro.

"Yeah."

He shakes his head. "You know, come to think of it, I think bringing the priest was a bad idea. You should have just let one of those lackeys the judges hire do it."

And he walks out.

Great, now my best friend thinks I'm an asshole.

# 16

## LILLITH

I sit on the rocks, watching the waves crashing down below like a sledgehammer leaving white foam in its wake. The sun sets on the horizon while the waves ripple gently like it was pulsing under the streams of orange light of the sun. It feels hot and then the wind blankets a peaceful coolness on my skin. The perfect balance.

Not too hot.

Not too cold.

Behind me is a dark mansion with concrete walls and bright neon lights lining the floor like a fortress under the shadows. A direct contrast to the light.

When I look to my right, there is the dock where the electronic lifts hold two stealth-looking boats. The shiny black tops of the solar panels reflect the light coming from the sun.

To my left is the view of the City of God. Tall skyscrapers with dark tinted windows reaching far into the sky. No light pollution. The air smells purified, but it is all an illusion because where it may seem to be a sense of peace, I know the truth.

People may view the island as their savior. Their goal the government convinced them to achieve. Ultimate fulfillment to be disease and problem-free.

But even hell can mirror the kingdom of God. People began to rely on the advancement of technology to solve all their problems. It seems like the answer until it controls you.

A place created by a government showing humanity the error of their ways in order to correct the damage done to the planet. They removed religion, freedom of speech, and the freedom to share information. Containing resources by putting a price on it and labeling it with rules.

Churches were condemned. People were banned from practicing any form of religion because it didn't conform to ideals. Presidents and governments were removed to form a new government. A government where members did not need any form of monetary help to create a new order.

Selling promises to the rest of the human population, knowing that under the new system, people on the mainland who lived to work could never reach the island without sacrifice.

Women who didn't fit natural ideals of what was beautiful could never live here because they were deemed impure by the wealthy. No alteration of the human flesh was allowed because their offspring would not be given the same traits.

"Do you always come out here by yourself?"

I turn to see Killian's friend standing with a bag on his back. He seems different. Where Killian is serious in his demeanor, his friend is the exact opposite. His expression reminds me of someone who just finished smiling. Playful.

"Sometimes. When I want to think."

He walks closer and sticks his hand out. "I'm Ciro by the way."

I look at his hand, reach out, and shake it. "Lillith Sin—Lillith."

I'm not used to having a different last name, and I honestly don't feel comfortable using either one.

"It's nice to meet you, Lillith. I'm sorry I didn't introduce myself, but you were wearing a mask at your wedding, and it seemed awkward."

"Your friend wears a mask, and you talk to him."

He smiles and nods. "Good point. I guess my reason is kind of lame, isn't it?"

I shrug my shoulders and look out at the sunset. "You don't owe me an explanation, Ciro. You have no reason to get to know me."

He surprises me by sitting next to me but maintains a respectable distance. "You're married to my best friend. I think that is reason enough."

I rest my arms on my knees, drawing them closer to ward off the chill from the wind as the sun dips lower. I still find his reason to be pointless. Why would he want to get to know me? I'm no one special. I haven't been introduced to any of Killian's friends, and I think it's for a reason.

"It isn't a love match, you know. It's probably why he didn't introduce me to you or the...others. I guess that would be awkward."

Knowing his girlfriends that he lets in the house so he can screw reminds me of the way I grew up with my father. At least when I chose a person, I had enough respect to keep things personal and honest. Ethan may have never made me feel the way Killian makes those women feel when having sex, but at least he never made me feel like I was unimportant.

I shiver but don't want to go inside just yet. It was peaceful until he showed up, talking about the man I'm trying to escape from mentally.

I hear rustling and a zipper being lowered. I turn my head, and my eyes widen when he leans close to drape his jacket over my shoulders like a blanket of warmth. He smells different—spicy—and not in a bad way, but it's not Killian's smell.

I grip the edge of the black jacket to keep it from sliding off my shoulders and meet his brown eyes. "Thank you," I say nervously.

"Where are you from?"

I'm surprised by his question, and a small smile tugs at my lips. "Here."

He shakes his head and points at my face. "Your eyes are different, and your hair is dark. It's...unusual.

I arch my brow. "Unusual," I mock.

He smiles, showing me his white teeth. "What I meant to say is that I've never seen someone look like you before. On or off the island."

"Are you calling me ugly and that I'm not good enough to live here?" I tease.

He gives me a throaty laugh, and I laugh along with him, but then his expression turns serious, and he stares at me for a second too long.

I blink hard, and my thoughts become a muddled mess because I have never had a man laugh along with me and then stare at me like I did something wrong.

"My mother was Armenian," I say quietly, looking away.

The thought of my mother causes a pang inside my chest because I never got the chance to know her. She never got the chance to hold me because she was dying after giving me life. I never knew her smell or her laugh.

"I'm sorry for staring at you. I..." He pauses and takes a deep breath. "I'm sorry, but you're the most beautiful woman I have ever laid eyes on, and I mean that respectfully."

My eyes water, and I give him a sad smile. "I wish I wasn't," I whisper.

"You said *was*."

Grateful he changed the subject, I nod. "My mother died giving birth to me. I was raised by a man who was more annoyed by my existence than being his daughter. And when the opportunity came, and he fucked up, he sold me to your best friend for a large sum of money. All because I was born with this face. It was either your friend or my father's, but I think he'd rather sell me off to your friend as long as his fuckups were kept hidden."

"I'm sorry, but one thing you don't have to worry about with Kill is that he isn't a bad guy. He has a heart inside there somewhere."

"Kill?"

I heard the girls he was having sex with call him Kill, but I wondered why.

"It's what we all call him on the mainland. Kill is his alias. His handle. It's what all his friends call him."

"Oh, I didn't know that."

"He didn't mention that, did he?"

I shake my head, then stand, handing him his sweater back. "Don't worry about it. I'm kinda use to it."

He takes the sweater in his hands and stands up with a confused expression. "Used to what?"

"Not being anyone's anything." I point my thumb behind me. "I should be heading back."

He looks at the ground. "Yeah, me too." He raises his head. "I have to get to my side of the island. It was nice talking to you, Lillith." He leans close. "But you can count me in."

I pinch my brows together and ask, "Count you in?"

He grins. "As your friend."

"Oh."

He turns around and walks away toward the dock to the second boat. I watch him leave, thinking about what he said. So all his friends call him Kill. I wonder what he wants me to call him since I'm obviously not close to him that way.

# 17

LILLITH

I'm fresh out of the shower, and I'm applying moisturizer when I hear the sound of my bedroom door open and slam against the wall.

*What the hell?*

I tie the white robe around my waist and walk out to the bedroom to see who is the crazy asshole barging into my room.

I stop and freeze, looking at Agnes's worried expression with Killian towering over her. He is wearing his black mask with the upside-down cross that reads No God—the same one he wore when I first met him.

"What's wrong? Are you trying to freak me out? Because it's working."

He steps inside the room, causing Agnes to step aside while he closes the door. "Have a seat on the bed," he demands, but his voice is hard.

"Why?"

"Because I asked you to."

*Um, what?* What am I, a slave?

"You didn't ask. You demanded. There's a difference. Now what is it that you want?"

"I said to sit on the bed, wife," he demands with a hint of annoyance.

I sigh, not wanting to push him because I don't know how far he will go in punishing me, and walk toward the bed. I take a seat and close my thighs together for modesty.

He steps closer until he stands right in front of me. "You know what? I changed my mind. I would like you to stand."

I roll my eyes and stand until my face hits the middle of his chest. My head tilts, and I can see the barcode on his throat and the hard angle of his jaw under his mask. His jaw is set tight. He's upset. I can feel the anger vibrating off him and wonder why.

He takes one step back and angles his head. I can't see his eyes or his face, but I can feel his gaze shooting daggers at me. "Take off the robe."

"Excuse me?"

"I said... take off the robe. I want to see what I bought and paid for."

I flinch like he slapped me. My head turns toward Agnes, but she makes it a point to look away. I blink rapidly, knowing I don't have anyone in my corner. No one by my side to save me if this goes south.

I knew the day would come when he would want to see all of me or what I look like without my clothes. I lower my head, focusing on the red wood on the floor, and undo the tie at my waist. The center of the robe opens, and I close my eyes and let it slide over my shoulders, hearing it pool around my feet.

I feel the cold air of the room blanket my skin, causing the tiny hairs on my arms to stand. My nipples harden, and it's not because I'm aroused but from the cold.

I open my eyes and raise my chin defiantly, staring at his

mask, not caring anymore that he can see me as naked as the day I was born or that Agnes is in the room.

"That will be all, Agnes."

"Yes, Mr. Cross."

She leaves the room and closes the door with a muffled click. I can hear his audible breathing under the mask like he just finished running a marathon.

"Turn around."

I do as he asks, relieved to give him my back. "Why are you doing this?" I ask in a shaky voice.

His hand slides around my neck, wrapping his fingers around my throat and pulling me close to his warm chest, leaning close enough to my ear that I feel the smoothness of his mask on my skin. "Because I can." He pushes me toward the bed, and I place my hands flat on the mattress to keep from falling face-first. "Get on your knees and stick your ass out."

I turn my head, my hair tickling my elbows to see him with his head cocked, waiting until I can get on all fours. I place my knees on the bed like a dog, but I keep my head turned, watching him, feeling his eyes staring at my bare pussy and ass like I'm a piece of art he is studying.

I try to bring my knees together. "Stop," he snaps. "Keep them open." I try, but I'm wet. Him watching me like this is turning me on. I'm open to his gaze, and I can't see what part he's looking at, but I feel his eyes everywhere. Every inch of my skin feels like it's being lit on fire.

I hear his boots on the wood floor when he steps forward and grips the globes of my ass, spreading them wide, and I gasp. "You're wet."

My elbows shake, keeping me from jutting my ass out more. Seeking what, I don't know. I think he likes his women in this position, or maybe he doesn't like what he sees. He fucks women from the mainland who are, according to Ciro, his friends. Maybe he doesn't like what he sees. Maybe he was curious or dreads having to sleep with me, and he's trying to figure out how he'll get through it.

Maybe he's in love with the dark-haired girl I have caught him with, and he is trying to figure out how to get through it to keep up the pretense of staying on the island by having to sleep with me.

But all the thoughts scrambling in my head pause when I feel the bed dip when he places his knee right behind me with my ass in the air. I whimper shamelessly when I feel my arousal leak down the insides of my thighs. The feel of his cock in his pants when he presses it against my pussy. His fingers dig in the skin at my hips, holding me tight against him while he grinds himself over my slit.

"Mmm, you feel that, Lillith? I think you're making a mess."

I feel my pussy throb against the pulsing of his cock through his pants.

"Tell me, are you horny, Lillith? Do you need to be fucked?"

I want him to fuck me. Hard. But I would never admit that to him. My pride won't allow it. I'm not like the women who spread their legs begging to be fucked by him. He already proved to me what and who he wants and that person is not me.

"No," I grit, trying to hold back a moan.

He pushes forward and rubs my sensitive flesh with the fabric of his pants. I close my eyes, struggling not to grind my hips, letting him know that my words are lies spilling from my lips.

Please, God.

He leans over, snaking his arm around me, and his fingers hold my neck. "Liar," he whispers. "I can tell by how wet you are that you want me to fuck you. I bet you want me to fuck you like I do my friends, but here's the thing between you and me, you're not my friend. You're my wife, and you do what I say." He releases my neck and pulls my hair back hard enough so my neck arches. "Don't you ever take a man's jacket to keep you warm that isn't mine." He slides his other hand and cups my pussy from behind with his warm fingers. "This... is mine," he growls, releasing me and then pushing himself off the bed.

I turn into a sitting position on the bed, watching him adjust himself in his pants trying to make sense of what just happened. He was spying on me. He bends at the foot of the bed, and I see the robe being tossed in my face.

"What the hell, Kill?"

He stiffens, and in a menacing voice, he says, "Don't you ever call me Kill. Only my close friends call me that."

My bottom lip trembles, and I bite the inside of my lip to keep him from noticing. A surge of anger mixed with hurt filters inside my veins like I'm about to breathe fire aimed to burn. Fuck him.

"I get it. I'll be the body you paid for, but don't you ever come at me like that again. Trust me, the last thing I want to be is anything of yours. Now go and fuck your friends."

"Gladly."

I bite the inside of my lip, watching him leave my room before letting the sob escape my throat. The tears spill, and I grab my robe, walking to the shower. I turn the knob until it's scalding. The water heats my skin, almost burning. I slide down the black tiles, drawing my knees up and letting the sobs consume me. I sit there until the steam clouds the glass.

Opening the shower door, I see a razor and grip the handle in my fingers. I walk up to the mirror and bang the plastic part of the razor against the black marble of the vanity. Tears blur my vision, but I don't care.

*Bang!* The blade slides out in the sink. I pick it up, not

caring that it slices my fingers. Blood drips down my arm when I hold it close to my face, looking at my reflection in the mirror.

*Knock. Knock.*

I turn my head toward the bathroom door. "Go away!" I yell.

I hold the razor steady in my fingers a centimeter over the skin of my face, and the door bursts open. "Mrs. Cross!"

I drop the razor with a gasp, turning to face Agnes as she rushes inside with a look of horror. "Please leave me alone," I cry, holding my hands up.

She closes the distance. "Shh," she coos, wrapping her arms around me. My  shaking fingers smear blood on her neck while she holds me. "My beautiful child. Don't you dare."

Agnes has been nice to me lately. I refuse to eat at the dining table with Killian since the night I waited for him. I stay in my room and read the novels that I didn't get to read back home. I've shared my favorite ones with her, even if she always gives me curt answers and seems indifferent. But I got her to open up one night, and she told me her favorite characters. She's the only one I hold a conversation with and the last person I thought would hold me right now. No one has ever held me like this, not even my father.

"What the fuck?" Killian's voice booms behind Agnes.

I bury my face in her chest, smelling her sweet perfume mixed with copper from the blood dripping down my fingers, not wanting to see him. "Call the doctor, Killian. Now."

"What—"

"Don't question me, boy. She needs a doctor."

I hear him growl and then his voice as he talks into his watch on his wrist. "Get over here, now."

Agnes steps back and holds my hands in one hand as the blood continues to drip down my skin like red rain running down a windowpane.

Killian steps forward with a towel and applies pressure to the wounds on my fingers. I wince at the sting of pain like a million needles hitting me at once.

I see him tilt his head, and I know he's staring at the razor blade sitting on the metal opening of the sink. His head lifts, but I make a point to look away, not caring that my hands are still shaking. I appreciate Agnes draping a clean robe over my naked body.

He wraps the towel tighter over my fingers, and then, in one motion, he lifts me in his arms like a bride. "Agnes, tell the doctor to meet me in my room."

"Right away."

He carries me down the hall, my head falling against his chest. My hair dripping wet. "I got you, okay." When we reach the door that must be his bedroom, he looks at the screen on the wall. "One second, let me lift my mask, baby."

He reaches with one hand and lifts it, and our eyes meet for a split second before he bends his head slightly, and the screen scans his prosthetic eye.

"Access granted, Mr. Cross," the automated female voice says.

# 18



I'm lying in the middle of his soft bed with black and gray sheets. The bed is the only furniture in the room. Smart panels on the walls change color to reflect the time of day, creating a soothing, ever-evolving chromatic effect that evokes the sun's cyclical movement across the sky. The room's ambient intelligence adjusts the lighting to create an atmosphere as he moves around the room.

The adaptable materials in the bed modify the level of firmness, guaranteeing a restful night. A thin, unnoticeable layer of cloth laced with nanotechnology regulates temperature, creating a microclimate of comfortable warmth or refreshing coolness at the press of a button on the bedside console. It currently reads REGULATING.

The walls are covered in projected holographic screens, each featuring a different image. The themes range from tranquil natural landscapes to digital art galleries. With a wave of your hand, you can turn any area into a calming retreat, putting the world's splendor at your fingertips.

After Dr. Archer cleans and applies a specialized glue on my cuts instead of stitches, I notice he gives Killian a hard stare before he leaves.

He pushes off the wall with his shoulders and begins to remove his boots, bending at the waist to undo them.

"What are you doing?"

He straightens and removes the mask from his face. He placed it back on when the doctor arrived, but the whole time I was inside his room, he kept the pressure on my fingers with the towel, and I kept my eyes closed.

"I'm going to take a shower, and then I'm going to bed with my wife," he replies curtly, walking away.

After twenty minutes, I see him pad his way in from his bathroom, which I noticed has no door. I'm not going to lie and say I didn't want to see what he looked like without his clothes on because I do. He is always covered except for his neck and hands.

I couldn't see him in the shower from the bed. All I could do was hear the sound of the water from the shower as it hit the tiled floor. It sounded peaceful, like rain.

I snuggle deeper in the mattress, holding the sheet up to my neck because I'm completely naked. He hasn't said a word about the elephant in the room, and I'm grateful. It's not something I want to talk about right now.

All I want to do is watch him as he walks around his room with a black towel around his waist, dripping wet from a shower. He has a raised red scar that runs down his chest to the side of his ribs, disappearing in a swirl of inked demons tattooed on his skin.

The other side has scriptures and clouds with his last name wrapped around in a cross. His skin reminds me of a black-and-white art book. Books are hard to come by on the island.

The ones I have been able to buy were from Ethan. He said people on the mainland hold on to them and sell them. Like banned items being sold on the black market.

The judges banned anything printed because it was detrimental to the planet. Digitizing information was beneficial, but the purpose was to control what information could be read. Also, making it expensive to get.

Killian presses one of the panels, and it opens. I'm amazed at the advanced technology in his house. I also notice that no one cleans, but the floors remain spotless.

"How come the floors don't get dirty?"

He turns, giving me a side profile of his face, and I notice his mouth lifting in a grin when he drops the towel, showing me his perfect ass. My body grows hot, and I'm hoping the screen by the bed doesn't detect my body's temperature.

"Because they don't need to be."

"How is that possible? You need to press a button, or someone needs to come clean them. Sanitize them."

He slides on a pair of tight boxer briefs that mold to his strong thighs and narrow hips. When he turns around to face me, my eyes immediately travel south to the huge bulge between his legs. *Okay, he's huge.*

"Not this house. I designed it that way. The floors are equipped with a technology that steams, sanitizes, and cleans themselves. It saves time and money. I'm not the type to hire people to clean floors with chemicals the judges make money on because they ensure they are safe for the planet."

"You don't agree with them?"

"I don't follow their vision."

Hm. Killian doesn't like authority. It makes sense, but I also gauge that he's smart as hell. Genius-level smart.

"Did you create it? Just like the boat?"

He pulls the sheet gently, and I lift my hands, feeling the cold air caress my skin.

His eyes roam my naked body, and a flush creeps up my cheeks. "Holy shit," he mutters. My eyes lift when he slides into the bed, automatically feeling the warmth from his body.

We face each other, and he pulls the sheet over my shoulder, making sure I'm comfortable. I keep my hands together so the cuts don't open under the gauze.

"Yes. That's what I do."

"What is that exactly?"

"I create new technology, but I also create the kind the government cannot control. Freedom."

I swallow thickly because that means he's a god to the antichrist. Now, it makes sense. That is why he hides out here in his dark estate.

"What do you like to do?" he asks. I bite my lip as I think about it. No one has ever asked me that question. He slowly pulls my bottom lip away from my teeth with his thumb. "Don't bite that pretty skin, gorgeous."

My heart begins to beat faster, and my stomach flutters when he calls me gorgeous. It means more for some reason when he says it, making me forget how mean he was to me earlier.

"I like to read books."

His lips curl into a smile. "Aren't you a little rebel? What kind of books?"

"The banned kind. Physical books."

"How did you get them?"

He knows they don't sell them on the island, and there is only one way to get them—from the mainland.

"I had someone bring them without my father finding out."

"Living dangerously," he teases.

I giggle. "You should try it. It helps pass the time. You can read about relationships, love, and children. You live one life, but you can live so many through the characters in books. The fun part is that you can choose which world, and if you don't like it, you can find another one, and no one gets hurt." I slide my pinky finger on the side of his face where his temple is. "Right there. You bring them to life, and they can become part of you in your mind. It's a way of freedom when you feel trapped in the life you are currently in. The best part? No one can take that from you."

"What type of books?"

"Romance, suspense, erotica."

He arches a brow. "I like the last one."

I let out a laugh. "I'm sure, but I don't know how you would feel about three guys and one girl."

His face grows serious. "Make sure that stays in the book and not in your mind."

"Why? I figured you were into that stuff. Literally."

His expression goes dark, and his right eye shifts like something sinister possesses him. "Never with you."

"Oh." My lips turn into a frown.

And just like that, the moment is ruined when it comes to the topic of sex. I may be pretty, but I'm not his type sexually, and I have to accept that. His answer is clear. *Never with you.* He didn't have a problem having sex with two girls at the same time.

He reaches over and touches the screen by his bed. Turning off the lights in the room, the neon lights on the floor flick on. I'm hoping he doesn't feel like he has to babysit me, so he has me here in his room.

"Cross?"

"What is it, Lillith?" he says in a tight voice.

A single tear slides down my cheek at his hard tone. "I just want you to know that I wasn't trying to kill myself. I-I wanted you to know that."

Silence.

But I felt it.

His judgment.

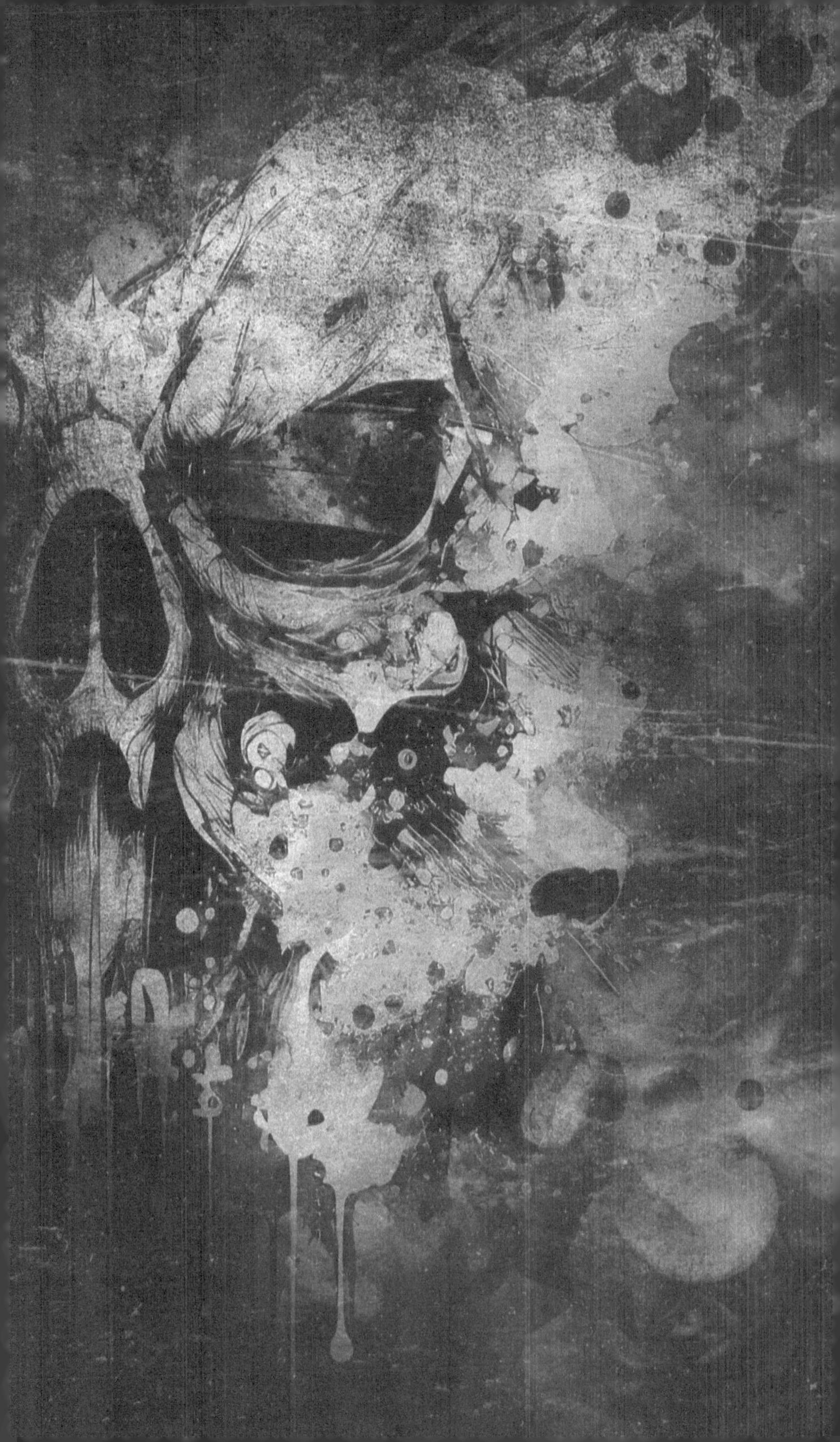

# 19



It's been three days, and I refuse to let her sleep in her room. Agnes said she was about to cut her face when she barged in on her. And it was because of me and the shitty things I said to her. The things I made her do.

How could someone so beautiful want to destroy what people would kill for? Agnes was right about her. I see the way the old woman looks at her when Lillith isn't looking. She likes her.

So does Ciro, and I acted like a jealous asshole when I saw through the outdoor camera the way she smiled at him. I lost it when he draped his jacket over her shoulders. I know Ciro wouldn't try anything, but I also made it seem like I don't care about her in that way.

"It's race night. Are you bringing her?"

I zip up my bag and drop it on the floor, unplugging the drives and scanning what I need. "Yeah, she can't stay here alone."

I refuse to tell him about the other night and her trying to cut herself. I check her fingers when she sleeps to make sure they heal like they should. I also watch her, memorizing every curve of her face and the shade of her full lips. I even smell her hair when it's spread out on the pillow.

She's perfect.

And I'm a monster.

"Why? Is everything alright? Is someone threatening you?"

I pick up the bag and hand it to him. "No. Not yet anyway. She needs to be with me at all times, Ciro. That is all you need to know."

"Good. I think she's nice. Has she ever been to the mainland?"

Shit, I've never asked her. I just assumed because of the book thing. That also reminds me. "Hey, do you still have that contact who gets all the physical books?"

He snorts. "Yeah, but what the hell do you need physical books for when you can hack the vault those evil assholes have locked up and get them for free digitally?"

"Can you call the guy or not? It's for Agnes."

I hate lying to my best friend, but I don't want him to think more into it, and frankly, it's none of his business because the conversations I have with Lillith are mine, and no one needs to know what we discuss. Especially what she likes and what she's into. It's personal.

"Relax, brother. Of course. What do you need?"

I tell him, and he laughs. "Alright, I got you. I'm sure I'll have them before we leave. I'll make room for the boxes."

# 20



I have never been to the mainland. My father told me it's forbidden, and that I couldn't get off the island for safety reasons. I heard his associates talk about the mainland and how they need to regulate it so they can help others to the island.

I know it's bullshit because the population on the island only increases when someone is born or when someone is let on because they work for someone.

Since I've already been on one of Killian's boats, I know my way around. I sit on one of the couches and stare at my phone.

Maybe I'll run into Ethan. I shouldn't think about him, but he was an important part of my life. He was so heartbroken when I left. I hope he's doing alright, and as sad as it sounds, I hope he's found someone to spend time with. It would be selfish of me not to want the best for him.

It doesn't matter if Killian calls me gorgeous or pretty. I've been called that by many. He's probably just being nice because he knew I broke down and wanted to cut my face. He knows what would happen if I succeeded. I wouldn't be able to show my face in upper-level society ever again. I'd probably be banished like he was.

Scanning the interior of the second boat Ciro came on, I didn't count on him bringing guests. Guests like the three girls currently giving me dirty looks while Ciro and Killian are busy navigating the boat across international waters.

The dark-haired girl I've caught my husband fucking twice before we were married strides up in a short skirt with ripped fishnet stockings and a shirt ripped in the center, exposing her bra and the small swell of her breasts. She sits opposite me in the seating area, crossing her shapely legs encased in boots that reach to her thigh. "So how's married life?" she asks with a knowing smirk.

Turning my head to the side, I let my hair spill over. I decided to change my look by straightening it and wearing a full suit with knife boots that hit mid-thigh. I give her a sarcastic smile. "How's single life?" I shoot back.

She snickers sarcastically. "You've got a bite."

"You don't want to find out how hard."

The blond one plops down next to her, wearing a similar outfit, except her shirt is tied to her waist, exposing her stomach. "Damn. You have a sharp mouth from that beautiful face."

"She's not that beautiful."

"Shut the fuck up, Blair. You know she is." The other girl with brunette hair and a ripped jean skirt sits on the other side and turns to face me. "I'm Sydney by the way. You already know Blair." *Bitch.* She points at the blonde. "And this is Sarah. We all grew up together. Then we met Ciro, and Ciro introduced us to Kill."

Blair leans close to Sarah and plays with a strand of her hair while the boat picks up speed, cutting through the waves. "We've been tight ever since."

"That's nice. You're all tight and shit."

Blair smiles coyly. She reminds me of Elvira, old but still looks young in a weird way. It's like you can't tell her age, and she's stuck in her mid-forties.

"Hmm. Especially, Kill." *This bitch.* She's baiting me for a reaction. Too bad she isn't getting one. She leans forward and calls out, "Right, baby? It's us tonight. Right, Kill?"

I look over, but he's distracted with Ciro looking over at something on a screen, and my stomach clenches. *He wouldn't.*

"Kill?" she repeats. "Right?" He looks up over at her with his black mask on that reads DAMNED. "Right, Kill?" she purrs.

"Yeah," he rushes out and looks back at the screen.

My stomach sinks, and I fist my hands by my sides, looking away. But Blair doesn't stop until she makes a point of taunting me. "Like I said, tight."

WHEN THE BOAT docks on the mainland, I step out and instantly scrunch up my nose at the smell. It smells like something rotten. What the hell?

"Smells differently, doesn't it, princess?" Sarah snips.

I'm about to step on the dock, but strong hands grip me by my waist and lift me in the air. "Be careful and stay close to me at all times," Killian cautions, placing me on the wood dock. I avert my eyes to look down the dark tunnel. *Right.*

"Got it."

His head tilts, gripping my chin softly with his fingers to turn my head back to him. "You alright?"

*No, you just agreed to fuck your friends or girlfriend later tonight right in front of me.*

"I'm fine," I chirp.

"Kill, come on. We're going to be late," Blair calls out, walking away.

"Let them wait," he snaps.

My head turns, and I see the hurt look in her eyes when she turns around.

She's in love with him. He probably feels the same, and I'm just a necessary evil in the way. I get it now.

"You have to get going."

He nods, and I follow him, understanding he could never be mine where it matters most.

We walk until we reach a sleek black classic gas-powered vehicle. *Wow.*

I smile as excitement runs through me. I've never been in one.

He opens the door and throws the bag in the back seat. I look over, and another vehicle is parked behind it on a deserted street. There is garbage and piles of metal everywhere.

I watch as Ciro opens the door, and Sarah and Sydney slide into the back seat of the second car.

Blair walks over to us and opens the door. She is about to sit in the front passenger seat, but Killian taps the roof of the car. She pauses halfway in the seat and she looks up. "Blair, go ride with Ciro."

"But?"

"I said, go ride with Ciro," he says in a stern tone.

She gets out and slams the car door, almost shoulder checking me as she stomps like a petulant child over to the other car. She opens the door with a harder force than necessary and glares at me before she slams the door.

I hear a string of curses coming from Killian, and he walks back around the car.

I already feel like I'm in the way and should have convinced him to let me stay on the island. "It's okay, Cross. I can ride with Ciro, and she can ride with you. It's really no trouble."

He opens the door harder than necessary and waits for me to slide in. "No."

Not wanting to make him more late than he is already to his event, I slide into the vintage muscle car, smiling to myself when I feel the leather and see the vintage gauges.

He leans inside and secures the seat belt over me; the heat and cologne coming off his body have me clenching my thighs together. He turns his head, his mask facing me. "Remember to stay close to me. Always."

"Always," I repeat with a smile.

He gets in the driver's side. My stomach somersaults in excitement when he places the car in first gear, and I hear the sound of the loud engine roaring and the tires screeching as it kisses the pavement, speeding down the road.

I look out the window, trying to catch the catastrophic state of the mainland. The buildings look uninhabited and deserted. Wires and metal poke out. There are tents, and people live in the street. Neon lights hang on what seems like old shops. Mechanical robots line the streets, picking up metal and tossing it into a huge pile with a single bright light.

"It's bad, isn't it?

I glance at him. "Yeah, I wish I could help." I look at all the people living on the streets, looking for food.

"You are. By helping me keep playing both sides."

I feel good about that but also sad that it has to come to that for him. He sacrifices his life to make it better for everyone living here struggling to live normally. Even if I find him attractive and wish for things to be different between us, I know in his eyes, I will always represent what he's trying to take down.

It's dark, and the roads are littered with debris until we reach what used to be a stadium with bright lights and people walking toward what looks like a huge event with floating droids and holographic screens. It reminds me of a darker version of the island, but at least here, people laugh and smile, living carefree in the chaos. They're not uptight with serious faces looking for more power and greed while people suffer in filth.

He maneuvers the car to park, and I love how his arms flex when he shifts gears. It looks like the car was built for him.

Blair walks over from the other car while Ciro lets the girls out from the back seat. Killian opens my door when I unclip the seat belt. "Ugh, what's wrong with her hands? Are they broken?"

When I step out, I meet Ciro's gaze. His lips are tight when Killian shuts the door. "No, that is what a husband does for his wife. He opens the door for her," he adds, giving me a wink.

"Stop being bitchy, Blair," Sydney chides, walking after Ciro.

Blair strides off in a huff. "Whatever."

After Ciro and Killian lock up the cars, they walk ahead, and I trail a couple of steps behind him with Sarah.

"I'm going to catch up with Blair," Sydney says, running up to her.

"He likes you."

I glance at Sarah, confused. "Huh? Who?"

"Your hubby, silly. He likes you."

"You mean he likes Blair."

She snorts. "I think you have it all wrong. Blair is obviously in love with Kill. Has been for years." The wheels in my head turn, thinking about the two of them. *No.* "I have never seen him hold the door open for a girl. Ever. Even though he wears a mask, and it can look creepy sometimes, you can tell he's always staring at you because that mask may hide his face, but it doesn't hide the spark of heat coming off you two."

There is no way. She is just messing with me so it can all blow up in my face. Her loyalty is to Blair, not me. We walk the rest of the way in silence until we reach a lift taking us all the way to the top. When the doors open, I hear rumbling and feel the floor vibrating like the earth is shaking.

*Vroom! Vroom!* My hair whips to the side, and I take a step back, watching two motorcycles pass with so much force, I have to place my hands over my ears.

The smell of something burning from the heat of the motorcycles burns my throat. People scream so loud it causes my ears to ring.

I smile when I hear the beat of the music and see a holographic robot coming out of the screen, dancing to the beat. It looks like it is hovering over the crowd.

The crowd goes quiet, and a guy on the microphone screams with his hands up. "He's here! The man. The legend. Kiiiiillllll!" I smile when In This Moment's "Beasts Within" makes its way over the sound system, and the crowd goes wild. The screen displays a live feed of Killian.

My eyes scan the entire setup. This is wild. He's like their dark hero.

Girls flash him their tits and scream, "I love you, Kill!"

Another one. "Marry me!" *Sorry, ladies.*

My eyes narrow when Blair walks up to him and wraps her arms around his waist. I look away angrily. My stomach clenches in knots, filling my insides with jealousy and causing me to slow down my steps, letting them walk ahead. He probably won't even notice if I slipped through the crowd and left. *I should have stayed on the island.*

I look and see an exit sign written in graffiti. GET THE FUCK OUT. The entrance side says MAKE SURE YOU COME INSIDE.

The judges banned cans of paint years ago. Maybe I can

find things here. Ethan told me they accept money if it's untraceable when scanned. I brought my phone that gives me access to a special account I had made for Ethan to use to buy me books. Hopefully, it's still active.

Before Killian can turn around, I step away in the whirl of the crowd among the chaos and make a run for the exit as fast as my boots allow me. I make it down the metal steps as people give me weird glances, but I make sure to look away and act like I know where I'm going.

When I return to the lot, there are all types of obsolete vehicles, some with different parts. I run between the cars, trying to get as far as I can before anyone notices I'm gone.

I pull out my phone and dial, hoping Ethan still has the same number.

"H-hello?"

I smile. "Ethan," I breathe.

# 21



"I can't believe you're here."

I glance at Ethan in his small car. "I didn't think you would answer me, to be honest."

"I'll always answer for you. What were you doing at the arena?"

"I was tagging along."

"With who?" He glances at my hand, and I pull it away from his gaze. "You're married."

"Yep," I chirp. I don't want to go into the details, so I cover my wedding ring with my hand.

He drives the car, and we stop at an old strip mall with various spaces selling different items mixed with living spaces on top. It's like one big mash-up.

One of the flashing neon signs catches my attention, and it looks like someplace where they conduct ancient rituals. I'm intrigued and want to go inside like it's calling me. I'm not superstitious or anything, but it could be fun.

It's better than watching my current husband pay attention to his side chick while I sit there and watch with my heart in my throat.

I point at the sign. "I want to go in there."

Ethan gives a little laugh. "Are you serious?"

I open the door. "Yeah, I'll be right back. You'll wait for me, right?"

"I'll be right here, Lillith. I won't leave you."

I smile warmly. "Thanks, Ethan."

I run across the street, avoiding people with their dirty clothes looking through the piles of debris. I reach the door and press the old, dimly lit button that makes a cracking sound.

Suddenly, a buzzer goes off. I pull the door open, and when I step inside, I cough at the weird smell of something burning.

"Hello?"

"I've been waiting for you, my dear." I pause, looking at an older woman sitting in the chair, staring straight ahead. I feel a rush of chills over my arms, and it's not even cold inside. I stare at her for about a minute, but she continues to stare straight ahead.

I wave my hand in front of her face. "I'm blind, not dumb, my dear. I can feel you."

Looking around the dirty shelves with candles burning and different symbols drawn on the walls under black lights, I glance back at the woman. "My name is—"

"Lillith."

*How did she know that?* A sudden awareness creeps over my skin. Like an electrical charge of energy causing my tiny hairs to spike.

I jolt when a black cat jumps on the table next to her with yellow eyes. It walks toward her and lies down. I didn't know people kept animals around anymore. Domesticated animals are banned from the island due to the spread of disease, but they are obviously allowed and kept as pets here.

"You can pet it, my dear. I'm sure your husband wouldn't mind getting you one."

There is no way she can see that I'm married unless she's full of shit and fucking with me. I reach out, and the cat rubs his head against my hand. I smile as I pet his head. His fur feels so soft and warm.

"They have a good judge of character, and it will be good to ward off evil. The kind that wants to destroy you and your husband." She points at the dusty old chair. "Have a seat. We have some things to discuss before he comes looking for you."

I sit, looking around the dusty walls. "Who?" I ask.

I glance at her when the chair groans as she leans forward and lowers her voice. I hear the words spill from her chapped lips. "The man linked to your soul. Your one true protector. You're the love of his life, even if he denies it."

"Ethan?"

He's the only one I can think of because my husband doesn't want me. He hasn't even kissed my lips.

She shakes her head. "That poor young man is more in love with where you were created than who you really are."

"What do you mean where I was created?" I ask, searching in her blank eyes for a clue that she's pulling my chain. They are the color of a pale blue sky.

"True evil can create beautiful things, but sometimes creating something that serves you can be your own destruction. You are pure-hearted. You can sense them since the day you were born. Your mother was a sacrifice for the greater good. You are the woman who will continue the lineage your husband wants to create. He is the creator, is he not?" *She's talking about Killian.*

Not in the way you think?"

She gives me a creepy laugh. "You have to be careful, my child, because when they find out about you and him together, they will try to destroy you. If they end your life, they will end his."

I shake my head. "I don't understand?"

"He can't exist without you, Lillith. He can't breathe without you. He just hasn't felt the air in his lungs cease yet, but soon, he will."

She's wrong. If it were up to him, I wouldn't be in his life.

"Thank you, but I'm sorry. You're wrong. I've seen it with my own eyes. I'm a means to an end. I have no one—I'm no one," I confess.

The cat rubs his head against my hand and jumps into my lap, purring.

"You are the beginning, my dear. The one with the mask will destroy anything and everyone for you. Have faith." She gets up, and so do I. "The love you have waited for is here to claim you." She dismisses me, disappearing into the back behind a black curtain. *Weird.*

Walking out, I look both ways before crossing the street. Ethan gets out and follows me to the passenger side. A deep rumble of an engine pulls up fast, then brakes hard with a squeal, blocking Ethan's car. The driver's side door opens forcefully by a pissed-off Killian.

*Shit!* He found me.

He rushes up to Ethan and growls, "Who the fuck are you?"

Ethan takes a step back, pushing me behind him. "D-do what you want to me, but leave her out of it."

"It's okay, Ethan," I assure him.

He turns his head. "Are you crazy? Do you know who that is—"

"Kill." Killian interrupts him. "And her husband," he adds.

"You're married to him, Lillith? He's dangerous. He's one of them."

I don't know what he means by "*one of them,*" but I have to go back.

Killian steps close in Ethan's face. "Give me a reason I shouldn't break your fucking neck right now." He points at me while he backs Ethan down. "Lillith, get in the car!"

Ciro comes up behind me and whispers, "Get in, Lillith."

"Don't hurt him. I called him," I explain. "I know him."

"No, you don't, princess." Killian replies. Cocking his head to the side, he holds a gun with a laser pointed at Ethan's head. "He's a scavenger. They try to woo women by getting on the island to give them money so they can run their own twisted operation back here."

"No, it wasn't like that with her," Ethan defends. "Please, don't hurt her," he pleads. "I love her."

I see Killian stiffen, and behind me, Ciro mutters, "Shit."

Killian presses the gun to Ethan's temple with a growl. "She's mine. If you go near her again, I'll shoot you on the spot," he warns. "The only reason I don't splatter your brains all over your pathetic excuse of a car right now is because she called you, and you didn't know. "

He pushes the tip of the gun off his head, causing Ethan to fumble backward, and tucks it behind the back of his pants. He turns around, walks to the front passenger side, and opens the door, but Ethan walks closer.

Killian points at him. "I'm warning you, you little fucking troll." Ethan places his hands up in mock surrender.

"Come here, Lillith," Killian demands, his voice laced with steel.

I walk over because what choice do I have? He will pick me up and toss me inside the car, and who knows what he will do with me.

"I'm sorry, Ethan."

# 22



I'm surprised Blair wasn't riding with him. She was already getting handsy with him at the arena.

When I slide inside the car, I remember to pull the strap and buckle myself in.

"Why did you do that? You didn't have to threaten to end his life like he was some sort of animal."

He shuts the door and turns the key to fire up the car. I see his hands on the top of the steering wheel, gripping it until his knuckles turn white. "Who is he to you?"

My tongue slides over my bottom lip, not knowing how to answer him without pissing him off further. How do I tell him that in a fit of jealousy, I ran away and called a friend to pick me up? The friend I lost my virginity to. A friend I've slept with more than once.

It looks bad, but I had no intention of ever sleeping with Ethan again now that I'm married to Killian. My circumstances are not what I envisioned in a marriage, but I'm wearing his ring. Trying not to make matters worse, afraid that he would kill Ethan, I decide to go the safer route. Telling the truth but not the whole truth unless he asks specifically.

"He worked for my father at the house."

He pulls out on the road, and I notice from the side mirrors that Ciro follows us. "Did you fuck him?"

I squeeze my fingers between my thighs and close my eyes. "Yes," I croak. "It was before you."

He laughs sarcastically. "So you disappeared and left with a man you used to fuck. Tell me why I shouldn't turn this car around and blow his fucking brains all over the place."

"The same way I don't use your gun and blow Blair and her little sidekick's brains all over the place," I quip. "Let's have at it. Let's turn around and line them up execution style. One for fucking me and the two for fucking my husband—which I might add I have seen with my own eyes. To top it off, she had her hands all over you at the arena, and you told her that you would meet her after for a late-night quickie while your wife was sitting right there." I raise my voice on the last part.

His head snaps to glance at me briefly. "I didn't agree to shit."

"Oh yes, you did." I laugh on a breath. "On the boat, you said yeah. She asked, and you agreed in front of my face because, in her eyes, you guys are tight and shit."

"I was distracted, and I'm sorry if you thought that. On the track, I thought it was you. I—"

He did?

I think about the conversation on the boat and know Blair is trying to hang on to what they had before. He was looking at the screen and probably wasn't paying attention to what was said. I didn't stay long enough at the arena to gauge his reaction.

"Look, I know I shouldn't have left like that. It was dangerous, and I wasn't thinking. Nothing is going on between Ethan and me. We are just friends. He was the only person I could talk to."

"I see that," he snaps.

He's pissed. The same way I was with Blair. Good, now he knows how it feels. It's not like he's made an effort to apologize, but I'm not like him.

"I'm sorry for leaving like that."

"Don't do it again. If you need to ask me something, then ask. If a woman tries to insinuate something, tell me. I'll let you know."

Yeah, but that isn't good enough. You didn't say you wouldn't. Only if you would.

Turning up the volume of Depeche Mode's "It's No Good," he shifts the car hard, pressing the gas.

Our conversation must be over.

I notice we're heading deeper into the mainland. The buildings are closer together. I look out the window where machines claw large amounts of metal into different piles from collapsed buildings.

The lights on the streets fade to a purple glow. The buildings on each side of the road begin to look similar to the skyscrapers on the island, but they have dark windows and look deserted. I notice the roads look more paved as the cars eat up the distance like we're in a more established area of the mainland.

Killian shifts the car, decreasing his speed. His hand reaches over to unhook the seat belt and tugs me gently toward him. The car slows down even further. He lifts me onto his lap, and I sit between his legs.

My hands begin to shake. I've never driven a car before.

Only electric cars are allowed on the island, and they are all self-automated. The purpose was to reduce accidents and have safe emissions. You could always shut off the self-automation feature and drive around, but no one does that.

Maybe that was how Killian's parents died in an accident. Maybe they decided to drive, but that wouldn't make sense if Killian is so skilled in driving both. They must have taught him. My father found no use in teaching me—or allowing anyone to teach me. When I asked, he said I should make better use of my time like finding a husband.

Killian places my hands on the steering wheel, and I shake my head, slowly telling him I can't. He places his hands over mine, entwining our fingers so we're both gripping the shiny black steering wheel.

He slides my hair to one side, watching the road while I settle between his legs, feeling the hardness of his cock through his pants. He releases one of his hands, keeping my other hand on the steering wheel. I don't think he has to change gears because the car glides down the street at the same speed.

The thrill of adrenaline runs through my veins behind the wheel of the powerful car sitting between his legs. I'm still upset at him, but right now, the excitement of being here with him has me forgetting everything except this moment.

I have to admit I'm jealous when it comes to Killian. I'm attracted to my husband, and I crave for him to touch me. The fact that I can't see his eyes or the expression on his face when he touches me drives me insane.

It's a dirty torture that makes me wet.

His hand slides between my thighs, and I gasp when he presses his fingers over the fabric covering my slit.

My heart flutters, filling with the sizzle of electricity right down to my pulsing clit. I'm hot under my bodysuit, and I want it off so I can feel his hands on my skin.

I can't release the steering wheel, and he can't hear me over the music when a moan escapes my parted lips. I'm shamelessly wet, and it feels so good when he touches me. The heat pools between my thighs while he rubs my clit, my hips grinding on his fingers, seeking release. The man knows what spot to hit, sliding his finger over the fabric and pushing it deep into my pussy. It is the only thing keeping him from finger fucking me.

My nipples are hard under the fabric. I arch my back slightly so my ass can rub against the hard ridge of his cock, letting him know I can feel it. I'm trying to keep my eyes on the road, not knowing where I'm going. I see Ciro's car pull in front of us, taking the lead, and I'm relieved.

The music shifts to "Adrenalize" by In This Moment. The goth metal rock filters through the amazing speakers of the car while he increases speed, circling my clit and adding another finger while I grind my hips into him.

I can feel his warm breath, causing chills to erupt over the sensitive skin of my neck. I'm close to coming, and I think he knows it. My hands grip the wheel harder, holding on, and my knuckles turn white when he pushes his cock against my ass.

*Fuck.* One more flick and he circles back around my clit with his finger. Another loop and another. *Shit.*

My thighs open wider, and he pushes one finger in with the fabric and rubs my clit with the other. *Right there. Please don't stop.* He doesn't. He pushes me into him with his hand on my pussy, rubbing his dick against my ass as he holds me. His fingers increase speed. My head sags against him, but my eyes stay on the road.

"Come for me, Lillith." He throws the car into gear, presses his foot on the gas, and turns the wheel to go around Ciro's car.

My eyes widen, and he touches the right spot to get me

over the edge of my climax. "I'm coming!" I moan loud, the streetlights flying past us.

It feels like I'm flying at the same speed. The streetlights seem brighter, but I know it's because my body got what it craves. Release.

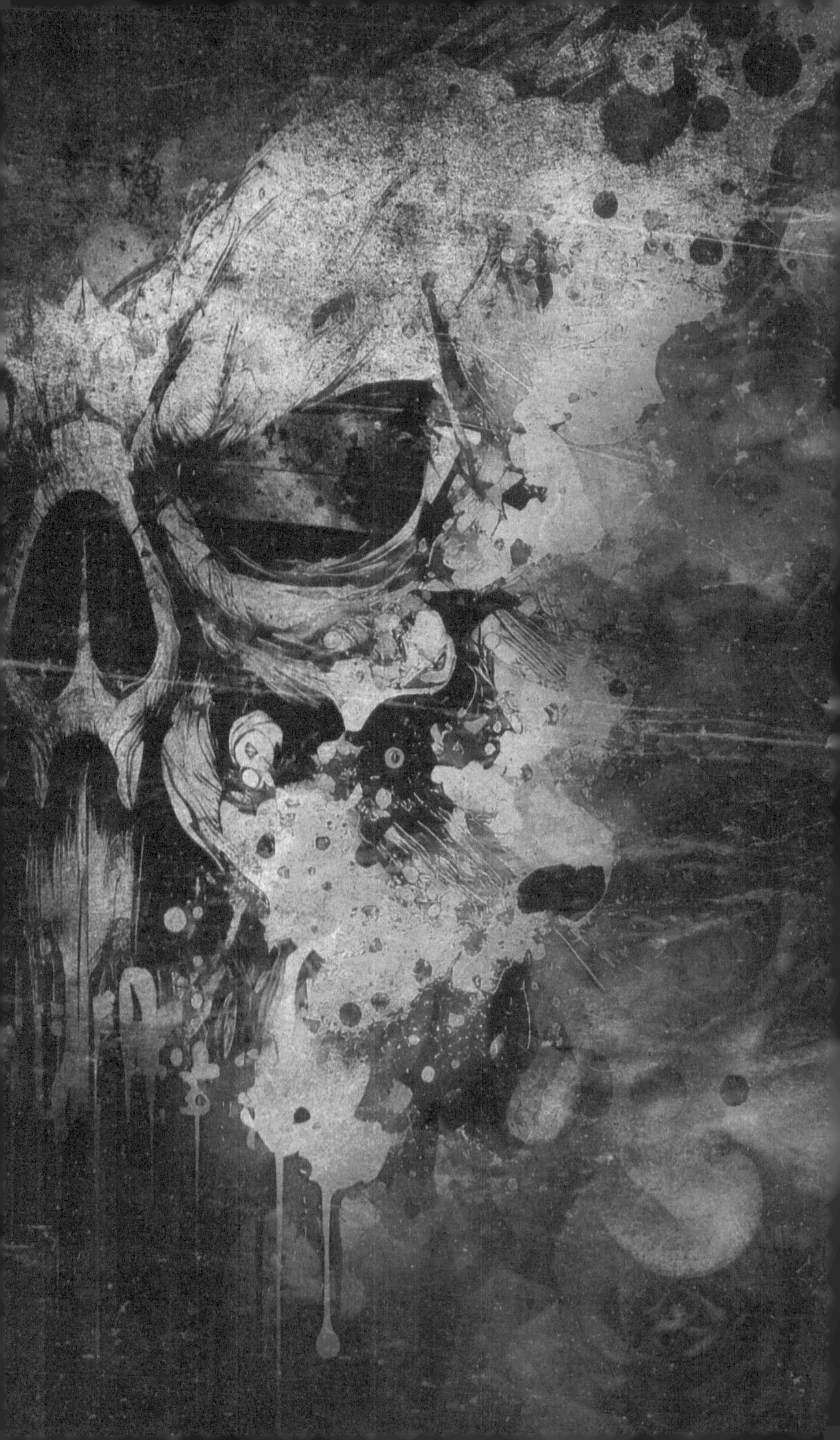

# 23

### KILLIAN

"**I** saw that you let her drive."

I look up after opening my bag to get one of my dress shirts and see Ciro's smirk. "Something like that."

We're at my place called the Cocoon. It is the hub I have on the mainland under a building. It is where I place the servers and hide them from the droids that the judges have patrolling the city. They use them to detect hackers to keep them from creating their own networks or grid, but they don't have the ability to detect anything once it's a certain depth underground.

I've breached their firewall and removed this location from their routes. To them, this location doesn't exist on the map.

"Dude, I can tell she was on your lap from the rearview mirror." He raises a brow. "Having second thoughts about the way you feel about her?" He leans on the wall by the massive screen pinpointing the location of all the droids patrolling the city tonight.

"She's my wife, Ciro. The point was to marry her and fuck

her so she can give me a kid. It wasn't to buy her flowers and take her on fake romantic dates. I think by me buying her off her father, she understands this isn't a love match. Things like that don't exist anymore."

"They existed for your parents. You weren't created out of convenience."

My jaw hardens when the subject of my parents comes up. They loved each other in the traditional way. They fell in love at first sight. The kind of love that doesn't exist anymore in this new world. Everything is based on interest, power, looks, and convenience.

"Look what that got them. I'm sorry, but look around us. The people we are trying to save from poverty, going hungry, and trying to free don't have time to think about love. I certainly don't." He pushes off the wall and plops in the chair in front of the computer. "She's nice to look at. I'm a man, and I know I'm married to the most gorgeous woman, but I can't lose my head just because she has a perfect face and body."

He shakes his head. "Yeah, that's why you were about to blow up her little boyfriend back there when you found them together. I know that guy is a scavenger, and he's a bottom-feeder who works on the island hustling for a buck, but it was obvious."

I zip the bag harder than necessary, almost breaking the zipper as I remember the rage I felt and what I said when I saw her with another man who was about her height. He wasn't bad looking, but the look in his eyes and how he stood in front of her like I was some crazy fucking psycho who would hurt her.

"What was so obvious? That my little wife is clueless when it comes to the mainland and ran away thinking she could escape me because she's a little pissed off that Blair was pouting like a jealous ex-girlfriend."

"The part where that idiot she was with is in love with her, and he obviously didn't know she was married to Kill." I roll my eyes, glad my mask keeps him from seeing that I'm jealous that asshole fucked my wife, but he continues. "I'm just looking out for you because I've never seen you lose your shit over a woman. I understand why you married her and are against the whole falling in love thing, but don't be surprised when she does."

What the fuck does he mean when she does?

"What the fuck are you talking about?"

"Exactly. Just because you refuse to deal with the emotion and are against it doesn't mean other people feel the same way. Some people know love exists, Kill, and when you've been dying to experience it from not having it your whole life, and someone gives it to you, you hold on to it. Don't be surprised when the person she falls for isn't you because you were too busy with your head up your ass."

"They will have to get through me first while I'm balls deep in her."

He scoffs. "No, he will just wait until you're fucking Blair or Sarah or even Sydney and her friends to make his move."

I lean close, my lip curling under my mask because I have a feeling my boy is testing the waters. I love Ciro like a brother. I know he had his heart trampled on, and it's one of the reasons I don't feel that way for any woman. Ever. But she's mine.

The way she came apart for me in the driver's seat of my car tells me she is. It also tells me she doesn't love that asshole she was with. She wouldn't let me touch her pussy if she was because Lillith believes in the fairy tale.

"Are you trying to warn me that it will be you? The shoulder for her to cry on."

He chuckles. "Why, so you can put a laser to my forehead and threaten to blow my fucking brains out? I think I'll pass on that one, but if you don't want her–" He shrugs. "I don't mind keeping her warm for you."

I slam my hand down on the table and get in his face. The mask is between us, but my forehead presses into his. "You've been my best friend since my parents died and I came here seeking answers. We promised to have each other's backs. I respect you. I care about you and have given you anything you've asked, but if you or anyone touches my wife, I'll end them. Got it?" I say through clenched teeth. "She's mine."

# 24



**M**y pants are ruined. We parked inside what looked like an abandoned warehouse surrounded by metal debris on the other side of the mainland. I was surprised to find it disguises what lies beneath. It's like a different world from the one above.

People who are a part of his circle live free. Walking in the dark hallway, people kiss underneath the neon glow of the lights, the only thing beating the darkness of the spaces. There are rooms and a wide-open space where there is a large screen.

Music plays while people drink and dance, having a party like they don't live in a fucked-up world full of oppression from the takeover of technology. The remnants of a war against the people. Jobs that used to allow people to work so they could provide a stable living for their families have been replaced by artificial intelligence. Roads and security are provided by droids, leaving people without a way to make money. Technology constantly evolves, outsmarting the mental capacity of the human brain.

Countries of the past didn't count on the fact that producing more droids and electric-powered machinery would reduce the need for natural resources, destroying the planet.

It is why the City of God was created by the rich.

A way for the rich and evil to live on so they wouldn't be held responsible for their mistakes. And you avoid being responsible by taking away the freedom of someone's voice.

Looking around the mainland, watching people suffering with limited natural resources living among programmed machines, makes you realize one thing—the people who allowed this to happen are the true destructors of humankind. It's like watching a new automation and you're being wowed by how easy it will make your daily life. You're taken in by the ability to have more time to do other things. They convince you by how easy it all seems, not realizing they want to take over and eliminate the need for you to exist.

No voice.

No faith.

Only the need to follow the system created in a dark world. A world where there is no light in the end. Just an endless cycle of classism. No actors or singers needed. There is an AI for that. An efficient replacement that can produce more without mistakes.

After removing my black suit, I walk out of the room, and I'm left in my stockings, thigh-high boots, and a black long-sleeved button-up that reaches right before the edge of my boot mid-thigh like a short dress.

"I have no underwear on," I point out, looking at Killian as I step out of the room made of concrete walls with only a bed draped with white sheets.

He left me here when we arrived and showed me where I could freshen up. After the car ride and the most amazing orgasm, he was quiet. I hated that I couldn't see his face to judge his feelings, and I didn't say anything because I didn't want to push him away. Too many emotions ran between us. Things neither of us had the right words to express.

I watch him tilt his head to the side the way he does when he's thinking. "Then don't open your legs."

My cheeks flame. "That's not funny."

He can't be serious.

"I didn't say it was."

There is a knock on the door, and he turns away to open it.

"Hey."

I roll my eyes. She just won't quit, but I refuse to be part of their little love quarrel. He doesn't talk about her or mention what is really going on between them. I'm not going to pry it out of him. He bought me for what I look like, not to listen to my feelings.

"Is everything alright?" I hear him ask her with concern in his voice.

He cares about her. That much is obvious. He will always have feelings for her in his weird way. Maybe what happened in the car is his way of getting me to lighten up so he can do the deed and be done with it. He doesn't talk to me like that. If anything, he seems annoyed that he has to deal with me.

At first, I wondered if he brought me along because he cared that I broke down. Wanting to keep me close because he was human, and he cared that I was tired of people using me.

But he's like all the rest. I'm here because he's making sure I stay pretty enough. I'm no use to him if I cut my face.

It also makes sense that he has me sleeping in his bed but makes sure not to hug or touch me. Every night, he slides in the bed and gives me his back, making sure I can't see his face, but in the middle of the night, he turns unconsciously, and I lie on the bed in the softly lit bedroom wishing he could see what I see. That he's beautiful.

"I was hoping you wanted to hang out after you're done with Ciro," she purrs.

You know what? They can have each other. I get up and pull the door open not surprised that her tits are practically spilling out as an invitation.

She gives me a sly smile. "Hi, Lillith. The girls are hanging out dancing. You should go. Maybe make some friends. Kill and I will catch up with you later."

*Meaning, I'm going to fuck Kill and need you to get lost.* I glance at Killian, and he's quiet. Needles prick my throat because I hate myself for caring—for letting him hurt me, for letting both of them get to me—because he doesn't correct her or tell her to fuck off.

He's waiting for me to show that her being here bothers me. *Fuck him.* Memories of them fucking play on a loop in my mind.

*The way he touched her.*

*The way he never touched me.*

He only looked at me like I was...nice to look at but not good enough. I'm never good enough. I wasn't for my father. He was quick to get rid of me, and I haven't heard from him since.

*No one cares for you, Lillith. No one cares if you live or die. Just like no one cared about your mother. No one could ever love you. Killian will never love you.*

"Yeah, I think that's a great idea. You two catch up. I'm sure it's been a while."

I turn and walk away, letting a tear fall down my face as I head toward the sound of the music.

I'M ABOUT to reach the chaos where bodies dance to the music. The sweat gleams off their bodies as they sway to the beat with cups in their hand. Probably alcohol.

Another thing banned on the island along with recreational drugs. You can tell people here are loaded. Girls are making out with each other, guys behind them grinding against them. It smells like sweat, smoke, and alcohol, but they are all in their element. This is how they cope. How they have fun. I look to my left, and there is an open doorway. I bet it's quiet, and hopefully, no one is in there so I can lick my wounds in private.

I notice a couple fucking near the exit. The guy thrusts inside her while her legs wrap around his waist. Her tits are in his face while she leans against the wall. *Ugh.* He could at least take her toward the other side where no one can see them, but I guess that's the point, for people to watch them. I guess some people get off on others watching.

Maybe Killian likes to be watched. He wasn't mad that I walked in on him and Blair. Then I think of them right now. He's probably fucking her in the room. I basically told him that I didn't care when I walked away. And he didn't come after me.

When I walk through the doorway, I notice that the music is not as loud, and it lets me listen to the voices in my head.

*He wouldn't go after you. He thinks you find his face repulsive. He thinks you're shallow, Lillith. You know why you're here. You're nothing.*

I look around and notice an opening in the room. A small circle surrounded by metal allows the outside air to filter in.

I see metal pieces of old car parts with seats strewn around, making a makeshift circle. I take a seat, looking up. There are no stars in the sky like on the island. The light pollution clouds the sky, not allowing the stars to shine through.

"Why do I always find you sitting out alone?"

I turn my head, watching Ciro coming closer with two cups in his hand. I pick up some pieces of glass from the ground and throw it, letting it hit the metal in the center of the circle. "Why are you the one always finding me?"

He takes a seat and hands me a cup with something in it. "Don't worry. It's safe. You must be thirsty or hungry."

He reaches into his pocket and pulls out a pack of peanuts. I take them because I'm starving, and I don't think he would drug or hurt me.

"Why are you being so nice to me?"

He leans back on the seat next to me. "Do you question all your friends when they're trying to hang out with you?"

"Who said we were friends? I thought Cross would have told you to stay away from me or whatever," I tease, popping a peanut in my mouth and squinting my eyes when I taste the saltiness."Too salty?"

He laughs, and then he turns serious. "Wait. Why are you calling him Cross?"

I swallow the salted peanut without chewing. "These are not allowed on the island. Way too salty. To answer your other question. He warned me not to take another man's jacket, and I'm not allowed to call him Kill. So I went with Cross."

I tilt the cup and take a sip. The fire spilling into my mouth causes me to spray it like a hose when I sputter. "What the hell is that?"

"Alcohol."

"Yuck! How do guys drink that stuff?"

He bellows in laughter. "You'll have to get used to it." *Uh, no thanks.* "There are different kinds. I'm sure you would like the sweeter stuff." I raise my hand, spitting on the ground. "No thanks."

I've never had alcohol or anything that is deemed bad for you by the judges on the island.

"I'm sorry. I thought you could handle it." He takes a sip of his own cup, but his brown eyes are on mine. His blond hair sticks out in a big, hot mess.

Ciro's nose is small but slightly crooked, like it was broken at one point. He has a scar on the left side of his lip. It looks like Ciro has gotten into a lot of fights.

"You keep looking at me like that, princess, and I swear I'll take my chances with my best friend and let him kill me."

I shake my head and look away, embarrassed. "Why would he do that? He's kind of busy at the moment."

He slides a couple of peanuts in his mouth, and I hear him crunch them with his teeth as he studies me. "Busy how?"

I grab the cup and take a sip, holding my breath as I swallow the concoction. My eyes water as I feel the burning liquid slide down my throat. I swear I can feel it causing a fire in my stomach. When I finish chugging whatever the hell he gave me, I wipe my mouth with the back of my hand.

I take a deep breath and glance at Ciro's playful smirk. "What?"

"Nice try. How is he busy, Lillith?"

He's not going to drop it. I was hoping me chugging the alcohol would change the subject.

"I left him with Blair. She seems to know what he needs. She said I should go hang out with the other girls at the big party you guys have going on. She and Cross would catch up with me later."

He gets up from the chair. "What did he say?"

"Nothing. It's not like I can tell if he's happy or sad since I can't see his face."

He sticks his hand out. "Come on." I look at his hand like it's a bomb about to detonate. A wave of dizziness hits me, and I think it's the alcohol. I must have drunk it too fast. I tilt my head, looking at his playful expression.

"Come with me. Let's go have fun."

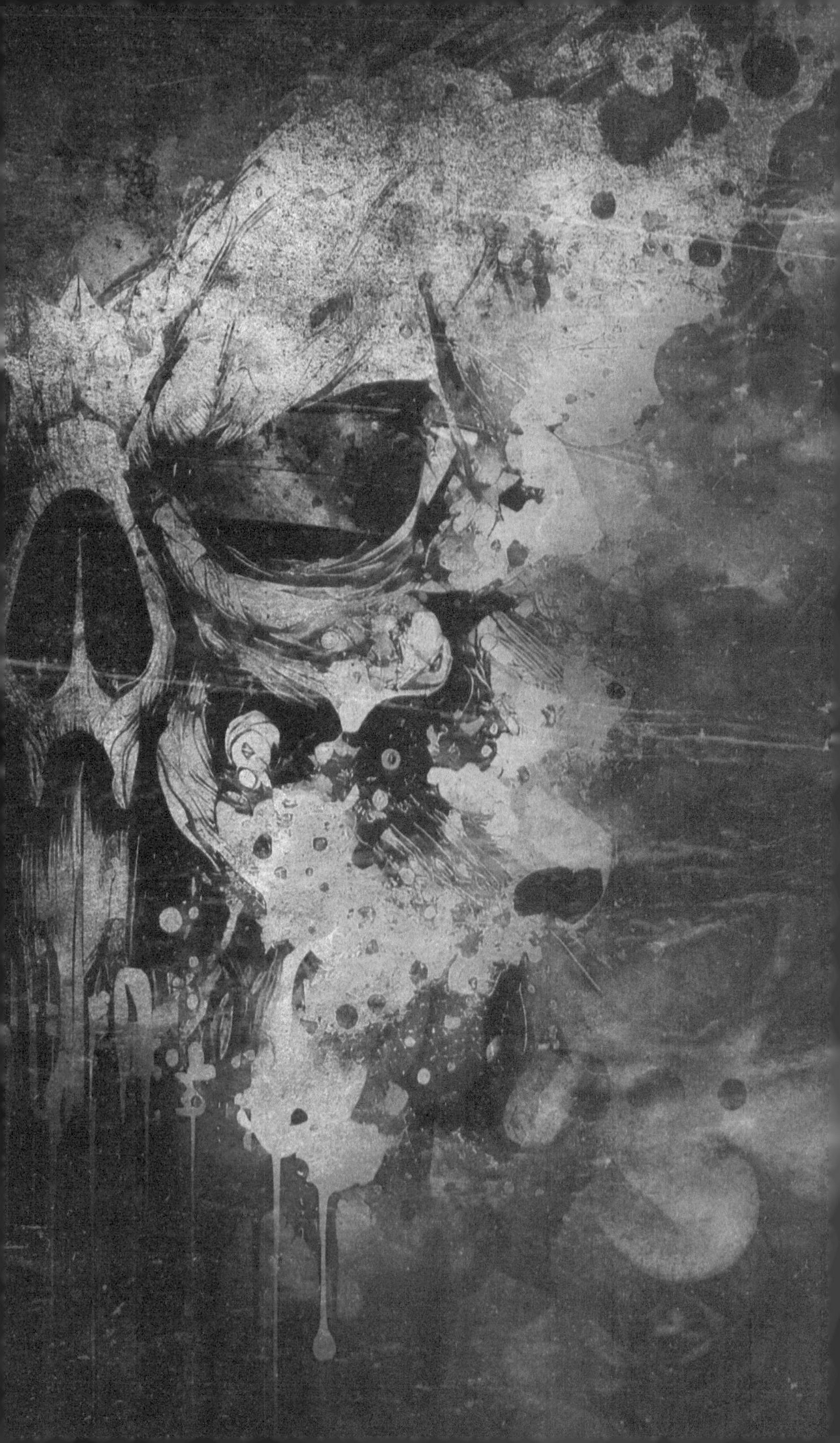

# 25



**"W**hat do you really want, Blair?"

She tries to walk around me, but I block her path. She places her hands on my chest. Before, I would have welcomed her touch, but now, I feel confused.

She looks up with a hopeful expression. "What's wrong? You know what I want, and she doesn't mind. She knows about us. She's watched."

I look down at her hands on my chest, and all I want to do is push them away. I take a step back away from her to create distance. "She's my wife and soon will be the mother of my child. I don't have time or room for anything else. You know that. I'm sorry, Blair. I care about you, but—"

"I love you," she blurts. "I'll do anything for you. I'll be anything you want," she says desperately.

After four and a half years, I don't want Blair to touch me. It feels wrong. I tighten my jaw and clench my fists at my sides.

I don't answer, and the air feels suffocating between us. I hate that I have to hurt her, but I'm relieved that I need to tell her. It's fucked up, and I hate that she thought I wanted more because I never did. My brain is muddled with different things to say, but I can't figure out how to let her down so that she understands. I don't want you? It was fun, but now it's over. I'm a married man? I care about you, but not like that.

"Say something!" she yells, but I can't.

Blair doesn't deserve to be treated like crap, but I hurt the woman I'm interested in and let her walk away thinking the worst. That I'm fucking Blair in the room while she waits. Alone.

Lillith is always alone, and now she thinks her husband is cheating on her. Real marriage or not, it's cheating.

"I can't do this with you right now, Blair. Whatever you think we still have is over."

She gives a nervous laugh. "Have you slept with her?" She looks at me, and I'm thankful she can't see the uneasy look in my eyes when I think about Lillith.

Every time I'm with her, I think about her, and every time I'm away from her, she's still on my mind. That doesn't happen with Blair. I don't think about her when she leaves.

"That isn't any of your business. I don't question who you fuck because it isn't any of my business."

"Has she seen your face? Have you kissed her?" She has tears in her eyes. I honestly feel bad, but I know it's not enough. I loved Blair, but it wasn't the love you read about in old books or the love my parents had.

She shakes her head, and her eyes are fixed on my mask, hoping I can see the anguish in her eyes. "I think you are the most amazing person, and you have done what no one has done for me. You have given me a home here, friends, great sex, and a life. You are everything to me. You're the most important person in my life."

I noticed she never once called me beautiful. Only one

woman has called me that after the accident. One. And it wasn't Blair.

"I'm sorry, Blair, but things were never serious between us, and I'm important to a lot of people."

"Do you love her?"

I blow out a breath, making it obvious behind the mask. "I don't have room for an emotion like that. I'm not that kind of man. Not even for you."

She sniffs, and tears pool in her eyes. "You're no fun," she teases.

"I thought I was a lot of fun." I grin. "Come here."

She walks closer, and I hug her. She smells like cherries and some fruity drink mixed with alcohol. "There was never a forever for us, Blair. It was just fun, and now I have to grow up and be a man. A lot of people are counting on me."

She looks up and wipes her face. "I know. It's just hard to see you with her. I know she has to bear you a child, and that is so fucked up."

"She's been a pawn all her life, Blair. She was born and raised by them. She doesn't have a choice, and I'm using her just like they all have. She's lived secluded all her life. A prison is a prison. It doesn't matter where if there is no freedom."

"I get it. Is the network all set up?"

I don't like talking about my business or how I plan to undermine the judges and funnel resources that people need to survive. The network system I referred to as "The Grid" consists of a web of subterranean passageways that wind their way under the barren landscape. The tunnels are protected from the outside world by a layer of reinforced materials. The rescue of the people lies inside this underground maze, where supplies of food and other necessities are moved from safe storage areas to various distribution sites.

"Almost. I can't get into details."

Augmented reality is the technology set in place to control the planet. It was how it all started. The control. I'm working on a network that uses specific servers with obsolete computers. A dead technology I have found still works, and no one would come looking. I just have to finish setting up the firewall. It will be like the normal days or the past where there is a currency or peer-to-peer to pay for resources like organic food, services that offer a better way of life so people can work and live. They just need a head start without the control. A new era where humans control machines the way they see fit.

I watch as Sydney walks up to us, and her eyes immediately fall to my arm around Blair. *Fuck.* Sydney isn't the type to keep her mouth shut.

I remove my arm when she approaches. "What's up?"

She smiles and looks between Blair and me. "You two look cozy. Now I know why Lillith is out there and not here." She snickers, and I don't like the way her eyes are glossy. She's high. "No biggie. I just wanted to ask if you were okay with Lillith dancing with Ciro."

"Where?" I growl.

But I know that is a stupid question. She's dancing in the main room.

She giggles. "Your girl can drink. She looks like she's having a blast." She turns to walk away, but I fly right by her.

My fists clench as I practically run to the main room. If anyone has touched her, I'll kick their fucking ass. My mind is going a million miles a minute at all the possible scenarios. I shouldn't have let her go.

When I walk into the main room, my eyes scan the throng of bodies dancing and grinding on one another to "Blind" by Korn blaring from the speakers.

The lights flashing from the main screen cause me to focus on the crowd looking for her. A robot synchronizing the movements of the beat looks like it's reaching for the crowd with flashing lights.

My eyes keep looking for dark hair and turquoise eyes, but a commotion has my head turning to my right. Right on the stage in front of the screen, I see Lillith.

Ciro tells her to come off the stage, but she shakes her head, laughing. Her perfect white teeth glow from her beautiful smile. She's oblivious to all the attention on her right now.

I notice some of the guys we work with giving her appreciative glances. She's wearing my shirt, but I remember her telling me that she didn't have panties on, and I immediately spring forward. It's dark enough, but the last thing I need is for my wife to flash her gorgeous pussy to everyone in here.

"Come on, Lillith!" Ciro bellows, holding her hand.

She shakes her head and raises her arm, causing my long dress shirt to lift and show her pretty thighs.

When the guys turn and see me standing there watching her with my mask on, they cower and look away.

They know I'm here for her. I'm sure they already know she's mine. She doesn't look like anyone here. Her complexion is perfect. But those eyes and hair are a dead giveaway.

I stand in front of Ciro, and the smile wipes right off her face.

*I know, baby. I hurt you.*

I climb up on the stage, and she steps back, turning away from me, but I come up behind her, holding her close.

My hand slides up her thigh, not giving a fuck who's watching. I feel her soft skin. She tries to clench her thighs together, but I'm stronger. I want her, and I'm going to do something crazy to show her.

She turns to face me and bares her teeth. I can smell the alcohol. Fucking Ciro. He did it to piss me off.

"Did someone touch you?" I ask loud enough over the music.

"Why do you care?" She points toward the crowd, but those eyes are on me. "Go fuck your little girlfriend and let me have *my* fun."

I see the hurt in them.

I grip her by the back of her neck. The lights change to red as the song changes, causing our skin to glow as In the Moment's "I Would Die For You" plays. I pull her close, raising my mask to expose my lips.

I feel the eyes of everyone like a million spotlights.

Most people have never seen my face.

I can hear cheering and screaming, but it's all white noise. Lillith remains still, her arms hanging limp at her sides. Her fierce eyes aimed right at my mouth.

I dip my head close enough to her ear to make sure she can hear me. "Judgment is for the blind."

I pull back, and her eyes soften as realization dawns.

I take her lips in a crushing kiss, pulling her close. Our tongues clash together, savoring the moment. The moment I have dreamed of since I first heard her voice all those years ago.

I could never get close enough to see what she looked like, but I just knew I had to meet her. I heard her voice and had to see if she was as beautiful as they said she was.

I deepen the kiss nice and slow. Her arms wrap around me, but she's careful not to allow my mask to come completely off.

I want the kiss to go on forever.

She sucks my lips, and I slide my tongue over hers, and the kiss goes on and on. I want to be inside her, but not here.

I pull away, sliding my mask back in place.

"Let's go. You've had enough fun, and you're tipsy."

She nods, and I pick her up, letting her wrap her legs around me. I make sure her butt is covered with the length of the shirt as I carry her to my room.

# 26

LILLITH

It was him. The whole time. He knew who I was before he took me from my father. I lift my head from the pillow, and the pounding headache hits me in full force. I groan. What the hell?

Last night, he brought me into the room and put me to bed. I didn't realize how tired I was until my head hit the pillow. Then I remembered the kiss. The taste of his lips and the words right before it. *"Judgment is for the blind."* My words.

He didn't fuck her. He wanted me to claim him in front of her, and I walked away because I was stuck in my head.

"Here." I open my eyes again, thankful it's dark in here. He hands me a metal flask and a pill in the palm of his hand.

"What's wrong with me?"

He smiles. "It's called a hangover. You wouldn't know that because those idiots ban everything. It's a good thing, I guess. It's not good for you, but if you only leave the bad and not give a person the option, then that would suck. You're set up to fail anyway."

"I think I'll stick to the good, then because I feel like my head is being banged on for fun."

He chuckles. "Come on. Sit up slowly."

I push myself up on the bed and wince. He sits on the edge, and I notice he doesn't have his mask on.

I take the pill and the metal flask and look inside it with caution.

"It's water." I nod and swallow the pill, feeling the cold liquid slide down my throat like it's a dry desert, but my eyes never leave his face.

I can't stop looking at him. Seeing him without his mask is like a gift he gives very few people. Like an eclipse of the moon.

You have to be there at the right moment in time to see its beauty. Once it passes, it's gone.

I pass him the metal flask, and he places it on the floor. He slides the sheet away, exposing my naked body.

"What are you doing? I'm cold."

I was. It was cold, but then I remember taking a quick shower before bed. I can smell his body wash still on my skin.

"I'll get you warmed up."

"Give me the sheet," I demand when he pulls it away from my grasp.

He slides his hands up my thighs and settles between them on the bed. I watch as his right eye does that reptile thing. "I have a better idea."

His thumbs slide up where my hip meets my thigh, and I hold myself up using my elbows. "What are you doing?"

He smirks, and God, if only he knew how hot he looks.

"Has anyone sucked your pussy, Lillith?" I shake my head. "Never?"

"You're my first."

"Hmm. I haven't..." I raise my eyebrows, surprised. "Not after..."

His accident.

I smile. "I guess I get the new and improved version of you, then."

He smiles and lowers his head, licking my clit. I gasp, " K–Cross."

He stops and lifts his head. "Killian," he corrects me. "I want you to call me Killian."

I nod and watch him go back at it. He slides his tongue up and down my slit, and he sucks my clit into his mouth, swirling his tongue.

I toss my head back, sinking into the bed and sliding my fingers in his dark hair. "Oh God. Yes. Don't stop. Please, don't stop."

He releases my clit, and his eyes flick to mine. "I won't. I like to eat all my food."

My legs widen, and I grind my pussy on his mouth, and he groans. "Yes," I moan.

It feels so good. The way his tongue swirls over my clit has my orgasm cresting fast. It's like he knows how to get me there every time with no effort. The man's tongue should be banned.

He kisses the way he eats pussy. Now I'm going to want this every time I feel his tongue. My breaths come out short and quick when he goes harder and harder.

"Don't stop, Killian. Please. I love it when..."

He dips his tongue inside my pussy again. "Yes, that. Right there. I love it when you suck..."

He does it again.

Fuck.

I grind into his mouth and feel my arousal slide down my ass, making a mess of the white sheets. My head hits the pillow as my orgasm begins to build higher. He holds my hips but doesn't let up.

He doesn't stop.

I come hard. "Killian," I breathe. "I'm coming!" Tingles spread across my skin, reaching the center of my pussy. I can feel my walls spasm on his tongue.

He groans, making sucking noises as he licks me clean.

I watch as he looks down at my pussy and then places a kiss between my lips. He lifts his head. "Damn." He licks his lips. "You taste as good as you look."

My eyes meet his, his lips wet and swollen. "You kiss the same way you eat pussy," I say softly. "Dangerous."

I lean closer, and he meets me so we're at eye level, kneeling on the bed. He's so much taller than me. His muscled chest is carved like a statue dressed in sweatpants. His ripped muscles have tattoos all over his skin. Especially over the scars on the right side of his chest.

I slide my hands slowly over his abs, feeling every dip with my fingers and hoping he doesn't pull away. His eyes follow my fingers, feeling his hot skin until I reach his neck and then his face.

My eyes lift. "You're perfect," I whisper.

He slides a dark strand of my hair behind my ear. "And you're the most gorgeous thing I have ever laid eyes on." My heart swells, and my stomach flutters with butterflies. I slide my fingers down to the waistband of his sweats, but he places his hand over mine, stopping me. I stare up at him. "In time. I'm not in a hurry."

"But I want to..."

I want to give him the same pleasure he gifted me moments ago. I want to finally taste him in my mouth for the first time.

"You don't have to."

I pinch my brows in confusion. "But..."

"We have to go. We need to get back."

And just like that, the moment is broken.

# 27

## LILLITH

After getting dressed, we're in the car, heading back to the tunnel where the boats are docked to return to the island.

"Why do you drive these cars and not the electrical kind on the mainland?"

He has his mask back on that reads, *Fucked* with the F backward. He points at the radio. "They can't track these. They don't have GPS or chips."

"Is that why they really banned them?"

"Part of it. But mostly, yes. They banned them because they do fuck up the planet, but the batteries they need to build to operate the electrical shit is just as bad. It heats the planet either way. Solar is better, and there are other ways to generate energy. Natural resources that can be recycled safely are good for the planet. The judges don't like it because they can't turn a profit. They want people to pay for things that are accessible for free and let the AI tell them what's good for them. It's all about control."

The solar-powered boats. They make sense. You don't have

to pay to operate them. Why don't they use solar power for everything? It allows citizens time to come up with the money to get new cells or generate lights to power them.

"What made you want to help the people? You could easily be like everyone else who lives on the island and not care as long as you're rich."

"My parents. They started to help people on the mainland by sending them fresh food that was not altered or synthetic. The alternate foods contain harmful chemicals, but people buy them because it's what they can afford. It causes cancer and other types of diseases, but the need for people to consume to survive doesn't give them much of a choice. My parents bought an island to grow fresh and organic food and other resources to help the people. They hired people with certain skills on this island to send medicine for the sick. But someone got wind."

"They murdered them. It wasn't an accident, and they wanted you to die along with them."

"Now you're catching on. I wasn't supposed to survive."

"But you did."

The sun rises as we drive through the city full of broken metal. Automated machines pick it up and place it in other piles.

"Yeah, but it doesn't mean they won't try again."

"What are they doing with this place?"

"They're re-building a place where machines run every-thing, and only the people who survive will be able to work the limited jobs available. There aren't enough jobs on the island that allow people who won't spread disease to work. They're building hubs all around the world just like this one. Control-ling the population. Controlling how people think. Their choices. Like ants on a farm."

"And you're freeing them."

"Yeah. I'm trying, but I need to let them think I'm one of

them. It is why I live on the edge of the island alone and don't allow anyone in. But we will have to go and mingle. I have to make them think I'm incapable of continuing what my parents started."

I glance at him, admiring him more for what he's trying to do. "I told you I want to help."

He changes gears, and the car increases speed. "You are. You're the most important part of the whole thing."

HE PULLS UP at the dock. I wonder how he has been able to move like a moth, hidden in the dark where no one can see him or realize he's even there.

"Come on. We don't have much time."

He grips my hand, helping me out of the car and shutting the door behind me. I pull another one of his shirts he gave me down my thighs, almost reaching the tops of my black boots. Thank God he was able to get me short shorts to put on underneath.

We reach the boat, and Ciro and a couple of other guys are loading the second boat with boxes. Sydney, Sarah, and Blair give us curious glances, but I don't say anything. Let them think whatever they want. It doesn't matter. I'm here, and there is nowhere to go except with Killian.

"You had fun last night?" Sydney asks, giving me a wink.

The expression on Blair's face tells me that Killian was telling me the truth. He didn't sleep with her. At least not last night.

Killian comes up behind me and snakes a hand around my waist, placing his chin on my shoulder, and responds, "We did and this morning."

He pulls away, walking over to the other boat, and right when I'm going to follow him, Sarah steps forward with a sly smile. "I hope you can handle him. He's the type who needs to be satisfied, or he'll get bored like he always does."

I raise my brow because I'm tired of this shit. "I think it's the other way around. I'm the one who gets bored easily."

Blair slides another box onto the boat and straightens, pulling her top that is tied in a knot at her waist while giving me a bitchy look. "That's good to hear because you may be married to him, but it's all for us. Kill doesn't have time to fall in love. He isn't built like that. Remember that before you fall in love with him, thinking he will love you back."

My stomach drops because we're nowhere near there, and our conversation in the car held a truth to her words. He said I was the most important part, and nowhere did that include falling in love.

"That's enough, Blair," Ciro says, scolding her like a child.

She glares at him but curls her lip. "I'm just telling her like it is, Ciro. Don't lie to her. She already thinks she's above us."

"I said that's enough," he barks.

She smiles, shaking her head. She is so bitter, and I get the feeling the next words out of her mouth will make matters even worse. "Aw, Ciro. Why don't you tell her the truth? It's obvious why you defend her so much."

The guys they brought to help out pause but look away.

I look back and forth between Sydney and Sarah to gauge their expressions. There is something I don't know about Ciro.

My eyes finally land on him. I watch as he flinches from her words, and my heart breaks for him. "You've always wanted to be like Kill. To live like Kill. Think like Kill. You're his best friend, but shit, you can't even hide it. He's warned you, but you just can't help yourself. You always want what you can't have. Ever since you laid eyes on her, you're dying to fuck her.

You watch her. You follow her. You're waiting until she catches us fucking so you can make your move and not feel guilty about it."

"Stop it," I warn.

"Don't worry. Once he slips his cock in you, you'll get bored. Just like the last girl he had. He caught her fucking Kill with me and her friend."

I see the anguish in his eyes. His eyes darken in pain. "Stop it," I repeat. But she keeps going.

"We told him, but like always, Ciro doesn't listen. Kill can do no wrong, but he finally found something he wants more than anything." She lowers her voice. "To fuck you because he's in love with you, and he knows Kill could never love you."

I walk across the boat, and her eyes widen. I pull my hand back and slap her. "Shut up!"

Her hand flies to her face in shock. She lunges after me, but Ciro steps in front of me and holds her hands, keeping her from reaching me. "You stupid bitch. How dare you! You can give him a kid, but he will always come back to me because I accept him how he is," she snarls.

No. She just wants him because of who he wants to become. I set my jaw and clench my teeth, seething in anger. "No, if Ciro was in Kill's position. You're the first one on your knees begging to be his number one bitch. It's the power you want. You're no different from the monsters who raised me on that fucking island."

"What the fuck?" Killian's behind me, jumping on the boat.

I turn to look at him and shake my head. "Get your bitch on a leash. She needs to be locked up. Orgies are your thing, right? Better yet, why don't you go fuck her and whoever she brings along. You love to have her around so she can rub how you fuck everyone in my face, including her, since she's your number one choice. Because I know I'm not. I never was."

"What the fuck is going on?" Killian asks, looking at Blair.

"Tell her the truth," Blair demands, pulling away from Ciro's grasp.

"About what?" Killian asks in a sharp tone.

"Tell her you have no plans to love her in the true sense. Tell her what you told me."

It feels like a knife stabs me in the chest over and over. A hot and cold feeling slides up my spine, and I can't breathe. It hurts. He talks about me to her, but he never says anything about her to me.

Then I remember this morning. How he stopped me when I wanted to pleasure him. Maybe he felt guilty because he saw the way I looked at him. The way I said that he was perfect because I meant it.

"Tell me the truth, Killian. I would like to know so I understand my role in your life a little better. That way, we can air it all out. They can all hear it. What are your plans for me? They're dying to know."

"What do you want me to tell you, Lillith?" Killian asks in a tight voice.

"The truth. Don't string me along so I can be agreeable to you in bed. Tell me, is it true you fucked Ciro's girlfriend?"

I see his chest rising and falling faster and faster. His head turns to look at his best friend. "Yes," he chokes out. "It wasn't supposed to happen. I didn't think it was serious, and she told me they weren't together. It was a mistake, and he knows that. We're past all this."

"How about me?" I ask.

He gives a frustrated sigh. "We talked about this. You know why you are here, Lillith. Everyone knows what the plan is. I don't have time for love or some fairy tale. This is the real world. Look around. The last thing I think about is falling in love with anyone when people are suffering." He steps closer, and my throat feels like an invisible hand squeezes it. "Get it through that pretty head of yours. You may have been kept in a gilded cage for so long on a beautiful island that it has blinded you from what is really going on." He closes the remaining distance. "But it is the truth, and I'm sorry I can't be the man in your little fantasy world you read in a book."

Everyone is silent. All you can hear is the water crashing against the dock and the boat. I look away, my eyes staring at the boat that will take us back to the island, refusing to let the tears that have pooled on my lashes fall. "I understand," I say, my voice turning cold. "Please, take me back."

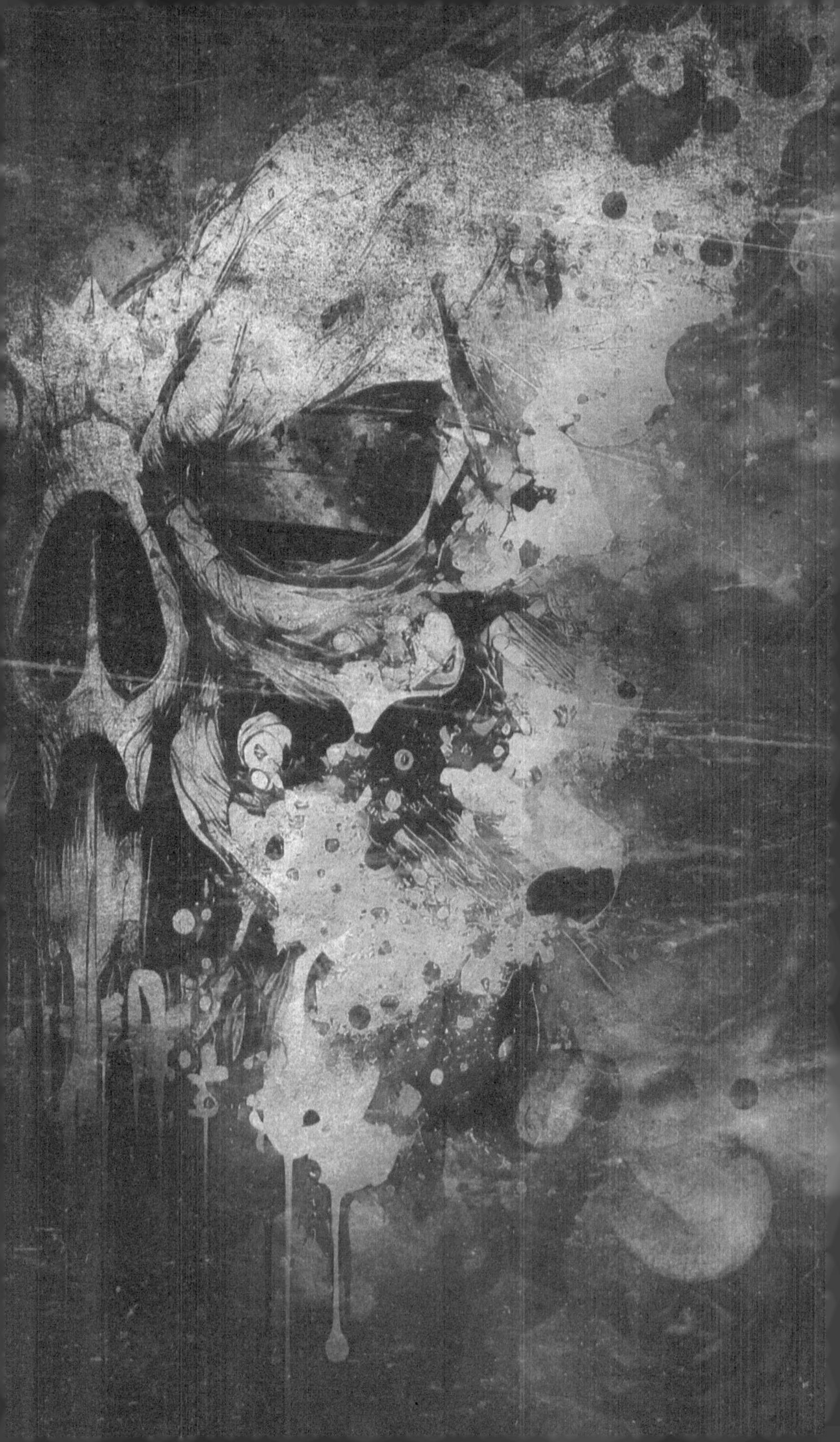

# 28

KILLIAN

’m in my bedroom, and since our talk at the dock, Lillith has avoided me. It's been two days, but I've left her alone. I know what I said was fucked up, but I couldn't take the tension between the people who have been helping me since my parents' death and I arrived on the mainland looking for answers.

After six months of surgery and therapy, it isn't easy to find out it wasn't an accident. Someone wanted the Cross family wiped out, and that included me. It has taken me years to build a grid and find the resources to help people.

Agnes appears in my doorway as I sit on the bed, looking at Lillith's empty side. "Where is she?"

"Mrs. Cross is in her room already asleep for the night. Is there anything you need, Killian?"

I stare at her and tell her the truth. "I need my wife in my bed."

She stands poised with her hands clasped together. "I suggest you go to her room, then."

A smile tugs on my lips, and I remove my mask. Agnes is

the only one of my staff who has seen my face. She took care of me after the accident, so she saw the before and after. She pretty much knows everything about me except for my feelings.

"You think that's a good idea?"

She looks down at the floor. "It didn't stop you last time when you told her to undress so you could see what you bought." She shrugs her shoulders. "You own her."

I acted like an asshole that day in front of Agnes, but I was jealous. Then she broke down and tried to do the unthinkable. I would never have forgiven myself if she had succeeded.

I've had Agnes keep an eye on her since we got back. I know what I said was fucked up at the docks, and it probably came out wrong. But since my parents' death and what my body went through, I want to avenge my parents and find out who was responsible, but I also want to finish what my parents started.

"I know I haven't put effort where she's concerned."

I haven't had sex with my wife. I haven't had sex with anyone since I married her.

"You haven't."

I get up and slide my mask over my face. "I'll be in Lillith's room tonight."

She steps aside. "I think that would be a great idea. She needs someone. I think she needs a friend she can trust."

I open the door to Lillith's bedroom. The smell of her light perfume hits me, and I smile, closing the door. That's the smell I miss on my bed. Her smell. I can't stop thinking about it. It's like a drug. One taste and you're addicted.

I remove my mask and place it on the nightstand my mother had especially made of wood. I'm glad I chose this room for her. My mother loved it when I was a kid. It's modern like the rest of the house's interior, but it has that historic feel at the same time.

I sit on the edge and see her plump lips parted and her long lashes kissing her cheeks. She sleeps peacefully, but I know that's the last thing she feels. She feels alone.

I slide the sheet down her shoulder, and her eyes flutter open. We stare at each other for a minute. Words are not needed. They never have been when it's just the two of us in bed, but tonight is different.

"Is everything alright?" she asks, her eyes glazed over with sleep.

"No."

"W-what's wrong?"

My eyes trail down her thin white camisole. Her pink nipples are outlined in contrast to the light fabric. Her flat stomach disappears under the sheet.

I stand and remove my long-sleeved shirt, then slide my pants over my hips along with my boxers. Her eyes lower, watching my hand slide over my semi-hard cock as I fist myself in front of her.

She knows what I want. She slides the sheet down, exposing her flat stomach, and her matching white panties come into view. I place a knee on the bed, helping her pull the sheet down her thighs.

She lifts her leg, and I hold her thigh so I can get settled between her legs. Those aquamarine eyes hold me when I slide my fingers to her hips and under the band of her panties. "I'm going to fuck you, Lillith. Soft at first. Hard. Harder. Until you can't take me anymore." I slide her panties over her hips and down her thighs as I continue to tell her what I'm going to do. What I need. "I'm going to come inside you. Repeatedly. Over and over, making your body mine. You tell me to stop, and I will because I could never hurt you, Lillith." I place a soft kiss on the tender skin of her inner thigh, and I hear her inhale. "I've wanted you since the first time I heard your sassy mouth all those years ago, but it wasn't the right time, was it?"

"I was sixteen."

"I waited until you were older. Until I finally had the balls to use your father's gambling habits and bad business decisions against him in order to have you." My hands slide up the sides of her ribs until I pull the strap over her shoulders so I can see her full breasts when I slide deep inside her so she can feel all of me.

"You wanted me?" she asks, her voice going all innocent.

*Fuck.*

I want her so much. So bad.

I was hoping she was untouched so I could be the one to pop her cherry. But I waited too long and didn't look the same as when I first met her.

I open her legs wider so the head of my cock crowns her entrance. I can feel how slick and wet she is, and I can't wait to be deep inside her, but I need her to know. "I didn't have to see your face that day in the garden to know I wanted you. Now that I have you, I'm not letting you go."

She rises on her elbows to see the head of my cock brush up and down her slit, getting her ready for me. Her tongue peeks out, wetting her lips." Oh yeah, why is that?"

I grin. "Because you like me. You like me, don't you, Lillith?"

I brush the tip of my cock over her clit, wetting the tip.

"Yeah," she breathes.

"Do you want me to fuck you, Lillith? Do you want me inside you?"

"Yes."

"How bad?" I ask, pushing the tip in a bit, and my wife rotates her hips like a greedy little whore. "You have a greedy pussy, baby. First, my tongue." I slide in a bit more. "Now, my dick."

She gasps. "Killian."

I arch a brow. "More?"

She reaches for me, but I shake my head, slowly stopping her. "Words. I want you begging for me like you did for my tongue."

"Please, Kill. More."

"What did I say about you calling me Kill?" I slide in half-way. Her pussy grips my shaft tight, and I'm trying to hold back. I want to fuck her hard so bad.

"Ahh!" She arches her neck. Her chest rises and falls. Her nipples aim at the ceiling, begging for my mouth. "More, Kill," she pleads.

"Such a bad girl. You want to be punished. Are you ready for me to fuck you like a bad girl?"

She's gasping for air with my dick still half inside her. She is so fucking tight. I might come on the spot, and I haven't even started.

"Oh God. Yes," she moans.

I raise myself above her with one hand pulling out slightly. Her eyes are on me, and I watch her spread pussy under me, about to take it all.

In one hard thrust, I push inside her. I hear her loud whimper and close my eyes because she's so fucking tight. I give her a moment to adjust.

"Are you good?" She nods.

"You feel amazing." Her lips turn up in a smile.

I look down at where we are joined and lift her leg over my hip and begin to fuck her hard. I thrust hard inside her wet pussy, watching her tits bounce up and down. I slide a hand over her throat, and her eyes hold mine. I move hard and deep, feeling her tight pussy slide over my hard length with each thrust.

I grunt.

She moans.

It was like she was made specifically for me. When I stare into her eyes, I know neither of us will forget this moment. Our first time falling into each other and I don't want to ever get up. I want to stay right here...with her.

I pull out of her, feeling the loss of her body, and flip her around. I slide my cock in her in one hard thrust and hold her back against my chest.

"Killian," she moans.

"I know, baby, but I want to have you like this. Do you know how bad I wanted to fuck your tight little cunt when I first saw you bent over for me?" I slide two fingers where we are joined, spreading her lips while I slide inside her wet cunt. I swirl my finger over her clit.

Her head sags against my shoulder. I slide my hands over her breasts, feeling how soft and heavy they are. *Fucking beautiful.* She meets me by pushing back with each thrust, and I groan.

"Lillith."

"Yeah?"

"I need you to come with me."

"Then fuck me."

I push her flat on the bed and grip her hips and fuck her. I fuck her hard, banging the bed against the wall.

"Killian! Yes!"

I smile. Our skin slaps against each other as I pound into her. She gets up on all fours, and I keep fucking her until I feel the tingle at the base of my spine. I fist her hair, arching her neck. I feel her pussy tighten, and I know she's going to come.

I don't relent. I keep fucking her. In and out. The slapping of our wet skin fills the room.

"I'm coming!" she screams.

I feel her pussy contract over my cock, and it pushes me over the edge. I come on a roar, spilling inside her while I push my cock as far as it will go.

I flip her around, and her eyes widen. Her chest rising and falling.

"Killian?"

I look down at her swollen bare pussy dripping with my cum. My good eye focuses on hers, holding the blissful look on her face.

I slide inside, and I whisper, "It's not over, Lillith. I've waited long enough to break this pussy in." I frame her face, dropping my elbows on the bed, and lick her lips. Fucking her slowly. Her hands grip my shoulders. "There was nothing wrong with you having sex, Lillith." I lower my voice. "It was because his dick was small and didn't know how to get you off." Her eyes widen when she realizes I'm referring to the doctor's questionnaire when she arrived.

I slide in and out of her, watching my cock disappear. Her legs are spread wide. Her fingernails dig into my skin with every thrust. She grinds her hips, and I almost lose it, coming for a second time.

"How do you know that?" she breathes.

"Because I made you come and bleed a bit from me taking you too hard."

She presses her ass into the mattress so she can see my cock sliding in and out of her pussy.

"It felt good, and I want more."

"Are you sure?"

She nods. "Fuck, yes."

I slide her legs over my shoulders and thrust in deep. "Good. Now, hold on."

# 29



I turn in the bed and stretch my right arm, but I feel the cold sheets instead of feeling warm skin like last night. I peel my eyes open, knowing I will find the empty spot where Killian slept after hours of hot sex. Because whatever last night was, it wasn't him coming to make love to me. He was honest about the way he felt about me and told me what I didn't want to hear. The truth.

It hurt. The words that rolled off his lips slammed into me, forcing me to accept the reality of what was happening around me. Because deep down, I hoped for something different. Even though fate twisted both our lives in a negative way, I hoped something good could come out of it. The same way life drove him down a different path for the greater good to help those suffering from a system devoid of humanity.

I hoped he would see the real me and not what society wanted him to see so he could use me. I look around the room, feeling the weight of his abandonment like a slap in the face. I reach over and check my phone and frown because I can't even call him if I want to. He never gave me a way to reach him if I needed him.

I slide out of bed and wince at how sore I am between my legs from last night. I wish I could smile like a woman who was deliciously used by a man who found her captivating, but all I could do was cry inside. My purpose is loud and clear. I'm just a vessel. The same way my mother was to my father.

A shell.

After I shower and scrub his scent from my skin, I walk toward his office. I hope to find him there before finding Agnus for breakfast even though I don't have much appetite.

When I reach his door, I take a deep breath, hoping I don't find him there with Blair or anyone else, but I shouldn't get my hopes up. I press the button on the screen for the door and see him behind his desk, looking up at the augmented screen with a bunch of codes falling. It looks like he's creating some sort of grid.

His head tilts, and all that stares at me is a dark mask that reads No Fate. "What is it?" he asks.

*Asshole.*

I did not want to look stupid or desperate for coming here, seeking his attention. He is obviously annoyed I sought him out. My pride kicks in.

"I would like to go shopping. I need a couple of things," I say sternly.

He leans back in his chair and folds his tattooed hands together over the glass. "Is it urgent?"

"Yes."

He waves his hand, dismissing me. "Fine, go."

"I need a way to pay. Or do I still need to ask my father? Maybe I could get a job."

He chuckles. "I bought you from your father so that isn't going to work. And you don't need a job because you were working last night for me so that would mean I would have to foot the bill. Especially since you're Mrs. Cross." Leaning forward in his chair, he reaches for a late-model clear phone and hands it to me. "This is for you, dear wife. Be gentle."

I walk closer and take it from him, gripping the sides of the device and wanting nothing more than to snap it in half. If he only knew that I hate being dependent on him. Anger boils in my veins. I'm tired of being subjected to a man's power.

I know he's treating me like this because he wants to make sure the message is set in stone. What he doesn't want to say in words, his actions are more than enough.

Last night meant nothing in the light of day.

I'm sure I wasn't enough to satisfy him. He didn't even stay the night, and after he was done, he didn't kiss me. Now that I think about it, he gave me his back. I was exhausted, and all I remember was reaching out and feeling his skin, but he never turned around to hold me. He probably waited until I fell asleep to slip out of the room.

Tears prick the back of my eyes. You can't make someone love you. I thought he was different. He was the mystery man I could never forget at the party when I was sixteen. The one who intrigued me with his words. I thought that him confirming it was him meant that we had some sort of connection. I couldn't have been more wrong. I was a target.

A thought flickers in my mind. What happens to me after he gets what he wants from me?

I take a step back, hating that I can't see his face. I want to see his expression, but at the same time, I don't because I'm scared of what I would see.

Indignation flares up inside me at his tone because I'm not a woman who takes advantage of a man with money. I wish I could say the same for him, but that would be pointless. He'll just remind me of all the reasons he can't love me.

"I'm not like that, but of course, you wouldn't know what I'm like."

He tilts his head to the side in that creepy way he does when he has his mask on. "I think I know exactly what you're like. Especially...how you taste."

I don't want to fall for his shit or allow him to intimidate me. He has his mind made up on what he thinks of me. I cross my arms over my chest, device in hand, and square my shoulders.

"What happens to me after I give you what you want?" I ask.

He knows I mean after I give him a child. The tension suddenly becomes thick and stifling. My stomach plummets because the silence tells me what I feared. What do men do when they get what they need? They eliminate and move on.

Just like my father. After my mother died giving birth to me, I overheard that my father had already brought women into the house, and he didn't bother with tradition in giving my mother the respect a husband gives when he loses his wife.

"I let you go."

I curl my lip. If he thinks I would willingly leave my child behind, he is out of his mind.

"I'm not abandoning my child."

"I don't think you have a choice. You leave, or I get rid of you."

My eyes pool with tears, and a knot lodges in my throat.

Why does he have to be so cruel? He blows hot and cold with me, and I have done nothing.

"Why?" I ask in a shaky voice, hating that it betrays my feelings.

"Because that is the way it has to be, Lillith. Your father knew your fate when I offered to bail him out. And besides, I would have no use for you." A stubborn tear escapes, sliding down my cheek from the corner of my eye.

"What if I can't do it?"

"Do what?" he snaps.

"Get pregnant."

"I doubt that will be a problem. You were very willing last night. The doctor gave me a full report and said you were fine. Now, I have work to do. You can see your way out."

"I hate you."

I look down at my left hand and swirl the ring with my thumb. I haven't eaten much since I refused to eat at the table. Agnes brings my meal to my room, and even then, I don't eat all of it.

My clothes are a bit loose and so is the ring he gave me when we got married. A marriage I regret, just like the feelings I started to have for the man in front of me.

"Good to know," he responds dryly. "You're just angry because I can't be the man in your little fairy-tale books. We've already been over this."

I walk toward his desk once again and place the ring on the glass, another stubborn tear sliding down my cheek. He slides his elbows off the desk and leans back.

"I'd rather cut off my fingers than wear your ring, and trust me, you will never be that man for me." I place the device that is both a phone and a way to pay for things on the desk, giving it back. "Keep it. I'm good."

I turn around and leave without a backward glance as my heart breaks into a million pieces.

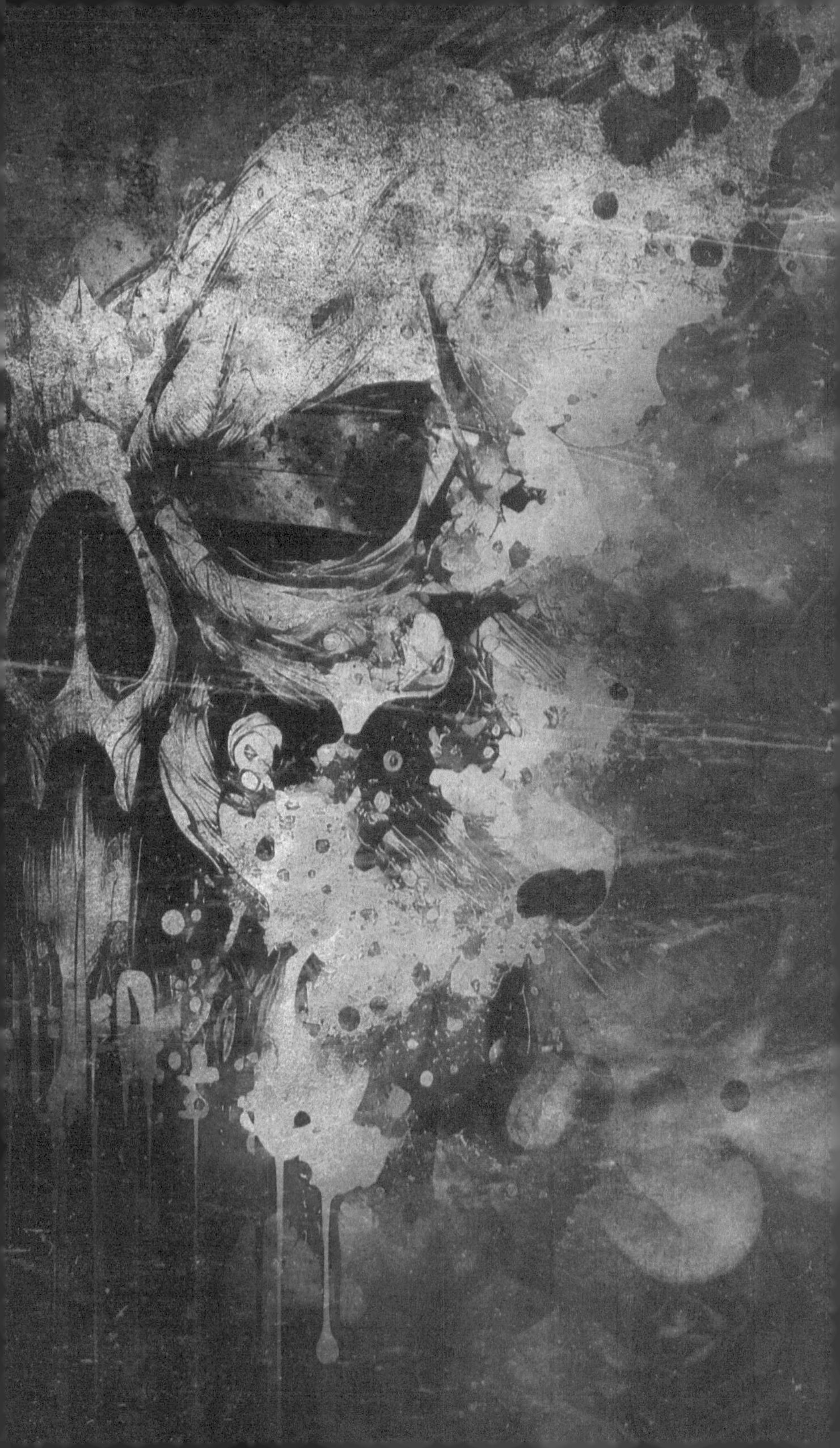

# 30



I stare at the ring she placed on my desk for hours after she left like a projectile waiting to slice right through me, but in all honesty, it has. My indifference blew up in my face. She hates me, and I can't blame her.

I've treated her like total shit. I told myself I was doing the right thing in distancing myself from her, but I was fooling myself. The look in her eye and the two tears I wanted to wipe away with my lips were like a knife twisting in my gut, making sure the wound wouldn't close.

"What's up, brother?" Ciro asks, walking into my office and taking a seat.

I'm a horrible husband.

"Nothing."

I'm about to swipe the ring off my desk, but Ciro is quicker and picks it up. He holds it up in the light.

"Is this what I think it is?"

"My wife's ring."

I use the word *wife* to remind him that she is married to me, even if she regrets it.

It was like a punch in the stomach, hearing her tell me I'm the last man she would want to be married to and that I could never be that man. Last night, I tried to stay, but I knew if I did, I would end up falling in love with her, and it scared the shit out of me.

"Why isn't she wearing it?"

"She wants me to send it to be cleaned."

Ciro snorts. "I doubt that. What did you do?" I snatch the ring from his fingers and slide it into my pocket, hating he's touching something that now belongs to her. But Ciro is a nosy motherfucker and looks over, raising his brow when he spots the phone and payment device I set up for her.

"Does she need that cleaned too?"

Dick.

I snatch the device away from him and hold it in my hand, knowing her dainty fingers touched it just moments ago.

"What do you need?"

"I need you to stop being an asshole to Lillith."

He taps the augmented screen, pulling up the location grid and hacking into the street cameras. He pulls a close-up image of her getting out of the Rolls-Royce I bought to take her around wherever she needs to go. The image of her face has my stomach tightening in knots.

She's been crying. A lot. Those beautiful turquoise eyes are puffy and red. I did that, and I want to go back and erase it, but I can't. I get all fucked up inside when she comes near me.

One look.

One word.

That is all it takes for me to fall under her spell.

But then I get angry because out of everyone, she is the only one who can dig inside me. She sees what no one has been able to—the real me.

I watch my best friend through my mask, and for the first

time, fear claws my gut. He's in love with her. And all I have done is push her away.

"Hack into her phone and add the account I have set up for her. Don't make it seem like it's from me. Ghost it."

"She will think her father never closed her personal accounts when you know he did the minute you wired him the rest of the money."

"If she knows it's from me, she won't use it, and she will be penniless out there."

"Then why did you let her leave, knowing she was going out there broke without a way to pay for anything?"

"Don't question what I do or how I handle my wife," I grit.

He gets up from the chair and storms out. "Where are you going?" I call out.

"To go get my friend! She needs me." His voice floats from the hallway.

I get up and pocket her device. He thinks she's his friend, but she's *my* wife.

# 31

LILLITH

"Please scan," the voice says from the machine, lighting up as it waits for payment. I tap my phone, and it turns green. "Payment accepted." I sigh in relief, glad my father wasn't such an asshole to close my account.

I took the ostentatious car that Killian left for me to travel around the island and went to a boutique shop to pick out some nice things to wear. I have always stuck to wearing black and opted for a blood-red suit that I think would pair nicely with the black boots I love to wear with everything.

I have tried to find them in different stores but haven't had any luck. It has been so long since I've gone out shopping for myself. I used to always have things sent to my father's house, but with the way things are going with Killian and me, it feels like living with him is a death sentence. I feel trapped inside a prison. Physically and mentally.

I walk out into the afternoon sun shining bright in the blue sky and spot the car I arrived in waiting at the curb. I approach it, and a man wearing a dark gray suit steps forward.

"Good afternoon, Miss Sinclair or, should I say, Mrs. Cross."

I squint my eyes and look into brown eyes and dark hair, scanning his face to see if I recognize him, but I can't place him.

"Do I know you?"

He shakes his head. "I know you, but I don't think you know me. I'm a friend of your father's. I requested an introduction, but your father was always busy." He sticks his hand out. "My name is James Hendricks."

I look at his outstretched hand and hesitate to place my hand in his, but I don't want to seem rude, so I shake it. His hand is firm, but the way his eyes darken has alarm bells going off in my head, screaming to run the other way. He slides his thumb over the top of my hand, and it feels forward and highly inappropriate. Even if it's just for show, I'm still married.

I pull my hand back and square my shoulders. "It was nice meeting you, Mr. Hendricks, but I have to head home. My husband is waiting."

He smiles, but it doesn't reach his eyes. I expected that. If he knows my father, he isn't to be trusted, and there must be a small moral bone in my father's body that hinted to him that it was never a good idea for me to meet this man.

James Hendricks is a tall, attractive man, but his demeanor makes him unapproachable. When you look into his eyes or watch his expression carefully, it's like watching a shark with cold eyes circling his prey, knowing he will strike but not knowing when.

I turn to walk toward the car when he asks, "How is your husband? He doesn't venture out much, does he? I'm kind of surprised he would let a woman who looks like you out alone. You never know who might snatch you up." He lowers his voice, and my skin pimples despite the heat. "You never know who might be lurking, looking for something as exquisite as you to sweep you off your feet and take you out to eat."

I don't miss the innuendo. James Hendricks is a pompous asshole.

"I wouldn't know. Maybe he's sure that wouldn't happen since I was properly fed my breakfast and dinner. He never leaves room for seconds."

His right eye twitches slightly at my response. Whoever this man really is, all I know is that he doesn't like Killian.

"Is that right, Mrs. Cross?" He places his hands in the pockets of his pants and rocks back on his heels. "If you ever get bored of eating or looking at the same thing, I work on the fifth floor in the next building over. I would love for you to join me for lunch or dinner. Maybe even both."

"I'll let my husband know and get back to you."

"Are you ready?" I look over at the sound of Ciro's voice, giving him a surprised smile. Ciro glances over at James and then back at me, but I don't miss the way James looks over at Ciro with his jaw set and eyes narrowed.

"He's from the mainland?"

I walk over to Ciro, giving him a look that says go along with whatever I say.

"My husband hired security for me when he isn't able to go with me on the days he has to work."

"Ah, yes. What is Killian Cross up to these days? One wonders what he does in that dark mansion. It is a wonder that the house was already here before the pandemic and technological revolution."

I shrug. "I wouldn't know. Maybe you could ask him when you see him."

*Which is never, asshole.*

James Hendricks represents the stark divide between the privileged and the majority of the mainland struggling to survive. Where people are living in the dark surrounded by drones tinged with an undercurrent of oppression and surveillance, the island itself is a picturesque paradise with a perfect landscape and beautiful people on the outside displaying excess wealth. But where there is wealth, there is madness underneath.

"Of course, when I see him."

I slide inside the car, releasing the breath I didn't realize I was holding when the car pulls away.

"Who the hell was that?"

I forgot that Ciro showed up. He sits in the front even though he isn't driving.

"What are you doing here? How did you find me?"

He turns around in his seat and gives me a smirk. "I'm not going to answer you until you tell me why you are out here all alone and not wearing your wedding ring." I roll my eyes at the mention of my wedding ring. "Come on. We're friends, remember?"

"You're more friends with Cross. Why don't you ask him?"

"I did."

That has me looking straight at him, nervously licking my lips. "What—"

"He didn't say." *Of course not. He doesn't care.* "However, I did tell him that he needs to stop being an asshole to you."

"How do you know he's being an asshole to me?"

"That's easy. What he said to you at the docks."

I look down at my hands clasped in my lap, remembering what he said, then last night, up until a few hours ago. I guess it's obvious. Everyone knows the truth about Killian and me in his circle, but out here, out here on the island, people wonder why I would choose Killian. I bet they think something is up. I know I would, and James Hendricks is sniffing close.

I meet Ciro's gaze. "I guess everyone knows, huh?"

"Knows what?"

I tear my gaze from his and look out the window, heading

to another set of stores between two massive skyscrapers. "That I mean nothing," I say absently.

The worst part of having everything at your disposal growing up is to look around you and know that you mean nothing to anyone. To know that you are kept around for someone's convenience. Like an object to be used and then discarded.

My father did it, and so will Killian.

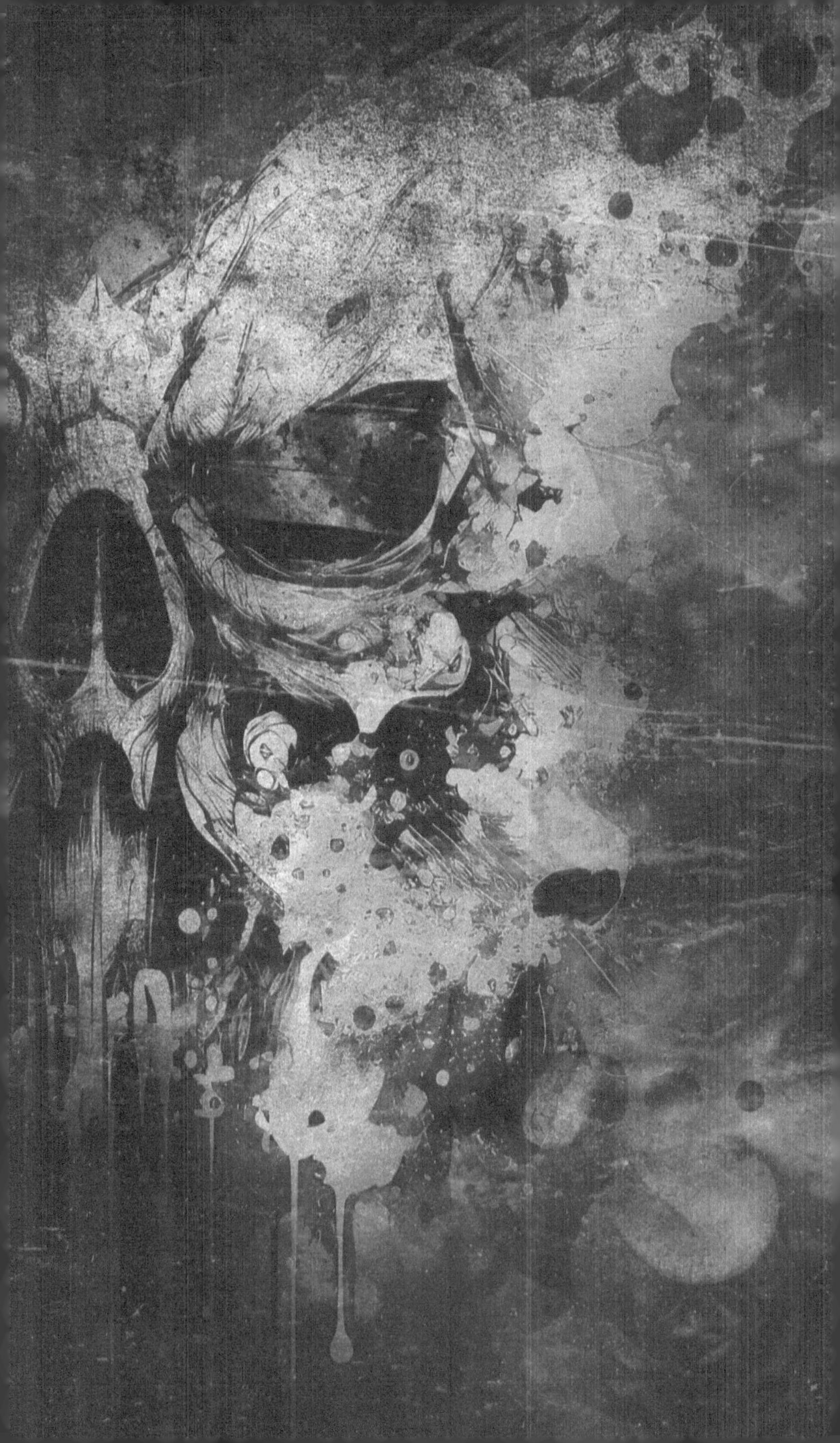

# 32



"How did you get in here?"

I swivel around in the dynamic chair created by the rich for the rich to look at James Hendricks's smug face. I lean back and fold my hands behind my head like it's my own office.

"I have my ways, but you should know that by now."

He stomps forward after pressing the button that slides the automatic door closed.

"What the fuck do you want, you freak?"

"I should ask you the same thing. Since you seem so inclined to ask my wife if I venture out." I watch the surprised expression wash over his face. "I also want to know how much you value things like your hands. Especially your fingers."

"How did you know I saw your wife?"

I sit up and begin fucking with the systems he has in place on his keypad. "Do you like monitoring your business? Do you like making sure no one touches something you value the most?"

"W-what are you doing? You little shit," he says, running out of breath. The cords of his neck pop out.

I press my finger hard on the key and reply, "Touching your shit."

I get up forcefully from the chair and round the desk, buying myself time so the virus I planted takes root inside all his systems. He takes a step back because one thing I know about James Hendricks and the judges he works for is that he's a coward and a snake. To be honest, I have never cared about what he's into or gave three fucks, but he touched *my* Lillith.

"What have you done?" His eyes widen as his systems begin to fail. I know the screen is glitching behind me.

"I have no idea what you're talking about."

"Is this about your wife? I didn't say anything to her."

"Are you sure about that? You didn't offer to fuck her or put your sleazy hand in hers?"

He raises his hand in mock surrender. "You can't be serious, Cross. I know she didn't marry you out of her free will, and everyone, including the judges, knows it. We were surprised when the officiate turned in the document indicating you got married. When they find out it was forced, you know what that means. You will be banished off the island, and she will be passed around, but I assure you, I will be the first to snatch her up."

"Are you a lefty or righty?"

A look of confusion crosses his features. "What?" he snaps.

"Do you write with your left or your right hand?"

He shakes his head, annoyed, and snarls. "My right. What does that have to—"

I snatch his thumb on his right hand and twist until I hear the crack of bone cutting off his words.

He clutches his hand and grunts through the pain. "You bastard. You broke my hand!" He tries to call for his security, but he can't because his system is fucked. On top of the fact that his right hand is out of commission and he can't scan it.

"Good luck jerking off, Mr. Hendricks."

"I'll end you, you freak."

I open my hands wide. "I'm right here. What are you waiting for?" I watch him grimace because the bastard can't take a little pain. Lowering my voice, I lean close. "Don't you ever touch my wife again, or I'll wipe you off the fucking planet. No one will know what the fuck you are when I'm done with you. They will have to scrape you off."

Lillith may have thought I didn't care because I watched her leave the house. We didn't say vows to one another when we married. One vow went through my mind when she pressed her soft lips on my mask. It was to protect her from assholes like James Hendricks.

# 33



I walk into the dressing room in the first boutique that caught my eye. All the clothes are basic tones of fabric covering half your body, but they look interesting and sexy. Not for Killian but for me. I want to feel beautiful. I'm tired of feeling sorry for myself and need to learn to live and stop dwelling on things I can't change.

I'm looking for the screen to turn on the light, wondering why the sensor didn't go off. The boutique has a dark theme, and the walls are the only stark white in the entire store. Everything else is black with chrome accents.

I finally find the screen on the left and press, looking up as the light turns on. When I turn to hang the clothes in my arms, I drop the clothes on the carpeted floor.

"How did you get in here?"

Sitting relaxed with his legs stretched out of his tall frame is Killian. The black mask he is wearing reads Kiss Me. *Very funny.*

"The same way you did. Through the door."

"Get out," I demand, bending down to pick up the three outfits I planned on trying on.

"Now, why would I do that?"

I huff. "Because I don't want to see you, and I have no interest in talking to you."

"You are so pretty when you're angry, but you're even more beautiful when I make you come."

My palms begin to sweat, and I'm thankful I have the clothes in my hands, but my thighs clench as I remember all the things he did to my body in vivid detail. I could be turning eighty years old, and I would always remember the night he made me his. But I deflect my feelings because I can't fall for him. He plans to get rid of me.

"I'm sure you have me mixed up with someone else. Since I met you, I have seen you fuck different women and make them come. Trust me, you have made it clear I'm nothing special. I'll be tossed out like a pile of garbage on the mainland."

I don't want to sound jealous even though deep down I was, but now I'm past caring. I left the house because it hurt too much to know why I was there, and I'm trying to figure out how to return. But he's screwing things up for me by showing up here.

I've thought of running, but where would I go?

"Try on the clothes."

"Leave."

He gets up from the chair and stalks closer. I step back almost to the door, looking up at him in defiance.

I should run, but I can't move. It feels like my feet are glued to the carpeted floor.

His mask ghosts my ear when he leans closer and whispers, "No." Awareness creeps in like a sneaky bitch down my neck. "Allow me." He takes the clothes from my hands and holds the first one up, cocking his head. "Where's the rest of it?"

I roll my eyes. "I'm not a droid."

"No because droids don't have clothes. Where's the rest of it, Lillith?"

"Are you worried I'll show too much?"

He lifts his mask over his mouth and darts his tongue out. Before I can lean away, he licks my lips like an animal. "Not at all. I want to make sure you can handle my possessive streak."

"What, are you going to hurt everyone who touches me?" I snort, rolling my eyes dramatically. "Why would you care? And stop licking me."

"You should see the last guy," he responds. "If I lick it, I eat it."

"Very funny, Cross."

"What did I say about calling me Cross?"

"Fine, Killlll."

I want to defy him. I want to push because he made me feel shitty.

He pushes me against the wall on the left, and I turn my face to the side. "You want me to eat you, Lillith? You want me to fuck you? I can smell how bad you want me."

I tilt my head and pin him with a stare. "Fuck. You."

He snags his bottom lip with his teeth, and I wish I could see the expression on his face hidden behind half the mask. When he pushes his body into me, I can feel the ridge of his hard cock.

"Trust me, nothing can take up space in my mind than the image of you taking my cock—only you." His hands slide up my tight pants, stopping at the curve of my waist. "Take this off. I want to see you try on the clothes I buy for you. Just make sure it covers your pussy. That's for my eyes only."

He steps away from me, and I swear if the wall hadn't been behind me, I would have crumpled to the floor. The scent of him clouds my vision. It's like he's a magician who can hypnotize me and make me do whatever he wants.

I strip for him because Killian Cross is a dangerous man. I can feel the side of him that is evil and doesn't relent when he wants something. He will do anything to get it. He waits in the dark. The same way he had been waiting for me all these years since we met unofficially, waiting for the right time. Just like now, when I thought I was on my own in the city, he shows up unannounced doing whatever the fuck he wants because he can.

He takes a seat, widening his legs and stroking his cock over his pants, letting me know he's still hard for me. *Dick.*

"Try on the first one," he says, adjusting his mask over his face. "The one I held up first."

"But you don't like it."

His comment was proof enough. Killian Cross is a jealous man when he wants to be.

"Humor me."

"Fine.

I should feel embarrassed that I'm completely nude, but I was nude last night after he came inside me five or six times in various positions. Positions I never knew existed.

"You're thinking about sex."

A shiver runs down my spine, and I shake my head, not wanting to tell him the truth, so I lie. "No, I'm not."

He snorts and then chuckles. "Come here."

I hesitate, but he calls me over with his finger. I slide my thong back up my thighs, and he chuckles louder. *Asshole.*

I'm standing between his legs, and the last thing I thought he would do, he does.

Fuck my life.

He slides the tiny fabric away from the apex between my thighs and dips his index finger between my folds, holding up evidence of the truth. "Liar." He tugs me hard enough so I'm at eye level with his mask. "Taste the way I make you feel, Lillith." He slides my arousal across my lips.

I can't move.

He holds me tight enough that I can't pull away but not enough to hurt me. I close my eyes and slide my tongue across my lips, tasting myself. Something I have never done.

"You may hate me like you say," he says, "but your body wants me. It craves me. Doesn't it, Lillith? That's why you're so angry with me. Why you took off my ring. Why you cry."

Tears burn my eyes because maybe he's right. Maybe I just can't get over the fact I want him more than he wants me. But want is one thing, and love is another, and I'm trying to protect my heart because he scares me. He scares me because Killian Cross is the only man who can finish breaking me into pieces and ruin me for anyone else.

"Killian, please," I plead.

"Look at me." I open my eyes. My vision blurs. He caresses my bottom lip with his thumb gently. "I want you too, Lillith, more than I should, and I'm sorry I can't give you the love you deserve. If I could, that person would always be you."

It didn't matter.

His words broke me anyway. Killian Cross shattered my heart.

I just hope I could survive the fall.

# 34



"**W**hat is your favorite romance novel?"

I look over at Killian sitting in his sleek matte-black car, heading deeper onto the island away from home.

He sent Ciro home in the Rolls after he had me try on every outfit I liked in the store. His words hurt, but I would rather him be honest than lie to me.

"I would have to say *The Phantom of the Opera* by Gaston Leroux."

"Why that one?"

"Because it's a sad love story. It's the only one I read where the protagonist rejects the greatest love in the end. He played music for her. Loved her. Would do anything for her. But she leaves him for Raoul. When Raoul didn't deserve her love. I think the phantom deserved it because he was a better person once he learned to love. He loved her so much that he let her and Raoul go so they could live happily ever after because that made her happy."

"You would have stayed?"

I nod. "I would have stayed. A love like that only comes once in a lifetime. That is why it's my favorite. All the other books have a happily ever after. Even if the man or woman dies in the end, they still loved one another. To me, the phantom always stood out, and in the past, they had adaptations of plays and musicals because the music is so beautiful. My favorite is the piano version."

"Is it?"

"You've never heard?"

He shakes his head. "No. It's not my thing."

"Oh. Of course not," I say and chew my lip nervously. "What is?"

"Are you asking what music I like to listen to, Lillith?"

"I am."

He slides his thumb over the screen, and "Imaginary Friends" by Deadmau5 plays.

Progressive house music. I shouldn't be surprised. Killian is a tech genius. I wondered how he could pinpoint my exact location and how Ciro showed up in the nick of time. I don't know how he's doing it, but now I know I'm always being watched.

I can't run away even if I have the balls to do it. He will always find me. There is nowhere I could run to or hide. Killian will always find me.

"We're really different, huh?" I ask.

He lowers the music so that it plays softly in the background as the stars light up the dark sky from the panoramic view of the moving car.

"Different is good."

"How so?"

"It means we could never be bored of one another. Different doesn't always have to equate to bad. You like things that are not easily accessible, that have meaning to you and history. It makes you unique because you like things that most people have forgotten exist. Books written by people who they thought were a lost cause. A lost voice. People like you keep them alive. You keep their stories alive."

I smile. That is the nicest thing anyone has ever said to me. No one in my father's house knew that I read besides Ethan or that I liked to read novels by great writers of the past.

"Thank you. I think you are a very intelligent man. "

He doesn't respond.

I want to throw in that he's gorgeous, but I know he wouldn't believe me. I wish he would take the mask off when he's around me. I want to memorize his face and expressions when he looks or speaks to me, but he doesn't feel comfortable around me.

The car stops at the edge of a road with a lighted path leading to the beach. When I was young, I once saw the beach because my father had to meet someone, and we were out. I was in the car and could never touch the sand or go in the water. I wanted to come on my own but was afraid of what I would find. What if I drowned? He jumps out and opens the door for me, holding out his hand.

We reach the sand, and I hear the waves crashing wildly on the shore as the wind blows my hair. All I see is the black sea with stars blanketing the sky. The sand covers my boots as my heels sink.

Killian plops on the ground beside me, drawing his knees up.

"Why are we here?"

"I thought you might like the fresh air and the sound of the sea."

I take a seat beside him, smelling the salty air. "I do. Have you ever been?"

He shakes his head. "No. Only my feet and then the accident."

I frown, thinking it odd that he built a boat but has never fully gone in the water. It dawns on me. Of course. The accident.

I turn my head. "Your eye. You can't go in?"

He shakes his head. "Never. I would lose the capability of my prosthetic. It's my own personal supercomputer. It transmits what I see to my brain."

"Is that why it shifts like you're a reptile?"

He laughs. "Yeah. I created it, and Dr. Archer implanted it."

"That's amazing."

"It's why they haven't killed me like they wanted to. I'm the only one who can control the technology on the entire island and the mainland. If they kill me, they're all fucked."

"How?"

"It will bring them back to the Stone Ages with landline phones. They might as well start training birds to deliver messages. I hacked the grid and created a world in the cloud. Augmented reality and security systems."

"You're playing both sides."

"Yes. Two worlds and I'm the key to it all, but they think I'm on their side regarding technology, and I go to the mainland to remove the lower-level hackers from tampering with their system. It's what they think I do anyway. Kind of like a bounty hunter."

That's why he gets away with going to the mainland. They just don't know exactly what he does there. He makes sure he covers his tracks.

"Why are you telling me all this?"

He sighs. "I don't know. So you can understand I'm not a monster. I'm the villain trying to kill the monster."

"Can I ask you to do something for me?"

"Depends."

"When we're alone, could you take off your mask?"

"Why?"

I tilt my head and murmur, "So I can see the way you look at me."

He turns to me, and I swear time stands still in anticipation. The stars and moon in the sky are the only light over his mask. I turn to face him on my knees, not caring about the sand.

My heart races when he's lifted the mask off, and I watch the emotions cross his features. It's like I'm looking at him for the first time. The dark beauty of him.

My eyes caress both the light and dark sides of his handsome face. His dark hair falls over one brow, and I fall under his spell.

"Lillith."

"Killian."

It feels like I can see his soul, and he can see mine. Our faces inch closer until we're mere centimeters away, drawn to each other like a moth to a flame. He's the moth, and I'm the flame, drawn to each other, knowing we will both burn in each other's ashes until nothing but the embers is left.

His breath is now mine, and mine is now his, needing each other like we're starved of oxygen.

Our lips crash, and I drown in him. My fingers slide into his hair. His hands slide down my body, tearing at my clothes. I grip the opening of his shirt, hearing the tear and the buttons pop. His soft skin with his tattoos under my fingers when I slide my hands underneath, seeking the feel of his skin. He doesn't stop until I'm left in my panties and bra. My hand slides brazenly inside his pants, finding the soft velvety skin on the tip of his cock.

"Lillith," he hisses.

"Fuck me, Killian."

I see the shift of his prosthetic eye shining like a mirror against the light of the moon. He lifts me onto his lap so I straddle him, sinking my knees in the sand as he leans back to free his cock. The warm tip crowns my entrance over my panties.

The wind picks up, causing my hair to fly in the wind behind me. I slide my panties over and impale his cock, causing him to groan.

A whimper escapes my throat, and I begin to ride him hard, but he grips my hips, holding me in place. I pinch my brows, and then I gasp when he flips me over so that he is on top.

He slides into me slowly, keeping his hands under my ass so the sand doesn't rub against our skin, and says softly, "My wife."

My fingers trace the outline of his jaw, feeling the stubble on his chin. The perfect shape of his lips while he drives into me slowly.

"Fuck me, Killian."

But he shakes his head, denying me what I want. I want him to take me hard, making it quick so I can get off, but he doesn't, and I want to hate him for it.

"Please," I beg, grinding my hips, seeking for him to move faster, but he pulls out and slides in slowly. Gently.

A delicious torture builds inside me, begging for release like a monster wanting out of his cage, but Killian won't do it. He won't let it. Not the way I want.

It will always be the way he wants.

Right now, it's soft and slow, and maybe it's hard and fast tomorrow. Quick, without so much as a single kiss. Always denying what is between us. The hunger for more.

I turn my head and look up at the sky like a deep abyss drowning out the pain I feel in my heart as he moves inside me.

It doesn't matter if he fucks me fast or slow, hard or gentle. The result will be the same—I will break apart for him.

He picks up speed, grunting. He knows I'm close. My pussy clenches him tight. I open my legs so he can take me deep, just like the dark sky. Dark and beautiful.

"I'm coming."

The crashing waves are all I hear when I come, mixed with the heat of him when he spills inside me. The wind causes a shiver to run over my sweaty skin, but I try not to look at his face.

"Look at me, Lillith."

My eyes meet his, hoping he doesn't see that I've fallen deeply in love with him despite everything.

Despite the fact that Killian Cross will kill me when I give him what he wants. It is why he refuses to love me.

Because it's easier to kill someone when you don't love them. When you don't care. A sacrifice for the greater good. What's one when you can save more?

EVERY DAY since the night at the beach seven weeks ago, Killian comes to me at night, fucks me, and always leaves after I fall asleep. He never stays longer than that. I guess it makes it easier for him not to get attached. The same way he figures the reason I don't want to wear his ring.

He says it was his mother's. Agnes talked about his parents once. She said they were in love and that the greatest gift was Killian. It seemed wrong to accept a ring from the woman who wore it when she received it from the man she loved. A man who was devoted to her for all the right reasons. Wearing it on my finger for all the wrong reasons feels like I'm shitting on their memory. Their life was taken, and I can understand Killian's need for vengeance. He won't admit to love, but he loved his parents, or he wouldn't care. He has a heart underneath his rough exterior. It just doesn't belong to me.

"Are you ready?"

I look up from staring at the ocean to Ciro, trying to figure out how to hide the truth.

I'm pregnant.

I haven't had my period in two months. Telling anyone that I am would put me and my baby in danger. I'd be on the chopping block, and my child would be at risk of being raised without its mother. I know exactly what that feels like.

"Yeah." I take a deep breath, knowing the rocking boat will make me queasy, but I have to get through it.

"Are you sure you want to do this?"

I look around and nod. "Please." When my gaze finds his, I hope he sees the desperation in my eyes for what I've decided to do. What I need to do. "You're my only hope."

I see him visibly swallow. "Like we talked about alright?"

"Like we talked about," I repeat.

I hear footsteps behind me and see Killian wearing his mask, dressed all in black as usual. He walks in front of me, and Ciro pauses, turning his head to the side and giving me his back.

"Let's go," Killian says in a stern voice.

He always gets serious when Ciro and I talk even though we are just friends. I don't think he's jealous because I have never given him a reason to be. I'm always around. If he leaves the house to go to the mainland, he makes sure I come along, never leaving me alone at the house. If I want to go shopping, he comes with me.

"Coming," I reply.

"I'm going to head out. I'll meet you guys at the docks," Ciro says, walking ahead to the second boat.

My heart begins to beat wildly in my chest, hoping I can survive the fall. We are all just trying to chase our dreams and love. I'm hoping to get away from mine.

The boat pulls away from the dock. Blair, Sydney, and Sarah are already on board, giving me weird looks because I refuse to go inside. I look around to make sure I'm alone and then at the dark sea as the boat turns, heading toward the mainland.

I'm surprised Killian hasn't said anything about me staying outside. I grip my phone and lean over the black railing, letting it slip from deft fingers into the ocean as the boat cuts through the water.

I look up, and a shiver runs down my spine. Is the water cold, warm, or will it not matter because I won't make it to the surface? Maybe something waits for me down there, sealing my fate before I can wallow in the consequences of my decisions. All the what-ifs. But it's not the what-ifs I'm concerned about. It's my future. My child's future. Its father has already made up his mind of what his consist of, and it doesn't include me in it.

I see it.

Every night he takes my body.

No love.

No hate.

Just purpose—his purpose.

I see the mainland come up on the horizon after staring at the water for the last hour and a half it takes to get there. Just a little closer.

I'm hoping the black skintight neoprene I'm wearing underneath keeps me warm enough.

*A little closer, Killian. Come on.*

The closer the boat gets, the seconds in my head tick by counting down the memories I have of Killian. Memories that I have to let go.

Tears slide down my cheeks as I grip the railing, feeling the metal underneath my hands.

One.

Two.

Three.

*I'm sorry.*

I jump.

The whoosh of cold water hits me like a thousand knives on my skin. The darkness grips me. The breath I'm holding so that my lungs don't seize as I try to stay afloat. The muscles in my arms and legs scream from my effort.

*Goodbye, Killian.*

# 35

## LILLITH

Five Years Later

There are spaces in your heart that open and close to love. You can hold on to it or let it go to make room for a new love. A love you never knew existed that came from within. A love that grew inside you like no other. An experience not everyone gets to enjoy.

It was the first time I realized what my mother truly lost. The love of her child. The true essence of beauty created from within. It's what I see when I look at my four-year-old son, Niro.

"Can I have this one, Mom?"

I look at his beautiful aquamarine eyes and hair so dark, it's almost blue, holding up a mechanical droid. It's old, but he likes to try to fix it so the other kids can play with it.

I look up at the woman with dirt smudges on her face, trying to cover my face as much as I can by pulling the hood of my sweater over my asymmetrical short haircut so she doesn't get a good look at me. I stand out when I show my face and so does Niro. It is like they know we aren't supposed to be on the mainland.

"How much?" I ask her.

"0.000174."

*Shit.*

"Do you take food or books?"

I need the digital currency for other stuff. Niro looks back and forth between me and the lady. He probably sees the worried look on my face.

"I can fix that?" He points.

He runs and fixes the lady's digital sign by resetting it, and it stops glitching.

I wonder how he figured that out at such a young age, but he does spend time with Ciro. It's just a couple of buttons and a master reset.

The woman raises her brows and nods.

"He can have it."

I nod my head in relief. "Thank you."

"Any time."

We step out of the store he wanted to enter, and I gently pull him to the side by his arm. "You can't do that all the time, Niro. Someone could follow us. It will attract attention."

He lowers his eyes and frowns. "I was trying to help. I saw the look on your face. It was sad, and I figured you couldn't pay."

He's right. I couldn't pay it. I know he wanted the little droid, but he can't draw attention to us.

After the fifteen-minute walk back to the little room above the fortune teller I went to years ago that Ciro was able to secure for us since I left Killian, I look into the little fridge to see what I can make Niro to eat.

It's getting harder, but Ciro has provided us with meals

from the runs he does with Kill. It's not easy, but he has managed to keep us hidden from everyone.

Killian thinks I'm dead.

"Hey." I hear Ciro come through the small door.

"Ciro!" Niro runs into Ciro's arms for a hug and their secret handshake.

He holds up a small box. "Look what I got you."

Niro tears into it while I shake my head. "Yes! My own tools! Look, Mom. I can fix things now."

"You're going to spoil him," I scold.

He shrugs, but I don't miss the look in his eyes. The look that tells me I mean more. The look I have to ignore.

"I got something for you." He pulls out a book from his pack and walks over.

I take it and look at the cover with my heart in my throat. "I heard it was your favorite."

I look away. "It was. A long time ago."

*The Phantom of the Opera.* I had a copy in my room at Killian's house, but I had to leave everything behind, and I didn't want to risk buying books here on the mainland in case Killian got wind someone was buying romance books from the only guy who could supply them.

"I was able to get a copy."

"How?"

He smiles. "I know a guy who knows a guy."

Meaning he made sure it couldn't be traced back to him.

"How did you know it was my favorite?"

"He talks about you... all the time."

My chest feels tight thinking about Killian. Ciro would tell me for months that he barely ate. The months of him hiding in his office. The hours he would spend every day on the water with his boat looking for my body.

He never came back to the mainland and would send Ciro

back and forth instead. I was glad when I heard that part because it meant he wasn't looking for me here. It meant I could be free, even if I lived with Niro in poverty like everyone else.

I look at Niro playing with the toy droid, trying to get it fixed with his new set of tools, and lower my voice. "Still?" I ask. "I thought he would have gotten over it by now. He could have kept his relationship with Blair. I'm sure having me gone made her happy. I know how much he cared about her and the others. He made sure to tell me how much everything meant to him."

"Lillith. He has never been the same since. He hardly talks to anyone. Even me. He's...different."

"So am I. I'm not giving up my son." I shake my head. "I'm not giving him away so he can raise Niro and then just kill me off anyway." My bottom lip trembles because I love Niro with every fiber of my being. "I wouldn't change any of it if it meant losing him."

Ciro wraps his arms around me. "I know, Lillith," he says. He tilts his head, pressing a kiss on my forehead. I rest my cheek on his chest, breathing in his manly scent.

Ciro has taken care of Niro and me the best he can. When he found out I was pregnant, he was there. Every step. He held my hand when the doctor helped me deliver Niro in this tiny room. He has always been there for us.

I look up into his brown eyes. "Thank you. For everything. For saving me. For saving us."

I know he's had to lie to his best friend all this time. It must have been hard keeping Niro and me a secret for so long.

"I would do anything for you and Niro. I wish I could do more. Give you guys more."

I lean back in his arms and smile. "You're too good to me."

His eyes caress my face, and I take the time to see the smile he always has for me. His hair has gotten darker since I first met him. It has turned a dark blond color. He always wears different colognes, so I can lean close and smell the one he's wearing, getting ready to tease him.

"Do you like this one?"

I snicker. "Where'd you rip this one off from?"

The corner of his mouth lifts in a crooked grin. "From a guy I know. Do you like this one?" I stand on my toes and lean close, smelling his neck. The scent is spicy and manly. I kind of liked Killian's, but I don't think that smell could ever be replicated. It's unique and all him. He dips his head and whispers, "I told him this picky friend I had was sensitive to smell."

I laugh because when I was pregnant, so many repugnant smells in the mainland would make me throw up everything I ate. Ciro would try to find me perfume and cologne to calm my stomach. There wasn't much to choose from, so I had to go with lab-created scents he could find.

"Picky, huh."

"Yeah, picky and gorgeous." I blush.

"Did you tell him how much of a pain in the ass you are?"

"Am I really?"

Holding up my index finger and thumb close together, leaving a tiny space, I tell him, "Just a little."

He laughs and slides my hair behind my ear, and there's that look again. He tries to peel back my layers with his eyes to figure out how I feel deep inside. I have been so focused on raising Niro the best I can and don't have time to feel or talk about the past. Like everyone else in the city, I worry about surviving the present and hoping for a brighter future.

"When's the next race?" I ask.

I need to make money. The arena is where you can make fast cash in one night. It's enough to keep us afloat for a month.

Ciro releases his arms around me and turns to see Niro playing with his droid. "I can give you money, Lillith. You don't have to race."

I get in front of him and meet his eyes. "I can't keep taking money from you, Ciro. You have done enough for me all these years. You have a place of your own you need to pay. You have been wanting to buy parts for your car."

"All that can wait, Lillith. You're more important to me than a stupid place I hardly stay in and a car I will hardly drive working with Kill."

"I won't let you. I'm going to race."

Ciro took me to the arena and showed me what really goes on down there. Motorcycle racing. I remember the day Killian took me there for the first time. The speed at which they were traveling was like a lightning bolt, making the ground shake as they zoomed past me. It took me a year to learn to ride, but I learned and am pretty good at it. When it means your next meal, you start figuring out how to go faster and faster until you're the best.

Kill was the best, but that was before, and this is now.

"You're going faster, and it's dangerous, Lillith."

"I've lived in danger all my life. A little motorcycle race going in circles hardly qualifies as dangerous." I lower my voice, clenching my teeth. "My own husband was counting down the months until I gave him an heir so he could kill me."

He whips around, making sure Niro can't hear what we are saying, causing me to retreat to the makeshift kitchen. "Don't you think I know that? Things are different with him now, but that doesn't change what you have to do. I wouldn't change it and would do it again. But you have to keep in mind that he will go back to the arena and race, Lillith." He steps closer, gently gripping me by the arms. "I'm trying to keep you safe. I love you, Lillith. You and Niro."

I avert my eyes because as much as I care about Ciro and all he is done for me and Niro, I don't love him that way. I know he's trying to make it seem like he loves me as a friend, but I see it. Ciro loves me like a man deeply in love with a woman who doesn't belong to him. He's Killian's best friend, and I would never cross that line.

Dead or not, I'm Killian Cross's wife, and I have his son. That will never change. It's stupid to hold on, but I didn't leave Killian to find happiness with his best friend. I faked my death to give Niro and me a chance to live. My life and the ability to ever love another man *was* the sacrifice.

"I know, and it's why you need to set up my next race. The bike's energy cell was upgraded to go faster."

"And if he gets wind and decides to race?"

"Then I guess you'll have to make sure he doesn't figure out who beats him," I tease.

"He will bring his A game, Lillith. This is how he tests the energy in things he builds off the grid."

I figured that was why Killian was so hell-bent on racing all the time. It was never for the money because it's obvious he has plenty of it. He would share his winnings with the guys in his crew, Ciro included. Now I understand why he won all the time. His bike was the fastest ever built off the main grid. Undetectable. There is also no way any network could track it.

"He may make the bikes faster with the cells he puts together, but I have skill. I know that track better than anyone."

"I get that, but still... if you push, he will push harder."

I move past him to put something together for Niro to eat the old-fashioned way, holding a pan and starting the burner. "That is if he decided to race. We both know he hasn't raced in five years, so there is that. There is no guarantee he will, but if he does, I'm ready for it. The money will be more than enough for a while, so it's a win-win for me *when* I beat him." I change the subject, holding the pan in the air. "Hungry?" I wince at what remains of the food he's able to get. It's not much, but it's the least I can do for the gifts he brought Niro and me.

He glances at the few items I have spread out. "Why didn't you tell me you needed more food, Lillith?"

I grip the pan, hating he noticed. Niro is growing, and he gets hungry more often, and I won't deny him a meal. There are many times that I skip a meal to make sure he eats.

The food that is easily accessible is still grown in a lab. It's synthetic and isn't good for the human body, but they will never tell anyone that. The government just says that it's good for the planet and humanity. *Shitty liars.* That stuff has chemicals and hormones that cause unknown diseases to form when you least expect it. There is no way I'll feed Niro that stuff.

I turn around, placing the pan on the burner and hoping he'll drop the issue. That is why I need to race. I hate depending on Ciro for things I can't get because I don't have untraceable money or the kind that is not linked to me. The only untraceable money is the digital kind won at the arena.

"Lillith." He calls my name.

"What?" I sigh, not glancing in his direction as I prepare the water to boil the vegetables.

"When was the last time you ate a decent meal?"

Three days ago, but I don't tell him that. Instead, I watch the bubbles form in the water of the pan in silence. Oil is not an option, so everything is cooked in the water Ciro gets me from the island.

"Move in with me, Lillith. You and Niro."

That has my head whipping around to face him. "I've told you no, Ciro. I have to do this on my own."

"You're so stubborn. He said that was your only flaw."

Blood rushes to my head every time Ciro reminds me of

Killian. It's like a dagger stuck twisting inside my heart, causing me the pain I have tried these past years to hide.

I grab the vegetables with more force than necessary and drop them in the pan, hearing them bubble. The sound reminds me of the anger bubbling inside me.

"Funny he says that when the biggest flaw is what he planned on doing to his wife after she was of no use to him."

"I know, but I think that is his biggest regret, Lillith. Making you think he would go through with it."

I slam my hand on the small table, the sound causing Niro to look up from where he sits on the floor.

My voice is hard, sucking back the bitter taste of Killian's past rejections. "You always defend him, Ciro. Did you know after I showed up and he bought me, I went snooping one night the third week I was there. I hadn't seen him or met him, but I found him. He was in another room fucking Blair. I know that because I saw them. He did it again while I waited for him at the dinner table. He was too busy fucking Blair and Sarah in his office to have the common decency to at least tell me to fuck off and go away." Ciro flinches, but my lip curls in contempt. Annoyed that Killian has the balls to say I'm stubborn. "He may be a great friend and a great lover to your little girlfriends in your crew. But you heard him yourself that day at the dock in front of everyone. He never cared about me. He cared more about the people counting on him, including you and the rest of your friends. It didn't include me. I wasn't trying to get him to choose. I just wanted to be included." I shake my head, hating myself for loving him despite everything. "So please... he can go fuck himself. He should be celebrating. In his mind, I'm dead. No more fucking the stubborn wife and leaving her when she falls asleep alone in the bed like a paid prostitute." My lip trembles on the last part, remembering all the lonely nights when Killian would leave me.

Ciro glances at Niro and then back at me with a sad expression. "I'm sorry. I had no idea it was like that."

My shoulders sag in defeat because it's not Ciro's fault. A sigh escapes my lips, and I finish preparing the food and quietly say, "That wasn't the worst part. The worst part is looking into the eyes of the person you love, and they repeatedly tell you they can't love you, wishing it was a lie."

"And I wish you didn't love him so you could give me the chance to love you the way you always dreamed of. Let me, Lillith."

A dull ache forms in the pit of my stomach, knowing it hurts him every time he is near me that I can't love him the way he deserves.

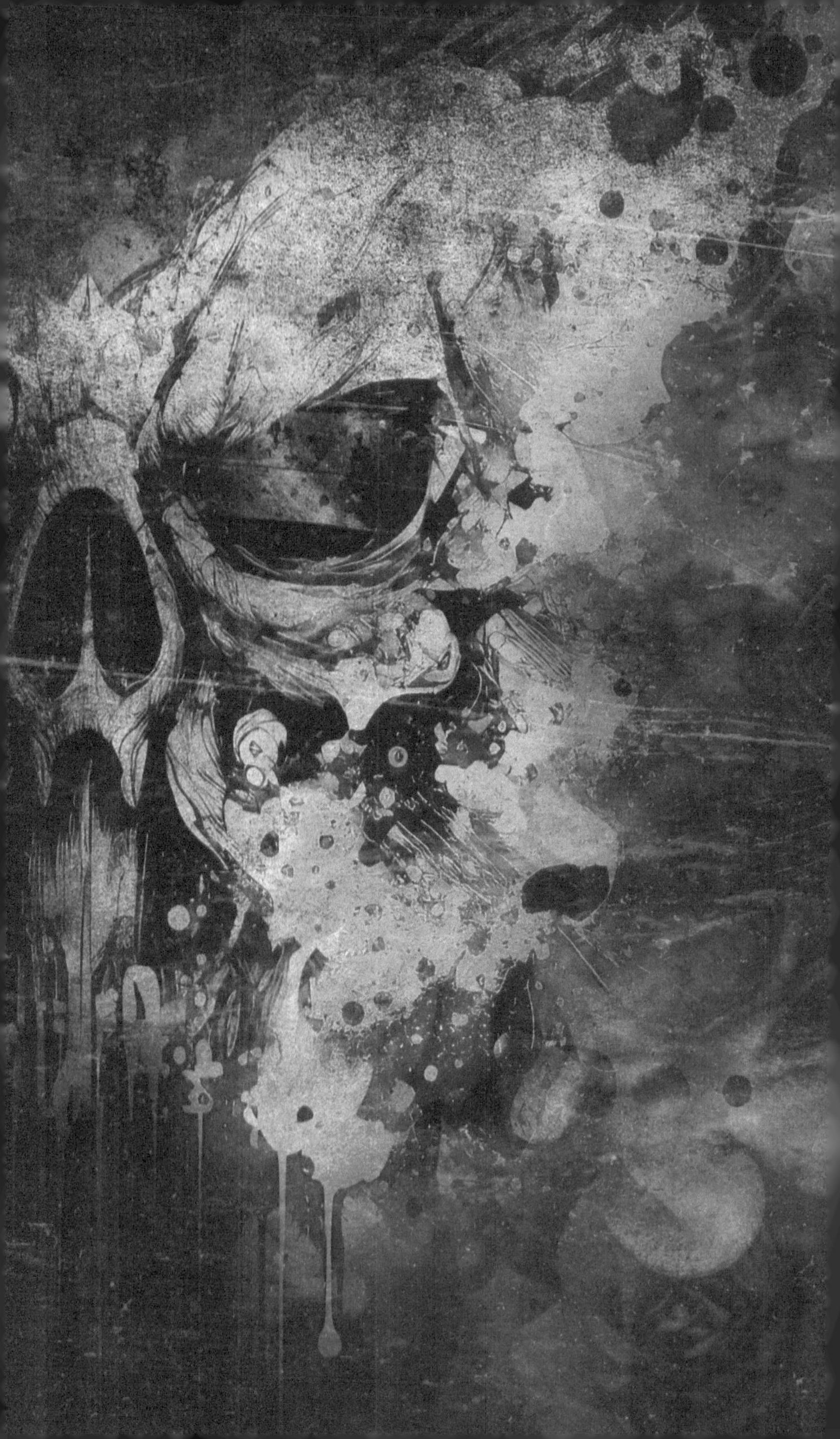

# 36

## KILLIAN

The noise of the spoon hitting the metal bowl on the table echoes in the dining room. I lower my mask when I hear footsteps to my left.

"I'm sorry, Mr. Cross," Agnes says breathlessly when she appears behind Blair. "I told her you were indisposed."

I raise a hand, silently dismissing her, and wait until Agnes leaves the dining room. "What?"

Blair saunters closer to the other end of the dining table, and my eyes narrow as she approaches the plate of food set across from me. "Don't you miss me—miss us?"

"No. Get out."

I know what happened is not Blair's or anyone's fault but my own, but a part of me died with her that day. I guess you don't know how precious someone is until they're gone. It puts things into perspective, and one thing is very clear—there is no Blair and me. Never was and never will be.

I watch as her hand toys with the back of the chair. "This isn't healthy, Kill. You need to get back and work on the grid. People are counting on you. I know it's hard. " She moves to touch the plate, and I slam my hand on the white table, causing her to jump and the metal to rattle on the table's surface.

"Don't touch her food!"

Blair jumps back and covers her mouth with her hand. Her eyes are glassy. "I'm s-sorry," she stammers. "She's dead, Kill. She jumped in the ocean, and it's been five years. You can't keep doing this to yourself."

I disregard her words because Lillith Cross will always be alive to me. Her smell, her touch, and the softness of her skin will always be with me. Nothing else matters.

I look her straight in the eyes, and she looks straight back at me. I'm boiling with fury at her, reminding me that my wife is dead. I clench my jaw so tight I grind my teeth. "To me, she will never be dead. No one will replace her, Blair. No one. I suggest you get the fuck out before I throw you out."

Her hands drop to her sides, forming fists. Blair loves to throw a tantrum when she doesn't get what she wants. She knows I won't fuck her. She can get naked, and my dick will crawl under my balls to hide. There is only one woman I want, and she's dead because I killed her. I killed us. She'd rather die than live a life without love.

"There's a race coming up. It can clear your mind. Since you've been gone, someone has taken over, winning every race for the past three years in a row."

That has my attention. A race would be good. It's not like I have much to lose anyway. I can push until I explode for all I care.

"Who?"

She shakes her head and shrugs her shoulders. "No one knows. She goes by the name Pyralis."

"*She?*"

"No one knows where she came from, but it's a woman

with a body like that. You know that no one alters themselves anymore if they want to get on the island."

"What does she look like? Maybe I know who it is."

Many people have been off the main grid for years because of yours truly. The judges and the assholes they employ have been a ghost for a while since I've stopped working on the network. Food and supplies are the only thing that I haven't stopped. If I start back on it, they will raise eyebrows and begin sniffing around me again. They assume it's me, but they don't have proof.

"No one has been able to see her face. She doesn't take off her helmet, and she's covered head to toe in black."

*Interesting.*

I pull up the network from my watch. The image appears on my prosthetic eye. The next race is in three days. I press the enter button on my watch.

The message appears. *Challenge Accepted.*

"I'll be there."

A smile forms on her lips. "So you're going to race Pyralis?"

She walks up to me, her smile getting wider, her face lighting up, and now that she is closer, I wonder what I ever saw in her. A shiver crosses over my skin. The kind when you find someone unattractive, and you have been intimate with.

"I said I'll be there."

Her gaze drops to the floor and then drifts up to land on my mask, and I see the desire in her eyes. "I miss you, Kill."

She's not giving up.

"I don't miss you." A hush tone wedges between my words. "I only miss *her*."

Her eyes lower, and her lips turn into a deep frown after hearing my rejection loud and clear. She mumbles, "I know."

I would have thought since I married Lillith, she would take the hint. Then my words play in my mind. The things I said to Lillith in front of them and in private, making me retreat inside myself. The guilt clawing to the surface for the way I treated her.

I grip the edge of the table and stand, walking out of the dining room without a backward glance. "See yourself out."

I HEAR a knock on the door, and I smile because this is the only room in the house that has a vintage wood door with a lock. They don't make them anymore. Only the kind that slides from within the wall with a press of a button.

"Come in."

"Mr. Cross. You wanted to see me," Agnes says, closing the door behind her.

I sit up from the bed, placing the book on the nightstand. "I wanted to ask if Lillith had any other favorites."

Agnes gives me a warm smile and tilts her head. "She did tell me once that she loved a book called *Shanna*."

"Did she have that one?"

"Here."

I nod, looking at the little shelf I had made for her books. I noticed when she died that she never opened the boxes of books I bought for her, but of course she wouldn't. Not after what I said to her that day. I left the boxes in her room out of respect, but I was hoping I could read another one of her favorites. I've read the Phantom of the Opera by Gaston Leroux five times. I remember when she told me it was her favorite.

Agnes moves toward the shelf and selects the one she mentioned. She hands it to me, and I smile, looking at the cover of a man and a woman in love like it's a prized jewel.

"I never took you for a reader of romance, Killian."

I snort. "You know why I want to read them, Agnes."

She sits on the bed and pats my arm gently. "Tell me."

I swallow thickly, touching the book like she would have. "If I read what she loved, maybe it would bring me closer to her even if she's gone. I want to read what she felt in those pages through her eyes."

"Is that why you won't stop using this room like it's your own?"

I nod. "Crazy, huh? My mother loved this room. Lillith loved this room, and now I love this room."

"It still smells like her."

"Like whom?"

"Lillith."

I place the pillow under my mask and smell it, hoping I could find the smell that belongs to her. I know that's impossible, but maybe it's in my mind.

She pats my hand and moves to leave but stops and says, "The greatest love never dies, Killian. It survives even when those we love pass on. It survives in the person who loved them the most. It's a gift. Like that book that belonged to her."

When the door closes behind her, I turn the page. *Chapter One.*

The sound of the electric motorcycles mixed with the roar of people screaming and dancing to the music sink into my bones. It's race day. The main event is about to start. The teleprompter at the back of the arena begins to play "Humble" by Skrillex.

I gently squeeze Niro's hand with my gloved fingers as I approach the racers' area. Ciro can't be here with me because Killian is racing tonight. I look to my left, and Ethan gives me a slight nod to keep walking.

After I had Niro, I ran into him one day outside the fortune teller's door and told him what I had done. He understood and was relieved we could remain friends, but Ciro doesn't like him and only tolerates him for my benefit. But right now, I need him to keep an eye on Niro while I race. Ciro usually watches him, but he will be with Killian's crew.

"I'll be in the same place like always," Ethan says loud enough for me to hear him above all the chaos.

I nod because I have a black helmet with a tinted black face shield, and he can't hear me. I look up at the device in my hand with an augmented screen. The untraceable kind we all have on the mainland. This is the main sport nowadays. I recognize a couple of the men from the island, heading to watch the race inside the dark glassed boxes up top when I first walked up the main entrance. They place their bets like everyone else in their imposing dark suits and dark glasses. *Hypocrites.*

I have found that off the island, this is their playground. Drugs, women, and betting. All the dirty shit they don't want people to know they are into is done here. They live double lives, so they don't think much of Killian when he comes and goes. Killian makes sure the things he's into goes undetected.

I watch as people dance to the music as they wait for the next race. Women with scraps of clothes that basically only cover their tits and pussy. The men have piercings and tattoos all over their skin, wearing skintight pants and chains around their necks. Intricate haircuts and their favorite racer's name painted on their skin. The men and women have my race name PYRALIS painted on their chest and stomach.

This is a different life than the one I grew up in, but it's reality, not the throne full of deceit they feed you on the island. The only challenge for Niro and me is staying hidden on the mainland.

I press the button on the headset in my helmet, and the screen pops up on the face shield so it can connect to the bike when I turn it on. The heads-up display gives me the speed and gears I can shift on with the amount of energy powering up the bike. An understated electric pulse, like a gentle electronic heartbeat, is an audible cue that the rider and the vehicle are ready to go. The propulsion system makes a quiet humming noise once in motion, similar to the background buzz of a scientific research facility. The low, soothing rumble serves as a seamless aural background that complements the sounds of the area.

I tap Niro's helmet; he gives me a thumbs-up, telling me he is okay with holding Ethan's hand. I motion to my heart with my fingers and make a heart symbol with both my hands, telling him I love you. My heart warms when he mimics the same thing.

*I love you, Niro. More than life itself.*

I make sure he waits with Ethan at a safe distance and walk up to my bike at the finish line with the other riders making obscene gestures with hands on their dicks, but there is one I notice out of all the others.

Kill.

His face is broadcast over the gigantic screen, announcing his return to face me and the rest. I try not to let my hands tremble under his scrutiny. He's wearing is signature mask with the word LORD in dripping red paint, but the L is backward.

I shake my gloved hands, feeling my blood pumping through my fingers.

I let out a shaky breath.

He can't see me.

He can't see you, Lillith. All he knows is that you're some chick named Pyralis.

But it doesn't shake the panic taking over me or the sudden drop in my stomach at him being so near me after so long. A shaky breath full of terror escapes my lips, reminding me of who Killian is and the fact that his son is only a couple of feet away.

I swing my leg over my bike and lean forward, placing my thick-soled boots on the paved road of the track as the motor-cycle's noise builds gradually. Like a conductor, the bike takes raw force and orchestrates performance. I let out a shaky breath when I turn my head slightly to get a glimpse of Killian's strong thighs over the beast of his black motorcycle. It lights up in blue with a soft illumination, recognizing his presence through advanced biometric sensors. His seat is composed of memory foam and responsive materials that molds itself to the contours of his strong legs, warranting optimal body positioning. His strong, muscled arms grip the handles, showing ever-detailed biceps. The tight black shirt he's wearing with the carbon fiber covering his spine in case he suffers a fall doesn't hide his six-pack or the muscles of his shoulders. His bike is a work of art, and I know from racing that he designed it. He built it.

His black helmet is in place over his head. He turns to the left and presses the screen on his watch, and I see the signal glitch on my visor.

Fuck, he hacked into my headset.

"Like what you see? I'm sure you'll like the view of the back when I smoke your ass."

*Asshole.*

I glance over to the sidelines and see Blair, Sydney, and Sarah cheering for him on the sideline with Ciro and their crew. Blair has his number and Kill painted on her face and chest. Anger and jealousy consume me like a wildfire, forming a red haze of fury.

I place my bike in gear, revving it to have enough power. The fuel cell is good, and I know kicking his ass will be fun. I lift my hand and turn my head in his direction. His helmet turns, and I stick my middle finger up and twirl it in a circle.

"Sorry, princess. I'm taken," he says through my headset.

My heart sinks, but I shake it off. He was never mine.

*He never loved you, Lillith.*

*He moved on.*

*You're nothing.*

I place the bike in gear. The robot on the screen widens her hands with red lights shining down at the crowd from her eyes. "Goin' In" by Skrillex makes its way through the speakers, and the race will start.

One

Two

Three

Skeletal hands widen like gates to a different hell, signaling to go.

I gun the bike, and it shoots forward ahead of everyone. I smile. Hell yes.

The traction catches from the back tire, and I smell burning rubber as I lean into the turns. I'm still ahead, but I see him on my heels. The crowd goes wild, and bets are increasing on the marker, causing excitement and chaos to erupt.

The next turn comes up, and he's gaining speed. I hate that I didn't watch him race so I could study the way he drives. I feel the heat from the tires coming from his bike. I move low, and he moves high, getting ahead.

Shit.

Shit.

*Come on, Lillith.*

I gain speed when I should be slowing down because it's the only way to beat him. He's hella fast, and the man can drive. The crowd grows quiet because it seems like I won't make the next turn. The rest of the racers have fallen behind. The other guy wiped out after the second turn.

His voice pops up in my headset. "Don't kill yourself trying to beat me." He brakes, his taillight flashing red like a beacon, and I have no choice but to brake. "Come on, princess. I can't make it easier than that. It would help if you talked to me." I switch gears, gaining speed and moving low. His voice is like a ghost in my ear, but his words gyrate on my nerves. Cocky bastard.

"How about we start with a name? That always helps."

I stay quiet, knowing he will recognize me if he hears my voice. I gain speed, but so does he. We are on the last turn, and the pot is up to two hundred thousand, and I need the money.

Knowing this is the only way I'll beat him, I pop the front wheel of the bike and hold it. The crowd goes wild, and I hear him curse as he slows down. When I know there is no way he could beat me, I let the bike drop and drop it into fourth. Then fifth.

"You're a bad girl, Pyralis."

I cross the finish line with him almost grinding his front tire on the back of mine.

Pyralis is still the champion. Some say that's cheating, but others want a re-match.

Shit.

They can't do that! I won.

"It's a race, not a stunt race!" one person shouts.

"She cheated!"

What the fuck?"

My heart begins to beat rapidly, and just when it couldn't get any worse, my bike shuts off, losing power. *Dammit.*

I look up toward the black box where the real criminals are seated. The ones who control everything. The screen flashes in big letters REMATCH.

I'm fucked. How am I going to feed Niro until the next race? How am I going to beat Killian without him finding out the truth?

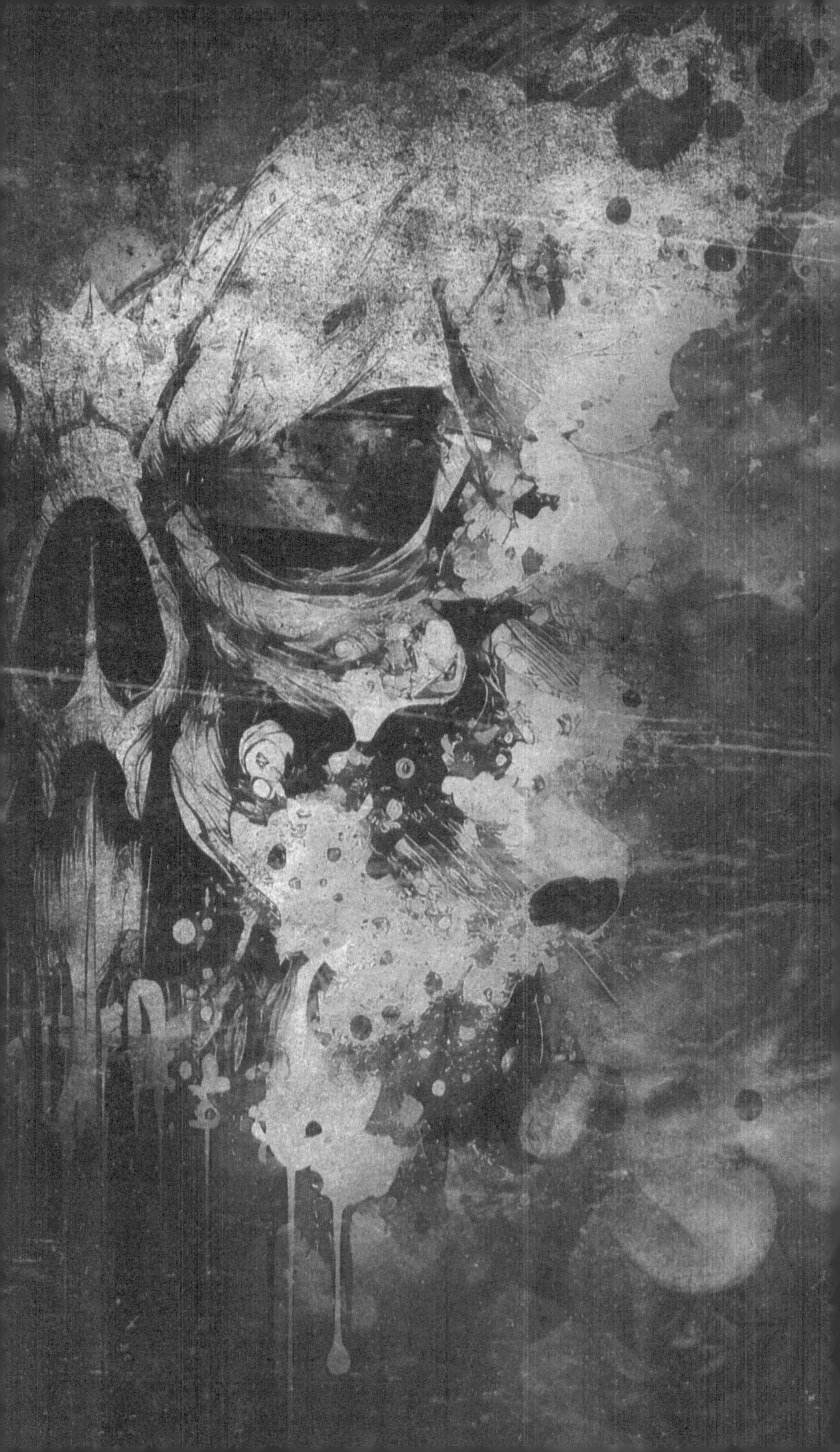

# 38

KILLIAN

'm waiting in my classic Cutlass parked on a dark street, watching the woman who beat me on the track. The one that wouldn't say a word through the headset. It didn't matter how much I pushed her or what I said. I couldn't bait her. But her body language said enough to have me sitting on a dark street after I sent everybody to the hideout deep in the city.

The way she moved was familiar. Her body, slender with wide hips and a small waist, reminded me too much of someone I dream about every night and think about every second of every day. *My Lillith.*

I know it's crazy to compare any woman to Lillith, but here I am. Curious. I saw that she has a little boy wearing a helmet. You couldn't see his face, and I wondered why. Who is she hiding him from? Who is *she* hiding from?

I wait until that twerp Ethan drops her off, and I look around the street, having a moment of déjà vu. The last time I was on this street was when I tracked down Lillith when she bolted from the arena in her fit of jealousy. My lips lift in a grin at the memory and the reason she bolted, but then I remember who she called, and it wasn't me. It was the asshole currently dropping off the woman they call Pyralis and her little boy.

The helmet is gone, but it's too dark to see their faces, and I'm parked too far, but it's her. I try to squint to get a better look while she waves to the short little asshole in his car before he drives off. I should go after him, but then I would miss my chance to find out where she lives and where she came from.

I have never seen or heard of her before, but then again, I've been gone for about five years and haven't set foot on the mainland.

I wait until she enters the building under the sign where it says fortune teller. *You've got to be kidding me.*

The little boy follows her inside, and I open my car door to find out what the hell she is doing going in there unless she reads people their future, but I doubt it's legit. Maybe she lives on the second floor like a lot of people do. They rent out tiny rooms to people who need a place instead of being on the street living in metal containers or abandoned trailers.

When I walk into the building, it's dark, and black lights illuminate the dark space. It used to be a shop with shelves selling novelty items, but of course after the shift in government, causing businesses to crumble, a new world took its place. People struggled financially because there were no jobs unless you worked for the rich.

Digital currency was used to buy what was necessary to survive.

There is a weird smell the deeper I walk inside. When I get to the back, I wonder why a woman would want to live in this shit hole compared to all the other shit holes I have seen in the city. I pause when I see an old woman seated in a chair. Her face is wrinkled with glowing white eyes, but she stares at nothing.

Is she dead? She looks like a corpse sitting there, not moving.

"It took you long enough."

She speaks.

"You're alive?"

She laughs. I hate to be a dick, but she sounds like a witch when she speaks, and I don't miss the hoarseness in her voice.

"You came here looking for something or rather someone? I want to warn you. She is not the same person you knew back then, and losing your shit will not help. All you will do is push her away right into the arms of someone else who is ready to be what she needs."

I pinch my brows in confusion, looking around and not believing I'm listening to this old lady. "Who the hell are you? You don't know me."

She points her finger at me, but her eyes are blank. "I know plenty. I know you are a pigheaded asshole who wears a mask to hide who you are, but you couldn't hide who you were. Not to her. I hope losing her has taught you something. I know exactly who you are, Killian Cross. I'm blind, not deaf."

She's fucking blind? It makes sense. Her eyes are white and lifeless, and she hasn't turned her head once. "You're crazy, and you need to stop listening to shit you don't know anything about."

She snickers. "Have a look. But I will warn you, she is more beautiful than you last saw her."

"I don't know who you are talking about because the only woman who matters to me is dead."

"Stupid boy. You know deep down that is a crock of shit."

"You're blind."

"I am"—she points at me—"but so are you."

I snort and walk toward the back door leading to the stairs, wondering why I'm still wasting my time talking to a crazy old lady. She couldn't have been talking about Lillith. Lillith is dead. Now I'm more curious as to who the hell that woman with the little boy is upstairs. I need to see her.

I make it up the stairs, and a line of sweat drips on the edge of my hairline as my heart pounds inside my chest, and I don't know why. Maybe it's the heat. It is hot up here, and this place is a shit hole. It is small, and something squeezes my chest, suffocating me, thinking of a woman raising a little boy in these conditions. Fucking government. A mixture of disrepair and hopelessness permeates the air and clings to everything in sight. The despondent monochromatic sky is seen through the blurry film that covers the windows. *This is the type of shit I fought to create the grid for.* Once painted in brighter hues, time has taken its toll on the walls, turning them a despondent gray. Paint peels off in flakes like discarded memories, exposing the raw, aged concrete underneath. Evidence of the passage of time and the neglect of its victims, cracks and holes degrade the surfaces.

Thinking about what to say when I barge in because knocking will not get me anywhere, I remember they won't pay anything out from the race until the rematch. Probably the asshole judges pulling their strings for control. The pot was high, and even if they don't know exactly who is under the helmet and suit, letting someone win that kind of cash so easily is not what they have in mind. I'm dreading the reason. What if they want to eliminate Pyralis because she's been winning? With me, they could never find who Kill represented in the city because I live on the island. The recluse with the mask who runs the mainframe for the government.

I check the knob of the old door, and it turns with a groan. I close my eyes when I pull. *It's not even locked.*

When the door swings open, I look inside, and I think my

heart ceases in my chest. My knees go weak. I think I forget to breathe because my vision blurs.

I walk inside, and the emotions rip into me all at once—loss, joy, anger, pain, grief, betrayal, love, and obsession.

*Lillith.*

# 39



I hear the front door open while I look around to make something for Niro to eat while he is in the small metal tub playing with his blocks. It must be Ciro. He's the only one who comes up here, and I left the door unlocked so he could come in. He is probably bringing more food since I didn't win the money.

Looking into the basket of fruits, I feel him standing there and sigh. "I'll figure something out. I know you're going to offer me to go live with you, but you know my answer. I can't."

Silence.

I know it hurt his feelings the first time he asked, and I turned him down, but it feels wrong. Especially now that Killian is back in the city and he's racing.

I smile, pulling out the last of the organic potatoes to make mashed potatoes from scratch. "Did you bring Niro and me something again and are afraid to tell me?"

When he doesn't answer, I look up and freeze. The potatoes drop to the floor with a thud. My hands begin to shake when my eyes meet the man who turned my world upside down.

His head is cocked, watching me with his matte black mask with the word PRETTY sketched on the top. His hands are folded across his muscled chest, and it feels like time has stopped.

Splashing water mixes with Niro's little voice. "Mommy, I'm ready."

I'm stunned. Frozen in place.

He found me.

*Of course he would, Lillith. It was only a matter of time before he did.* Beating him on the track sparked his curiosity. Maybe he recognized me, but that couldn't be it because he said he was taken. He moved on with someone else like I figured he would.

I wasn't anything special to him. I would be delusional if I thought I was. It was one of the reasons I did what I did.

I faked my own death.

Who would miss me?

No one.

It would be like I never existed.

My father sold me, and my husband planned to kill me. I was out of options.

"Mom," Niro calls out.

"Your son needs you, Lillith," Killian says in a lethal voice.

My eyes sting with unshed tears. "Please, don't hurt us," I plead. Raising my hands, I back away toward the little room with the tiny tin tub.

Does Ciro know he's here? Did he hurt him for keeping Niro and me a secret?

After getting Niro dressed, I walk out to the main area and hope that he left, but my life is not that simple.

Killian sits on one of the two old mismatched chairs

against the wall with his head tilted upward like he is looking at the ceiling.

"Mom, is that...?"

Niro recognizes Kill from the race and was excited to see him on his cool bike. He doesn't understand that Kill being here is not a friendly visit. He thinks Kill is some type of superhero.

I can tell by how he is beaming at Kill, not caring that he can't see Kill's face because he's wearing a mask. It probably adds to the excitement and mystery of it all.

"You thought I was someone else. Who were you expecting, Lillith? Who did you leave me for?" He raises his hand. "You know what? Don't answer that. I want to talk about the elephant in the room. Is he mine?"

He means Niro, and I never would have imagined that this was the way he would find out. I stayed up countless nights replaying this scenario for the past five years, not knowing if I wanted him to know. The logical part of me wanted Niro to know his father, and his father to know he had a beautiful son, but the other part told me that the risk was too high. He wanted to kill me after I gave him Niro.

If he is here to kill me, I can't stop him. He is too strong and well-connected. Silent tears slide down my cheeks, and I let out a slow breath between my parted lips to keep from breaking down and scaring Niro.

"I'm going to ask you again. Is he mine?" He gets up and looks down at Niro, watching him place his cheek against my thigh. "Is he, Lillith?" His voice breaks on the last part, and I think he is trying to keep himself from losing it. I could feel the anger coming from his voice.

I take a deep swallow, looking down at the dingy floor, knowing I have no choice. I need to tell him the truth. "Yes," I say reluctantly.

"Do you know what you have done?" he says, his voice cold like the dark side of the moon.

I lift my chin, looking at him scornfully. Pushing the ends of my hair away from my neck, I step back, pulling Niro with me. "I don't care. Now you know, and I think it's best you leave."

"I think we both know that isn't going to happen."

# PART TWO

# The Flame

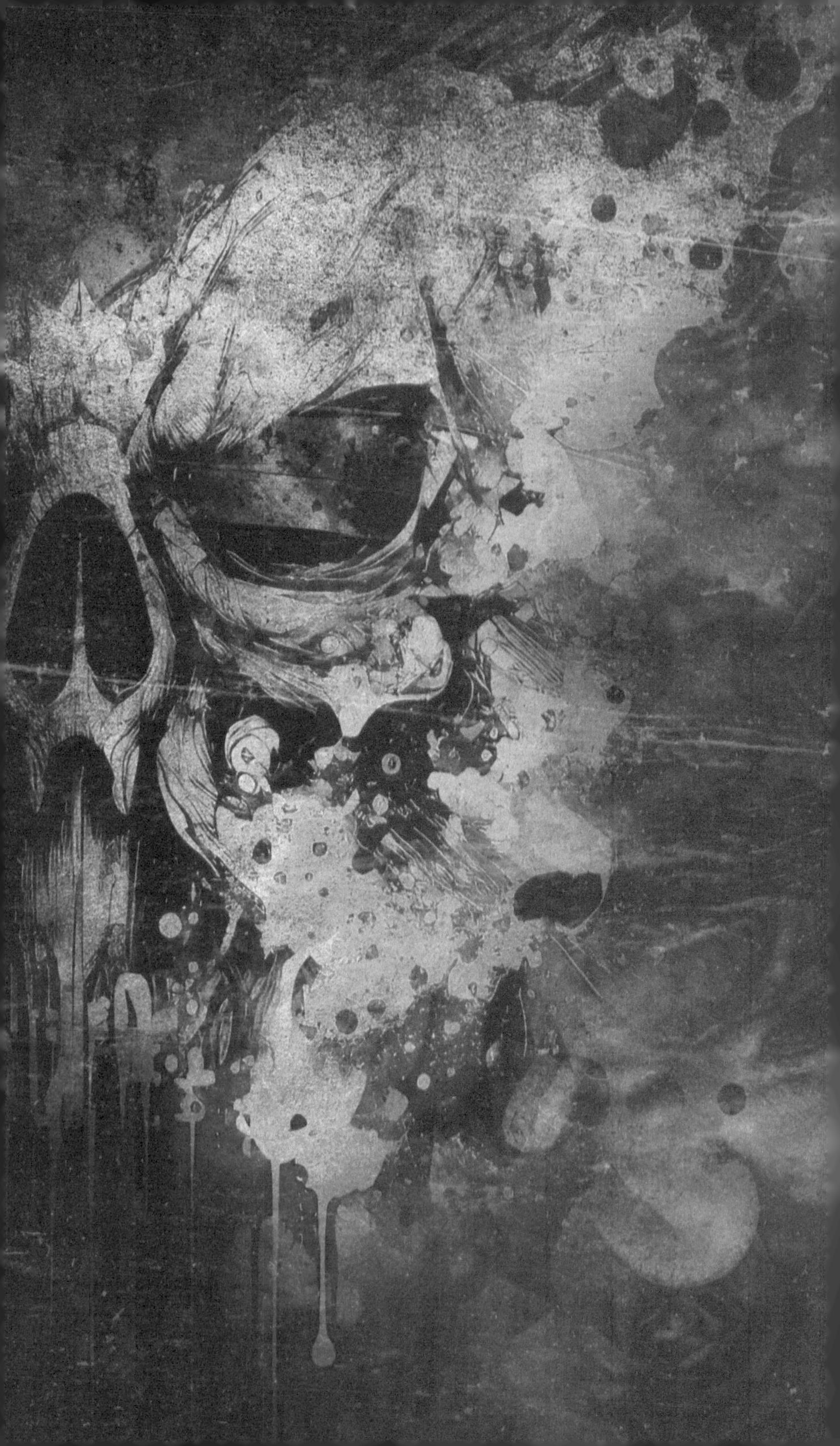

# 40

KILLIAN

*K*nock, *knock.*

I turn my head to the old door peeling with paint, knowing it is the only exit inside this shit hole. This just keeps getting better and better. My wife not only hid the fact that she was pregnant from me but faked her own death just to get away from me. The bonus is that she left me to be with someone else.

My mind races to see who is on the other side of that door. The question I ask myself is should I kill, hurt, or make that person disappear? She thinks I'm going to hurt her. I want to make her pay, but I won't physically. Even if the betrayal scorches me on the inside like a thousand knives cutting me apart, I could never hurt her. I can't.

*Knock, knock.*

I tilt my head in her direction. Her eyes widen, but she makes no move to open the door. I ask sarcastically, "Aren't you going to get that?"

I watch her eyes swing from me to the door and then back to me. Her hand holds *our* son's hand in her grasp. The resemblance is uncanny. He looks like both of us. He has her eyes and my hair. It was pointless asking her if he was mine, but I wanted her to tell me. My chest filled with pride, looking at the most gorgeous little boy watching me in bewilderment when I walked in with the same turquoise eyes as his mother. He's beautiful.

*Knock. Knock.* The knocking is harder this time, causing the old wood to groan.

The handle turning and the door's squeak as it is thrust open grates on my skin like pins and needles because I want to know who is behind door number one.

Darkness turns my insides cold when the last person I expected stands at the threshold with a surprised look on his face.

"Lil—"

"Having fun playing house with my family?" I ask in a seething tone, taking pleasure in watching all the blood rush from his face. *Motherfucker.*

"Killian, don't. It's not what you think," Lillith rushes out, taking a step forward and clutching my son.

I scoff. "Pack what my son likes and cannot be without. You have five minutes, Lillith. Don't try my patience."

She knows I want my son. If she thinks I'm going to sit here and listen to the bullshit excuses from either of them, they must be out of their fucking mind. She is lucky I don't shoot him in the head, but I have no interest in scarring my son for life.

My head snaps to Ciro, and I walk over, relieved that Lillith isn't going to fight me on leaving. It's better for her to think the worst of me right now so I can get her and my son out of here. This is no place for a woman and child to live. I'm surprised the floor beneath us doesn't cave in. There is hardly a place to sit on. I can't even imagine where they sleep. A sense of failure comes over me, imagining her and my son struggling for food and not having the basic necessities. The worst part is that my best friend knew the whole time, watching me mourn my wife in solitude.

"You have three seconds to get missing, Ciro. I don't know how long my patience will last. I haven't killed you right now because of my son."

"I did it for her."

I laugh. It's a deep, maniacal sound that bubbles out of my throat. I clench my teeth and back him up against the closed door. "What else did you do for her, Ciro? Did you enjoy my misery while you were fucking her...while you were fucking my wife."

He squares his shoulders, and I see it in his eyes that he would die for her. "S-she was afraid you were going to kill her. She wanted to raise her own child." *He's in love with her. Our friendship be damned.* "I'm sorry, Killian." He shakes his head. "This is what she wanted, and I wasn't going to deny her."

"We're ready." I hear her small voice behind me and turn around, meeting two sets of aquamarine eyes. "We will go with you. No questions asked." She looks at Ciro. "He had nothing to do with it." She steps closer and glances at me, clutching our son. "I begged him."

"And now she defends him. How touching."

We're on my boat heading back to the house on the island, and a million thoughts run through my head. The dates. The time. Hell, I don't even know my son's name.

"Are we going somewhere cool? I've never been on a boat before," he says in a soft voice, looking at his mom.

I look up from the screen. "We're going home...your home."

He scrunches his nose and tilts his head. "But I have a home."

I glance at Lillith, the worried look aimed at our son, and

reply, "That's not your home. Where we are going is your home."

"My name is Niro. What's your name?"

*Niro.* I like it. "My name is Killian Cross."

I'm not sure what a father does or what he says when he has lost a chunk of his son's life, and you meet him for the first time.

What do I say? Hey kid, I'm your father, and your mother kept you from me because she was afraid I'd kill her, but here I am, uprooting you from everything you have ever known because I showed up.

"Why do you wear a mask? Are you afraid people will think you're ugly?"

I almost choke on my spit and cough.

"Niro! That is not nice. Y—"

I hold up my hand, silencing Lillith. "I had an accident, so I wear a mask."

"How come?"

I grin. "Because I look different, and where I come from, people don't like people who look different."

"That's mean."

I glance at Lillith, but she averts her gaze when I answer, "I can promise you, Niro, I have seen worse."

"So she's alive," Agnes says, wringing her hands together.

"Obviously."

I pull up the security access system of the house, making sure Lillith and Niro have access but, more importantly, cannot escape without me noticing.

"She's...different."

Agnes noticed the same thing I did when I found out. Lillith is not the same woman I married. She has conformed to the way of life on the mainland. Gone is the privileged woman I married, and in her place is a survivor.

"I guess it's a good thing that you never announced her passing. You felt it. Didn't you?"

*I felt my soul evaporate.*

"Felt what?"

But I know what she means, even if I refused to admit it. I kept Lillith alive inside my heart. To me, Lillith never died. There was no use in telling everyone a part of me died that day. That she jumped into the depths of the ocean because she couldn't stomach another moment with me. I was inside my head and stupid for thinking I could until I figured out how I felt about her. About us.

In those dark moments, I wondered where her body was. Nothing and no one mattered to me but finding her that day. Hours and days scouring the ocean, hoping for a clue, a body, something that would lead me to her because I refused for us to end that way.

It is a shame she felt that it was the only way out, but I didn't give her enough reason to think otherwise. I know that. And now I know the truth. She was alive and living a life without me— with someone else.

Like some cruel joke.

A big kept secret.

"You knew that she was alive because you two are connected."

I snort. "Yeah, she was connected to my best friend and his cock."

Agnes straightens a pin in her graying hair. "You think she left you for him?"

The sting burning behind my one eye reminds me of all the

physical reasons. Maybe I wasn't appealing to her in any way. Not even my wealth, status, or way of life I could provide her mattered. Definitely not the way I look or the way we had sex was enough. But he was enough. He was enough to raise my son without me knowing he even existed.

A single angry tear betraying me snakes down my cheek, reaching the edge of my mask. "If she did or didn't, she went with him. She trusted him with her life and my son."

"The same way you told her everyone trusted their life with you. The way they counted on you and you would do anything to ensure their safety. With all due respect, Killian, who was ensuring hers? You?" Agnes's mouth pulls into a frown. "I hate to say it, Killian, but I don't blame her. She took a chance and asked whoever was willing to give it."

I nod. "She did."

"I'm sorry it wasn't you, Killian."

# 41

## LILLITH

Looking around the room that was once mine and Killian's mother, I notice it smells like Killian. It feels lived in and not cold like I would have thought. My eyes scan the little bookshelf, surprised that everything is still there. I thought Killian would have gotten rid of my things if he thought I died. Erasing me from his life.

The bed is made but looks slept in.

I turn my head when I hear the door swing open, and the man I have been running away from appears, closing the door behind him.

His biceps are bigger than the last time I saw him. I can tell he has been working out and has put on a few pounds of muscle. I watch him remove his mask, giving me his back, and observe his muscles ripple with the effort.

"What are you doing in here?"

Placing the mask on the table, he removes his shirt. "What does it look like? I'm getting ready for bed."

"This is not your room."

He turns around, and my eyes follow the swirls of ink all

over his skin, noticing the thin chain holding both our wedding rings around his neck. *He kept them.* They're his parents' wedding rings. I shouldn't think too much of it.

"This is our room. Now get in the shower, Lillith."

"No."

His lips lift, giving me a slight grin. "Okay."

*Okay?* Something is off. I don't like the glimmer in his eyes or the way he slides his gaze over my worn clothes. I take a step to the side toward the door.

I take another one, and then he rushes me. "Killian!" I yelp. He grabs me, lifting me over his shoulder. "Killian, what the hell?"

He places me in the shower with the water running warm. "You're *my* wife. I want you in the shower with me and in my bed. Our son is in the next room sleeping, and we have much to discuss. Lost time I plan on making up for, Lillith. Many nights without my cock inside you."

I look up, blinking away the spray of water falling over my face with a hot retort on the tip of my tongue, but I can't stop watching him peel the rest of his clothes off his perfect body.

My eyes fly to his face, where his prosthetic eye is getting wet, and I wonder if it will get ruined with so much water. He tilts his head with a grin, and I watch fascinated as it turns a dark color until it goes pitch black. I point. "Your eye."

"I had plenty of time to upgrade in your absence. I had a lot to think about since you jumped in the ocean. How could I have jumped after you without a water-resistant prosthetic eye? I'm your cyborg now."

He looks like man and machine merged into one. Like a droid. A very hot droid. But what now? He thinks I betrayed him with Ciro.

"What do you want?"

He lifts me from the shower floor and pins me to the wall.

"I want you naked, Lillith," he growls. "I want to feel what I have missed." He slides his nose over my cheek and rasps, "But I have to ask, did he fuck you good? Was he better than me?"

His words slide over my wet skin with its jagged edges. Then his words the night of the race grip me in its vise. "*I'm taken.*"

He's been taken since the day I showed up. Who knows how many since I've been gone, or maybe it's her. Blair. She was here the first day. The day in his office. On the boat. She was still there the night of the race. And he still has the balls to question me.

I lift my chin, blinking back the onset of tears from my bitter thoughts and feelings of the past. "I should ask you the same thing. Was Blair better the first time I saw you with her or the time I was waiting on you at dinner?" I release air from my lungs, making room for the feeling of hot coals in the pit of my stomach. I find my footing and push him away from me with my hands, relieved when he steps back. "We both know how much she's your favorite."

I step out of the shower and dry off, leaving him under the spray and hating myself for bringing up the past. He doesn't matter anymore, but it still hurts, and it weighs in my heart like a brick as I make my way to Niro's room. *We were ill-fated from the start.*

He could ask me a million times if I slept with Ciro, and I would never answer him. Why? Because I shouldn't answer a man who thought so little of me. A man who didn't think I deserved to live.

I'm lying down next to a sleeping Niro with the little droid he tried to fix clutched in his hand when my phone goes off.

> Ciro: Are you and Niro alright? Did he hurt
> you? Is Niro okay?

I smile, reading Ciro's string of messages.

Lillith: We're fine. I'm sleeping with Niro in his new room.

Ciro: Is he going to kill me?

Lillith: I don't think so. Why? Are you dead?

Ciro: Very funny. But I would, you know.

I pinch my brows.

Lillith: Would what?

Ciro: Die for you.

My stomach sinks because I know he would, but I wouldn't let him. He has been too good to me. He risked his life and friendship with Killian, knowing I could never be what he wanted. I could never be his.

Lillith: I wouldn't let you waste your life, but thank you. :)

Ciro: Your life could never be a waste, and why are you thanking me?

Lillith: For caring about Niro and me. For thinking I was worth something.

I'm about to place my phone on the wireless pad to charge when he sends another message.

Ciro: I love you, Lillith. You and Niro.

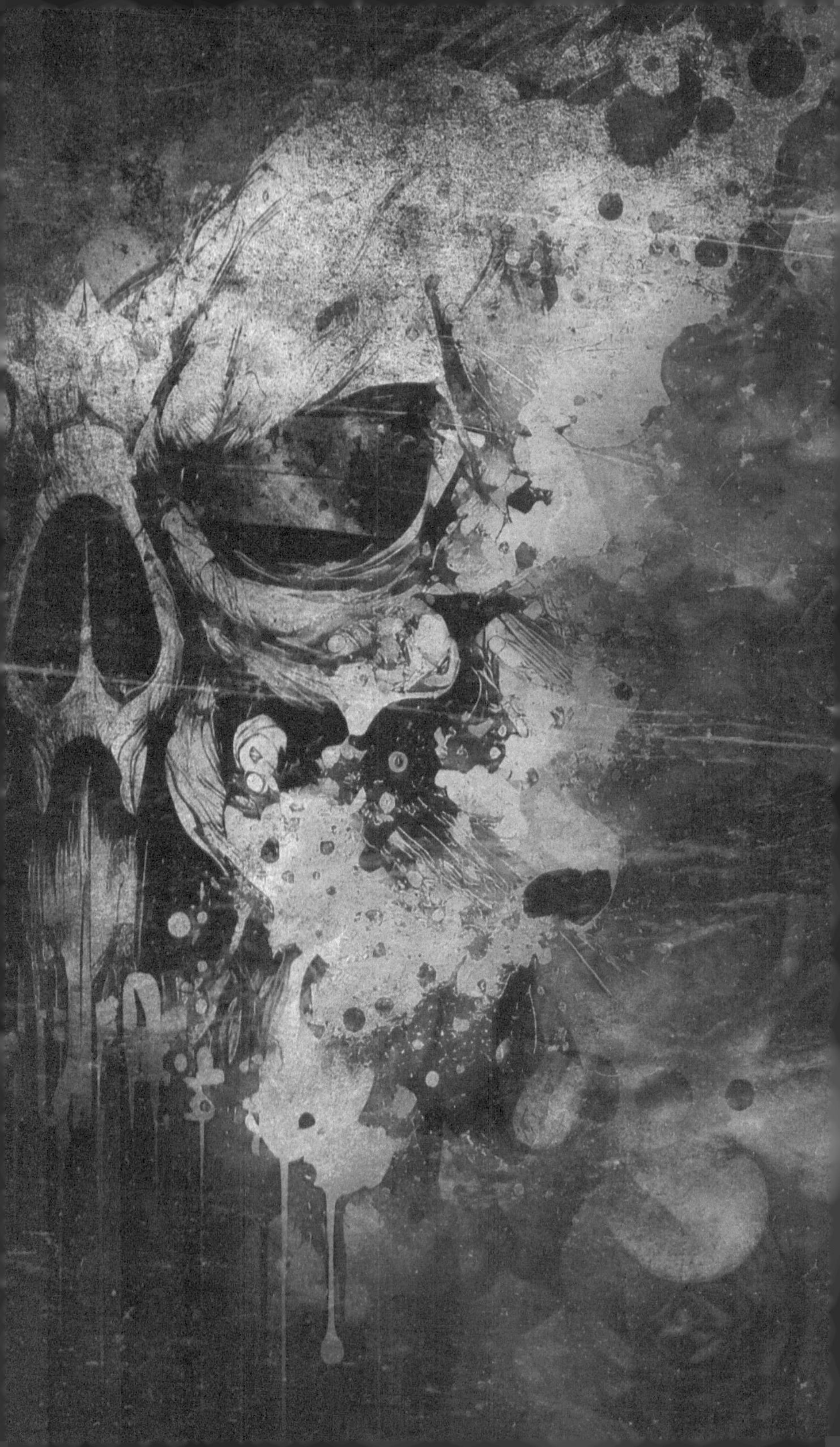

# 42

KILLIAN

I stare at my breakfast, replaying the last message he sent her. He loves her and Niro. I clench my hands into fists in frustration.

I went to check on her, knowing she had left to sleep with our son in his room after our little spat in the shower. They were both sleeping peacefully. I noticed only one bed in the tiny space when she returned to the small room no bigger than my bathroom.

When I saw her phone resting on the charger, I couldn't resist. I was hoping to find pictures of her and Niro.

Instead, I found messages I had no business seeing but needed to see. Crushing me.

But the little voice in my head gives me hope even when I don't deserve it. *She didn't respond. She didn't respond. She didn't tell him that she loved him.*

"Are you alright?"

My eyes lift, and all I see is her. The woman who has me in her grip. My eyes swing to Niro with pride, seeing my son in our home.

My family.

"Yes."

She points. "Your hands are clenching the table, and you haven't touched your food."

"How does he eat with his mask?" Niro asks his mother like I'm not sitting here.

"He lifts it about halfway and—"

Her eyes widen when I remove my mask, interrupting what she was about to say.

"I remove it when I eat and take a shower," I reply.

Niro tilts his head and stares at my face. I expect fear or maybe disgust, but instead, I get curiosity and...awe. It's like he's fascinated by the way I look.

"You're a robot," he declares.

"He is not. Niro—"

"It's alright, Lillith. Let him speak his mind." I glance at my son. "Do you think I'm a Uthean?"

"You look like you're half machine. Like the ones that fly and walk the streets but more human, so that makes you look... cooler."

"Y-you're not afraid?" I ask.

I'm not going to lie. I thought I would scare the shit out of him when he took a look at my face for the first time. It's common to see soldiers with robotic parts on their bodies. Civilians who have been injured from the war or hurt have been able to get prosthetic replacements, but not the kind that fuses with your brain. Only a lab-created cyborg, or Uthean as they are called, are the closest a robot could ever resemble a human.

He beams. "I knew you were some type of superhero on your bike but never a Uthhheen. Wait until I tell my friends back at home. This is so cool!"

This is *your* home, but I don't correct him. I need to talk to Lillith about how I will explain that I'm his father.

Agnes sets the food on the table, and my heart breaks. Niro looks at Agnes like she hung the moon because of all the food. Organic eggs, pancakes, bacon, and sausage are arranged on the table like a feast for a king. He watches, mesmerized as she pours orange juice into a cup, licking his lips.

"Mom? Can I?" Niro asks.

She nods with a look of guilt that crosses her face. He wouldn't have to ever ask for anything if she would have stayed, but we both know why she chose to leave. Why she chose him.

Niro begins to fork food into his mouth, and my lip twitches with pride. Pride that I have a son. Pride that I can provide a plate of food for him.

He smiles after five minutes and says, "This is good. Thank you."

"My pleasure."

"Can I send the leftovers to my friends back home?" he asks hopefully.

"Whatever you want, Niro. If that is what you think is best."

"Yes. My friend James would die if he saw all this food, and it tastes yummy."

I meet Lillith's gaze across the table and notice she has taken all but three bites off her plate.

"Is there something you don't like, Lillith? I can ask Ag—"

"No, that's okay," she interrupts and averts her gaze. "I'm not used to all this food, is all."

*Of course, if you were with me, you wouldn't have gone hungry,* but I don't say that. My intention is for her to stay with Niro and not run off with that asshole again. It is obvious they have been struggling. I'm sure he's offered food and money, hiding it from me, but she's stubborn. I'm sure she has refused. Her stubborn pride won't let her.

I watch her for a few more minutes, noticing that she has lost weight. She's still undeniably gorgeous, but I liked her thicker. She must have looked breathtaking while pregnant. Just thinking about it has me gripping my spoon a little too hard that it begins to bend. *He got to see her swollen with my son.* He was there, and I was robbed of those moments—moments I can't get back. I want to blame her and tell her to fuck herself, but I can't because I did this. I did this to us for not showing her love— for not believing in what we could have had.

I'M SITTING in my office chair looking at the grid I still need to finish. It needs work. I need to upload the program I created so that citizens on the island can have secure access to information they need to buy things from each other like in the old days. You made it, then you sold it. It is a win-win for everyone. All they have right now is the information to create, but it's useless without the tools and supplies.

"Incoming call from Ciro. Do I answer?" the automated voice asks.

I don't want to answer that asshole, but I have to. I've been in my head since this morning. I left Lillith and Niro with Agnes so they can get what they need.

"Answer."

His stupid face appears on the augmented reality screen, and I swear, murder is on my mind. I lean back in my chair, stroking the pads of my fingers over my mask. "What the fuck do you want? You have a lot of nerve, a big sack of balls, to call me."

"How is she... and Niro?"

"They are none of your concern. Now what the fuck do you want?"

"Her. I want her and him. Is that what you want to hear? I can't be without them. I can't breathe. I can't think."

This motherfucker.

"They are none of your concern, Ciro. They never were. Now tell me why I shouldn't hunt you down and blast your fucking brains all over the mainland."

"They're looking for her."

I sit up and lean closer, looking at his surroundings, and the inner demon inside me is relieved that he's in the Cocoon on a secured line.

"Who's looking for her?"

But I know the answer. The judges sent their minions to the island to see when I would show up, and now, they want a rematch. It's a rematch I have no intention of going through with. It's about money and the fact they want to know who the infamous Pyralis is. Ciro has done an excellent job keeping her hidden, coupled with the fact that no one knows outside our circle that my wife had supposedly died.

"You know exactly who I'm talking about. You need to bring her back."

"Fuck no," I growl.

"You don't want her, Kill. I'm not going to let you hurt her."

I chuckle sarcastically. "Who said I was going to hurt her? She's my wife, Ciro. He's my son. They don't belong to you. I don't care how many times you fucked her. I'll spend the rest of my life unfucking you out of her system."

"This is not a game, Kill. If they find out who she is, they will kill her."

Playing both sides is against the rules if you're a woman. Especially if she is mine. He's right, but I'm pissed off imagining his hands on her beautiful skin. Her moans. The smell of her hair.

I slam my fist on the glass of my desk. "Fuck you, Ciro. Fuck you for lying to me. You were my best friend."

"I still am, Kill."

I shake my head. "I think fucking my wife and lying to me about her and my son being alive throws our friendship out the fucking window."

"You didn't want her," he grits, baring his teeth.

I wish he was in front of me so I could break his fucking face. My chest rises and falls from the anger slithering through my veins like poison.

"I never said that. I want my wife and son; if you touch them again, mark my words, Ciro. I'll hang you off a fucking building after I slice you open so your guts spill. Not even the Utheans will know what they are scraping off the pavement when I'm done with you," I roar before cutting the connection, and his face disappears from the hologram.

"Hang him from a building? His guts?" My head whips up to see Lillith standing in the doorway. "A bit much."

I lean back, taking her in like a punch to the stomach. The tight black suit with gray stitching molded to her body like a second skin has all the blood rushing south to my cock. My eyes slide over her thighs until they reach her flawless face with her perfectly arched brow.

"I take it you found your things."

She slides her hands down her body over the tight fabric, and my nostrils flare, wanting my hands to follow. "I did. I was surprised you kept all of my stuff and the things you bought me."

"I had no reason to throw them out." She bites her bottom lip, and it's her tell that she's nervous. She steps forward, and I wave my hand dramatically. "Have a seat. We need to talk."

She sits and crosses her legs, and I swear my cock will burst like a pubescent teenager seeing his crush up close for the first time. I don't want to argue with her about the past, so I change the subject. She already heard me threaten Ciro, and the last thing I need is for her to think I'll do the same to her.

I remove my mask and press the button for the door to close automatically. "You cut your hair."

"Did you need to close the door to point that out to me, or are you afraid I'll run out screaming for help?"

"I wanted privacy. After five years of not being with you, I don't want to miss another moment."

"I'm surprised you noticed and haven't conquered the world, saving millions by now. I remember you telling me it was all you care about."

"Cared," I correct. "That was until I lost someone more important. Two, actually."

She licks the spot on her bottom lip and scratches the area between her brows. "Funny, it takes losing me for you to figure that out. To have a change of heart."

"I figured out many things when I thought you were dead."

"What do you want long term? I'm here and agreed to come here with you because of Niro. Believe it or not, it is important to me for him to know his father. It was one of the reasons I did what I did. I wanted Niro to have the opportunity to have both of his parents alive. We both know how important that is."

"Fair enough." I pull up the security feed on the house that detects body heat and spot Agnes sitting with Niro while he shows her some droid struggling to stay on. "I want you and Niro to stay. It isn't safe for you to go back."

"I heard."

That means Ciro called and told her. That is probably why she came here to seek me out. I have to admit, I'm insanely jealous. I'm possessive. I'm going out of my fucking mind, but anger and violence will not get her back.

"It means we need to attend public appearances on the island. It will keep them guessing and you off the radar."

"But not you. It doesn't take a rocket scientist to know that Kill is Killian Cross, and what if they find out what you really do on the mainland?"

"They don't give a fuck about the freak behind a mask. They see a woman as more of a threat on the track, making money. It defeats the purpose, and when they find out it is a woman from high society, it will create pandemonium. What gives hope must be destroyed. A woman beating the fastest and smartest man on the planet does that."

She smirks. "Who said you're the fastest and the smartest?"

"You've got jokes."

"I've got facts."

"The fact is that you're staying here and will need to act as my wife."

"What will your girlfriend think?" She leans forward and glances at the screen to watch the live feed. "Is she here some-where? I've been expecting her to pop out from somewhere and remind me how tight you guys are."

She's jealous. Just like I am of her and Ciro. Of anyone touching her. Too bad I'm not going to answer her. Let her think what she wants. I'll just have to show her. Remove the doubt I placed in her mind about me—about us.

"There's a dinner being held for a fundraiser tomorrow night. Be ready at seven sharp. Agnes will watch Niro. He will be in good hands. I'll make sure he has everything he needs."

"He wants a working droid. He likes fixing them and wants to learn."

I grin. "Like his father. I liked to fix things when I was a kid. I wanted to build things but realized everything was moving faster in the cloud. A network was rapidly growing and offering a better way of life. It seemed easier."

"Until it falls into the wrong hands after they find out everyone depends on it. Then greed and the need for control sets in. Using it against the people who need it to survive."

"Yes, but it takes one person to unravel it all. To release it or to create one just like it without anyone knowing it exists, and even if they find out about it, it's too late to control it." She shifts in her seat, crossing her legs over the other. My eyes follow the movement, desire rising like the tension in the room. Our eyes meet. "If you keep that up, I will bend you over this table and show you what you've missed."

I don't miss the blush on her cheeks, but it's mixed with the stormy look in her eyes. Her fingers slide the short chocolate strands behind her ear, waiting for the slick retort to slide off her tongue, causing my dick to pulse in my pants.

"Is that what you were hoping for since you found me? For me to spread my legs because you're Killian Cross. To fuck me and show me what I'm missing?"

"Maybe, or... maybe, I want to make love to you."

She laughs, and it sounds like music. I can listen to her repeatedly without getting bored of hearing it.

"You don't believe in love, remember? You never had time for an emotion so profound like that."

"Things change."

"So do people." She stands, watching me remove my mask, and I walk around my desk. "What are—"

I pull her in my arms, silencing her with a kiss. Her lips are warm, soft, and sweet against mine. Her fingers slide in the back of my hair when I cup her face softly in my hands. Our mouths fused together, exploring each other's taste. I press my cock into her, showing her what she does to me. My tongue slides in her mouth, and I'm in heaven. Her sweet breath mixed with the scent of her skin and her soft, straight hair.

The animal inside rattles to be set free. To take her hard. But not having her for so long taught me that these moments I can steal away are the most important. The little things like the soft kisses, the smell of her skin, a glance when she isn't looking, the sound of her voice, and the gift of her laughter. The little things that mean the most. The ones I missed and thought I lost forever.

The silence when you're alone is damning. It consumes your thoughts, gripping them in a vise. The real test is wondering—could I have changed anything?

But she's mine, and I'll kill whoever takes her from me.

# 43

LILLITH

"You look gorgeous," Agnes says when I turn to look at myself in the mirror.

I'm wearing a body suit with a mesh skirt. A black sash cinches at the waist. It reminds me of a black vintage gown, but the suit is neoprene and temperature-controlled underneath.

I found the latest collection inside a grandiose closet full of the latest futuristic designs. The pantsuits I found had sharp angles and uneven patterns to give it a look of an asymmetrical design. The high neck protects you from the elements by combining a high collar and an integrated hood. All the tops are fitted with built-in technology, like a built-in respirator for adapting to polluted air, pockets for storing vital items, and luminous strips for visibility in low-light circumstances.

The color scheme is subdued in utilitarian tones such as charcoal gray, deep matte black, or industrial metallic tints. All handpicked by Killian.

"Thank you, Agnes." I glance at the mirror, and she gives me a wry smile. "It takes a bit getting used to."

Wearing clothes you find in markets on the streets littered with holes was a lot different from when you were used to the most expensive fabrics bought with a single swipe of a device. I had to learn to sew and create clothes out of materials by hand. I had to find a way to blend in and fast when I arrived. Especially when I was pregnant. I had to fit in and ensure my face was always covered, living among the survivors. I lived in fear that Killian would find me. Every night, the fear would grip me, rendering me restless, hoping I could stay alive to raise my son.

"This is where you belong, Lillith." I turn to face her. "You belong with Killian. You're his wife and have gifted this family with a legacy. A beautiful son. Strong like his parents."

"I'm scared, Agnes." Needles prick my throat. "I've never been so scared in my entire life."

She smooths my hair with the palm of her hand. "I know, my child. I know you're scared, but so is he."

My bottom lip trembles. "He has nothing to be scared about."

"Oh, he does. Losing you is his biggest fear. When you get a taste of what you fear the most, you'll do anything, Lillith." She takes my hands. "You're the fire he needs, Mrs. Cross. Without it, he will cease to exist."

It's not the first time I've heard similar words. The fortune teller back on the mainland always told me he's coming. I learned to block her out because her words instilled fear like a dark cloud hovering over me, and I was waiting for the hailstorm to follow, dragging me to the depths of the darkest ocean.

I make it to the foyer at seven sharp. Killian turns around in his dark suit. A breath lodges in my throat; he looks handsome in his suit. His charcoal-colored mask covers his gorgeous face underneath but adds mystery.

A grin forms on my lips. BROKEN is sketched on top of his mask. Then he bows, taking my hand. Instead of kissing the top, he places it over his chest, his palm over mine. I step back, looking around to see if any other person is in the room, but it's just the two of us.

"I read that bowing before a lady is a sign of respect."

"It is," I reply.

He straightens and leans close. "I added the part where I place your hand over my chest so you can feel how hard my heart beats for you every time I look at you."

Warmth slides up my arm, wrapping around my heart and leaving flutters in my stomach. "You had me at the bow," I say softly, my hands wrapping around his neck. My thumb caresses the skin where his pulse beats. "I hope you're wearing this for them." My eyes trace the edge of his mask. "Because you don't need to wear it with me."

The back of his hand strokes my face, leaving tingles in his wake. "Maybe I want only one set of eyes on my face." I can feel the heat of his gaze awakening every nerve ending in my body, lighting me on fire. "You look stunning."

I blush. "Thank you. You look very handsome in your suit."

He lifts my hand softly. "In that case, I was hoping"–he holds my wedding ring in his fingers–"you would do me the honor and wear this for me?"

I nod. I didn't think of that. How would it look if we arrived at the fundraiser and I was without my wedding ring? As the wife of the richest man on the island no one has seen in years, we are bound to be the center of attention. I glance at his left hand and notice he's wearing his ring. *He asked because of the fundraiser.* He's playing nice, and I have the feeling I know why. The grid. Now that I'm back, he wants to continue what he had started.

Pushing my feelings aside, I know firsthand what people

are going through on the mainland—the despair and hope-lessness, the hunger and the destruction of humanity. Pretty soon, there will be more Utheans than people on the mainland.

He slides the ring on my finger, which feels like an internal in-between between two people–between former lovers who, in the eyes of the world, are still husband and wife.

We head toward the downtown area of the island. I haven't been here for so long that I almost forgot what it looked like. Some things have changed. A huge development with towers, homes, and gardens. Buildings designed in a synthesis of contemporary minimalism. A stark contrast to the mainland. The island can provide for its own needs, thanks to cutting-edge technology that generates renewable energy, treats wastewater, and cultivates edible crops. The vast solar and wind farms dotting the landscape power the lavish lifestyles of the rich. Modern aquaculture facilities and vertical farms ensure the availability of fresh vegetables and fish.

"It hasn't changed, has it?" I ask, looking at what is so easily built but kept from the rest.

He looks out of the driver's window of his Lamborghini Revuelto. "It hasn't... the few with the privilege live lives of unparalleled abundance, while the majority struggle to survive amid resource scarcity, pollution, and civil unrest. The island has always been a symbol of greed and indifference, sparking envy and resentment among those left behind. To me, his place is a symbol of evil. We need to remember which side we're on."

I look around, admiring the interior of the car. "This is different."

He turns on the next street, looking up at the Utheans inside an aircraft hovering above us. "Do you like it? I had it delivered when I found out we had to attend the fundraiser. We have to blend in."

"It's...a lot."

It's beautiful. It looks powerful like the man driving it. He presses a couple of buttons, and then the screen pulls up different driving modes. He pulls the seat belt so that it's tight across my body.

I turn my head, and he says, "Let's see what this baby can do."

"But the Utheans, they will detain you or give you a fine."

He chuckles. "I could afford it, and besides, I can erase the feed."

The car lunges forward, and I smile at the rush of adrenaline. My stomach somersaults, and I let out a laugh. The buildings rush by in a stream of lights as the car eats up the road.

A huge bright light shines above us, illuminating the interior of the car. "Excessive speed! Stop the vehicle!" The Uthean's voice thunders through the streets, following us above.

He takes a sharp right, and the tires kiss the pavement in a loud screech.

"Hold on, baby."

I close my eyes. "Just don't kill us."

"Says the one riding across the finish line on one wheel."

"I beat you fair and square."

He snorts. "I let you win, Pyralis."

"We'll see...won't we, Kill?"

He slows down and pulls out a device. His fingers fly across the screen. "Exit the vehicle!" The spotlight illuminates the entire car on the side of the road.

"We're screwed, aren't we?"

"One second," he says, looking at the screen.

"Feed detected." A female voice responds to whatever he is inputting. "Purging now."

I glance up and watch through the panoramic roof. The

light shuts off, basking us in darkness. The red light from the Uthean's laser turns green, indicating no infraction or imminent threat, and hovers past us. "Show-off."

"Did you think I would get us caught or, worse, endanger you?"

"Would you?"

Silence blankets us for a few minutes. There are times I want to tell him how he makes me feel. How the butterfly wings flap inside my ribs when I feel his gaze on me or when he's near, or how the touch of his skin ignites a booming fire within me hoping I don't go down in flames.

"I would have jumped after you in the ocean even if I didn't think I could save you. The answer to your question, Lillith, is no. I could never. You can rest easy at night knowing you're safe with me."

He drives the car forward until we reach a tall skyscraper. "That is good to know." I smooth the skirt over my thighs. "I can finally get some sleep."

My door swings open. "You can come to our bed, and I promise you, I'll rock you to sleep and keep you safe."

A warm chill runs down my spine, awakening a burning need between my thighs I thought I would never feel again.

"Mr. and Mrs. Cross," a man who looks like he would be my father's age welcomes us at the entrance when Killian makes his way to my side.

Killian stands next to me but doesn't greet the man in return. He has brown eyes and is wearing a nude-colored suit. He glances at me like a reptile looking for prey, wondering if what he sees is edible.

We are ushered into a room full of vintage and digital art for auction. It reminds me of the first time I met Killian and didn't know who he was. I calculated that day to the time of his accident, and it was before.

Goose bumps rise on my neck when I glance around the room. All eyes are upon us like I predicted. Women give me intriguing looks, and the men admire what they see.

My hand slides, gripping Killian's arm. "Let me know if you see anything you like."

I smile. "You remembered."

He remembered when I was engrossed in the painting all those years ago. It was the only thing interesting in the room until he appeared.

"Of course. I remember everything about you."

"Lillith." I turn, and my chest squeezes at my father's voice. "Father."

He glances up at Killian with a woman I don't recognize on his arm. He never brings Gretel to these things because she doesn't fit in with her looks.

"Mr. Sinclair, what a surprise."

"I could say the same. I didn't think you still came to these things. You were always the silent donor."

"I guess when you have married a beautiful woman, it would be a shame to keep her hidden from society." Killian lowers his voice. "You didn't think I would eat her alive, did you?"

Well played. So this is why he wanted to come.

My father looks back and forth between Killian and me with a tight smile.

"Where's Gretel?" I ask in contempt. "I thought you brought her to these things." I look at the woman with red hair and alabaster skin on his arm. She's not my father's type. She must be well connected or someone's wife he plans on fucking later.

"She's at home."

Interesting. I guess she is off the menu tonight and was sent to bed early. Some things never change.

"Oh, how unfortunate."

"How's married life?" my father asks with a sly grin.

He thinks I'm being tortured because, in his eyes, he married me off to a monster.

"It's wonderful. I have no complaints," I rush out before Killian can answer. "How's business?"

Bastard. Two can play this game.

My father visibly stiffens and is probably relieved when his friend Nicholas walks up. "Killian Cross," Nicholas says with an insinuating grin, then slides his gaze over me, not hiding the fact he's fucking me with his eyes. My father smiles. *Pig.*

"Nicholas, I see that your eyes are trying to get acquainted with my wife," Killian says in a lethal tone.

Nicholas raises his brows in surprise because he's probably never been called out before. My father chuckles, and so does the woman on his arm, but Killian isn't laughing. He's serious. A chill skates up my arms, feeling Killian's anger.

My father smiles at me. "What did you feed him, Lillith? He's losing his mind already."

"I can assure you my mind is not lost, and your daughter feeds me quite well." He pulls me close to his side, snaking his hand protectively around my waist. "I make sure to return the favor."

My father grins when Nicholas excuses himself, murmuring under his breath.

"It's been a while, Lillith. I haven't seen you around the island."

I don't miss his tone or the fear snaking around my spine. The way my father's eyes have a vacuous emptiness when he speaks to me. He's one of them, and I'm a defector in his eyes. He knows I'm loyal to Killian. He sees the way I allow Killian to touch me. The way I embrace it.

The woman smiles. The curve of her red lips lifts when she says, "They're in love."

She probably sees it in my eyes. The way I'm irrevocably in love with Killian, but she can't see Killian's expression to judge accurately that it's one-sided. The way he has me clutched to his side possessively, anyone would think the same thing. That we're in love.

But I know the truth. Killian expressed to me numerous times that he didn't have room to love me. To love anyone. Killian has one purpose—to save humanity from these monsters.

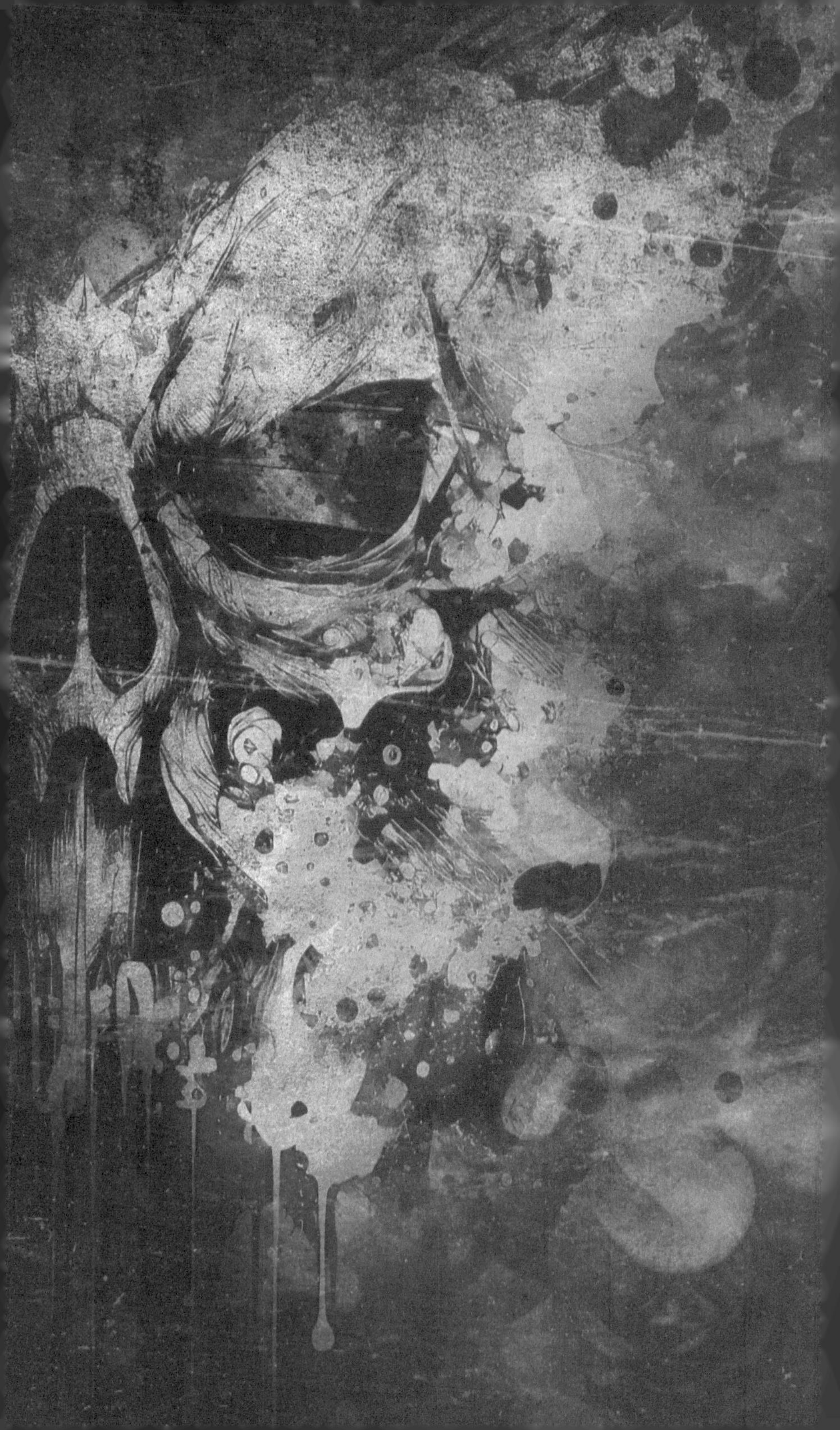

# 44



I left my wife to study art while I went to find my new target. Nicholas Hawke. Hawke Industries provides technological advancements for aircraft to go into space. After the government failed with NASA, a private company took over and realized there wasn't shit up in space that we could use. They found technological advancement through energy sources from our planet.

The problem was that they needed to understand how to use the technology, but I did. It is why they need me, but funding it is an issue. Greedy assholes stay greedy while others suffer. I find Nicholas alone, drinking alcohol out back in the dark by the open balcony, looking over downtown.

"I thought they banned that stuff."

He turns, holding out a flask nervously toward me. Nice try. I place my hands behind my back, sliding them under to retrieve my gun, then pushing the safety off and letting it heat. "I don't drink, Hawke."

He blinks rapidly, hesitating a moment. "You know."

I do know that they are watching Lillith closely.

He sighs. "They're going to take her from you, Killian. It's only a matter of time before someone sticks their cock in her and offers her a better life than you could give her." He laughs. "Everyone wondered why her father would marry her off to you. It's kind of sick if you think about it. His daughter has to fuck a monster like you." He points at me with his hand holding the flask. A grin on his pathetic face. "The judges are on to her, you know. You're saved because of what you know and what you can provide. The technology. It's what this whole thing is about. It's nothing personal. Women are transferable. Dispensable. I'm sure you have found enough on the mainland to keep you busy, considering what you look like underneath. She's nice to look at, and I'm sure one hell of a good fuck."

My nostrils flare. "You have a hard time comprehending, Nicholas. You think because you are close to the board of the judges, and you have an in with your shit company, you can walk up and disrespect my wife and tell me you plan to fuck her."

"I do."

I pull out my gun and see his eyes widen. "You're going to kill me, Cross, because I bent your ego regarding your wife?"

I turn the gun and make sure it's on the silencer setting. "I don't have an ego, Nicholas. I have a temper when someone threatens to fuck my wife or take her from me." He takes a step backward. "See... there's no reason to have an ego."

"We can talk about this, Cross." He reaches behind him for the railing. The lights shine down on his face, which has drained of all its color. "I get that you are overprotective of her." He looks over the railing, realizing there is nowhere to go but down. He looks at the gun with the laser aimed at his face. "I didn't mean...Christ. They know who she really is, Cross." He closes his eyes. "God–"

I tilt my head to the side. "There is no God. Now open your eyes, you filthy piece of shit, and tell me again what you planned to do to my wife." I pull the trigger, watching his head inflate, then half of it implode. The sound of a beam and then mush echoes. Half his head is missing, and his hands try to grope the railing. The right eye is protruding, half hanging out like a vintage slinky. "You must have a headache." I twirl the gun, watching his head twitch. "I can tell you had a problem with your eyes when you first approached us. My wife noticed it, too." I pull the trigger again, blowing the rest of his head off into nothing. His headless corpse drummed on the ground. I tuck the gun back in my pants and walk back inside to get my wife.

The room is full of curious glances aimed my way. Women shamelessly give me suggestive looks while on their husbands' arms. My eyes scan the room in search of Lillith. I smile when I find her admiring a painting, oblivious to everyone in the room. Even the men openly stare at how breathtaking she looks in her outfit. The skirt cinches her waist, flaring out like a vintage gown of tulle and lace.

Before reaching her, I walk toward the auction table.

"Yes, Mr. Cross."

"The painting my wife is looking at."

"Yes, sir."

"Make sure I win the bid and send it to my home along with every painting she has shown interest in tonight."

"Will you and Mrs. Cross be attending the auction?"

"I'm afraid I have a prior engagement."

People will soon notice Nicholas's headless corpse outside on the balcony. The last thing I need is to ruin my wife's night.

"Of course, as you wish."

"Do you like that the painting offers a view of the future, or are you rather intrigued by the present?"

"How do you know the difference?" she asks, continuing to study the twentieth-century painting.

"Depends on the latest philosophy and science. What calls to you. What you find important.

"Isn't that interpretive to the artist? The way they see it in their eyes. Their vision."

"It only matters to who bought it. They are the ones that have to look at it."

She giggles. "How observant."

"I'm just pointing out the obvious."

She turns to look at me."You bought it, didn't you?"

"I did."

"Why?"

"Because I can. Because...I want to own everything you find interesting. Whatever fascinates you."

"Anything?"

I lean in my mask, touching her, watching the goose bumps rise on her skin. "Show me," I whisper.

Once we are in the car, she points. "There."

I look over, and it's the closest area with a view of the lights coming from the mainland. "There?"

"Yes."

I drive the fifteen minutes until we arrive at a tall structure with a beam of light shining like a beacon over the dark water. It's a sensor for the geo-fencing parameter to safeguard the island.

She removes the skirt around her waist, leaving her with just the suit and her pointed boots, and begins to climb the ladder.

"Lillith, what are you doing?"

"You want to see what fascinates me or not?"

I lock the car, take my gun, and scan the area, noticing a

healthy presence of Utheans over at the building downtown where we just left.

I glance up and climb after her until we both sit on the edge with our feet hanging over the ledge. "There"–she points–"you see that?"

"I do," I reply, looking at the distance where the mainland is miles away, but it's unmistakable. Even from here, you can see the machines picking up metal debris.

"Getting food and supplies to those who need it. That is what fascinates me. Showing our son the good we have in our hearts, not taking anything for granted. I love that you bought me the paintings, but I could have used that money to feed them."

"I have plenty of money, Lillith. It's more complex. If they see us handing out food or buying supplies like a bunch of Robin Hoods, they will kill us. Then who will raise Niro?"

She lowers her hand, placing it on her lap, but I don't miss the tears that slide down her cheeks. "They're hungry." She sniffs. "They don't have clothes, and some don't even have a place to keep warm."

"I know," I say vaguely. "I'm trying. Alright?"

"You know they want the rematch, and I think they know who you are. They want to kill you, Lillith. You were never supposed to win."

"I don't understand. How?"

"I was supposed to beat you, and then they would have gotten rid of you because you are a woman from the island. They knew."

"I don't understand."

"Your father."

He wanted to make sure no one knew of our agreement. It was perfect. I got what I wanted, and he got what he wanted with the bonus that Lillith would die, and so would his secret. It would have jeopardized his ability to stay on the island. He never contacted her because he watched her every move. Someone told him about her on the mainland. They've been waiting.

It's the only way they could have found out, but who does he have on his side who would want Lillith dead?

"My father?"

"He wants you dead, Lillith. If it means the judges finding out he has a massive debt and is practically broke, he will have to move off the island. He is taking on debt fast."

"But how?"

"The races, Lillith. I bankrupted him, making him bet so I could get to you. Your racing bankrupted him further. He likes to bet on the mainland."

"The black box."

"Yes, when he started betting, I ensured he lost."

"Why?"

"He killed my parents, Lillith. You were collateral damage. At the time, I needed an heir to continue the plan and save the people, but I never knew I would–"

"Why?" she repeats, pulling away. She looks nervously at my gun and then back at me. Her bottom lip quivers. "Are you going to kill me? Is that why you brought a gun?"

"No, I'm going to save you."

# 45

LILLITH

How could you fall in love with someone who wanted you dead? Someone like me who would do anything because they want to be loved so bad they believe in the one who could paint you a clear sky with beautiful stars telling me about the moon, only to ruin it with a storm.

I glance up at his hand while he stands. "I'm going to save you, Lillith," he repeats. You're my wife and son's mother, and nothing else matters." He looks over and sees Utheans lighting up the streets. "Let's go home. Our son is waiting for us."

I swallow and place my hand in his, watching his fingers entwine with mine. I allow my life to be in his hands, hoping I survive.

"Is everything alright?" Agnes asks with an edge of concern when I barge into Niro's bedroom. Not caring that he is fast asleep, I press a soft kiss in his hair.

"Everything is fine, Agnes. She just misses him."

It's not a total lie; I do miss Niro. He is the air that I breathe. The reason. The purpose. I'm not used to being away from him.

I took the chance tonight because, through it all, I trust Agnes. I'm unsure about my life, but I know Killian wouldn't hurt Niro. Deep down inside, I always knew that Niro was safe with Killian. It was my life that I was worried about. This whole time, my life hung in the balance.

After holding Niro for a while, I walk into my old bedroom but pull up short when I see Killian on the bed with one of my romance novels.

"Our love is the most beautiful thing to witness when the flames we light inside each other burn together. It's what I love the most about us, but the fire is you."

"What are you doing?" I ask, watching him place the book in the empty slot next to the others. "You read them?"

"I did." He looks up. His prosthetic eye shifts in different colors from the light. "I had a lot of time on my hands. I thought it would be good. It helped with the pain of losing you. It was an escape when nothing else mattered." He slides his fingers over the spines. "So many ways to fall in love, and I wondered which was your favorite way... to fall."

"What are you talking about?"

"I wanted to know the answer to that question. Every night, I fell asleep reading the words your eyes read, wondering...which one was my wife's favorite. And if I got a second chance, I would peel your layers like the pages in a book until I found it." He swallows. "The way I could convince you to fall in love with me the way I did with you."

I step closer to the foot of the bed, speechless, taking in the room and imagining him reading the pages of my favorite books so he can feel me when I'm not there. My vision blurs when my eyes fill with tears. When he pulls the pillow from the other side and holds it under his chin. "It was on the sixty-seventh day that the smell of your hair left the pillow. I thought I died that day, but Agnes..." He wipes the tears falling from the side of his face. "She handed me *Shanna* from your shelf and said it was one of your favorites. I read it almost every night, thinking of you. I read the others, but when I saw you on that bike, something told me to follow you. I talked to this crazy lady telling me some prophecy, but when I saw you, my life was returned. My second chance."

"You saw the fortune teller?"

He nods. "Yeah, the blind one who isn't really blind."

"That is the one."

I peel my suit off slowly. Our eyes meet, and he asks, "What are you doing?"

"Peeling off a layer."

He grins. "Teasing me will get you into trouble, Mrs. Cross."

"I want to take a shower," I tell him, standing completely naked.

After our shower, he pushes me so my back is on the bed. His lips crush mine. Our tongues get lost in each other. His hands cradle the back of my head, holding me. Our breaths mingle between us. His words replaying in my mind when he told me he loved me. The days he spent reading my favorite novels were worth more to me than any painting he could have bought me. It was a connection like no other. A synching between souls. Something so simple meant the most in my eyes, like the time he spent thinking of me. Thinking of us. The pages he read only because I read them like a looking glass into someone's soul where their escape was your escape from reality.

We are all scared to love because it makes us vulnerable by revealing our imperfections and hoping for acceptance. Hoping that the person you love loves you back.

"I love you," I whisper.

He pauses. His hands slide under me. My chest rises and

falls. The tips of my nipples rub on his hard chest. The ache between my legs seeks his warmth.

"Say it again," he demands softly.

"I love you, Killian Cross."

He closes his eyes like he's savoring a moment or figuring out if it's a dream.

He pulls his cock out of his pants, hard and ready. Looking between my thighs, he groans when he slides inside me. "One of my favorite moments besides being introduced to our son is hearing you tell me you love me, Lillith. It is the greatest sound in the world, but this right here...being inside you is the best feeling."

I hold him tight, breathing in the scent of his skin. I wanted to be one with him, and we were. All night, he made love to me. He kissed and licked every inch of me like I was something sweet and addicting.

In the morning, he was already awake, flipping me over. Our skin would clap when he would take me hard. I gripped the sheets, digging my nails into the soft mattress, trying not to moan too loud. Niro was bound to wake up in a little while.

"I can't get enough of you," he whispers.

I smile when I arch my back and push my ass out. He groans when he slides in deeper. "Mmm...harder."

He slaps my ass, and I yelp. "You're perfect." He caresses the sting and then hits my ass again. Harder this time. "Mmm...more," I breathe.

He does it again and again, taking me harder. He pulls me up so that my back is against his front, grinding his hips and pushing his cock into me in a steady rhythm. His lips wander over the skin on my neck, his fingers gripping my short hair. "You're so fucking gorgeous." I close my eyes.

"I'm coming," I say softly on a moan. His hand slides over my left breast, teasing my nipple.

"Me too, baby." He holds me tight against his body, and our bodies move in a rhythm. He grips my chin, turning my head and taking my lips in his, drowning out our moans, and I'm lost in him.

"What does that button do, Daddy?" Niro looks up at his father, pointing at the screen on his boat. Niro sits on Killian's lap.

After breakfast yesterday, we sat him down and told him the truth about who Killian was and why we were separated when he was born. We omitted pertinent details like me jumping off the boat and my reason, but Niro was more in awe that his father was Killian.

"It tells us where we are."

"And that one?" he asks, pointing at another one with curiosity. His big turquoise eyes are like two marvels soaking up all the information Killian gives him.

"Does he always ask so many questions?" Blair asks with a hint of annoyance.

I hate that she's here, but so are Sydney and Sarah. Ciro is on the other side, far from Killian, working on a screen. They hardly speak to each other, and I know I'm to blame, but Killian says otherwise. He wouldn't go into details, but I have more important things on my mind like the jealousy eating away at me whenever Blair glances at Killian.

"It's what children do when they are with their parents. They ask questions."

"If you don't like it, Blair, you could have stayed at the Cocoon until Ciro arrived," Killian says, showing Niro something on the screen. He lifts his head. "Don't question my son to my wife again. Understood?"

Sydney and Sarah glance at each other, raising their brows. Ciro stops typing and slides his gaze to Blair.

Blair rolls her eyes, blowing air out of her mouth. "Whatever." Niro frowns, looking at Blair. Ciro sneaks a glance my way when I pluck Niro from Killian's lap. He knows I won't allow anyone to make Niro feel uncomfortable. There is no reason for Blair or any of the women who have slept with my husband to naturally be fond of Niro. He's a threat to them just like I am, but Niro is innocent and subjected to a precarious situation.

"He's fine," Killian says, straightening.

"Niro gets nervous around certain people," Ciro adds.

"That is not a nice lady," Niro whispers. "She doesn't like me."

"I wonder why?" I quip, looking up at Killian. I snuggle Niro close. "Come on."

I take Niro to the bedroom and pull a children's book with pictures out of my bag. Ciro's connection on the mainland got them for me. I would read to Niro most nights. We didn't have a network in the building to watch anything, so reading vintage books was a way to pass the time.

"That's my favorite," he says in a small voice.

"Is he alright?" Ciro asks.

I glance up and smile. "Yeah, he isn't used to all this."

Ciro nods. "I know." But I don't miss the look of longing in his expression. "I—"

"Does he need anything?" Killian pushes Ciro aside, removing his mask and crossing the small space. "I don't want to upset him or you in any way."

"Then deal with her," Ciro says in a hard tone before turning away.

"I'll talk to her. If she pushes back, she's gone."

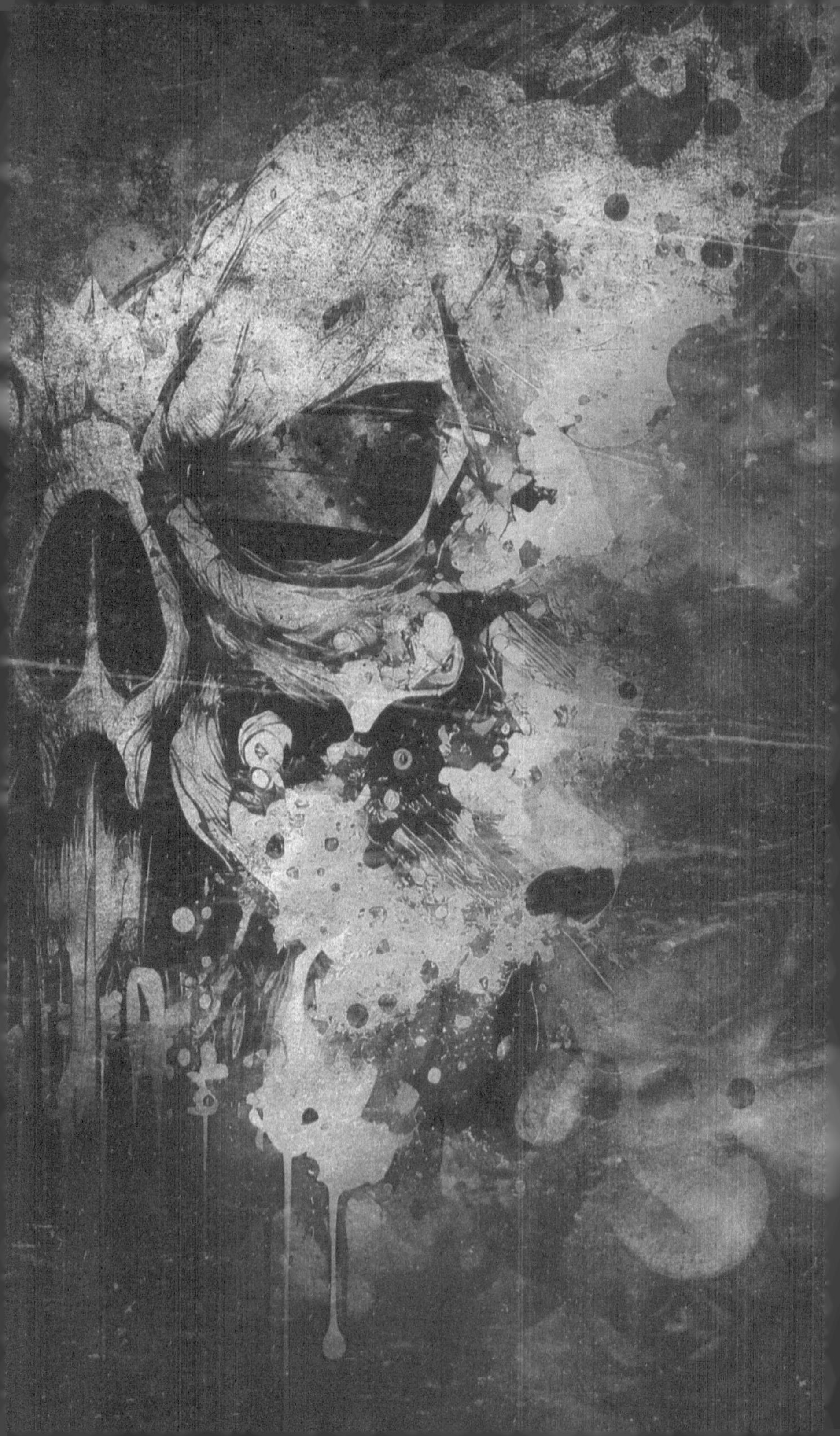

# 46

### KILLIAN

"A re they okay?" Ciro asks when I exit the room and press the screen, shutting the door behind me.

Fifteen minutes before we arrive at the dock, he wants to push me when I want to strangle him for the way he looks at her–at them. My family.

"They are not your concern."

"They have been for the past five years, Killian." He steps closer, almost in my face, but I have an inch on him. "Hate me or not, they are and will always be. I have been by their side, and if it makes you feel better, no, I didn't sleep with her. She loves you too much to allow another man to touch her." His jaw hardens. "But knowing that you didn't feel the same way made it easier for me. All she has to do was look at me the way she looks at you, and I would've." He steps back with a defeated look in his eyes. "I love her, and I don't give a fuck if that means we can't be friends because she's worth it. They're worth it. Think about that when you bring your past along with you so it can mock what you have always taken for granted."

I feel a weight lift off my shoulders, knowing she didn't sleep with Ciro or anyone. The same way I didn't. The thought of my best friend fucking my wife. The images that would play out in my mind.

Shame runs over me when I think about being with Blair and Sarah. What I put Lillith through. The way she must feel. The reason she took our son into the room so he wouldn't see?

"You're right," I say quietly.

He gives me a bitter laugh and slides his hand over his face. "I wish I was wrong."

"I'm in love with my wife, Ciro. I'm in love with my son. My family."

"That is why I'm still here, Kill. I'm not the bastard you think I am. I know you haven't touched another woman since Lillith left. But if you love her, I will stand by you both because I love her and want her and Niro to be happy. I want you to be happy."

He walks to the front of the boat as it approaches shore, the sensors going off.

"Hey, Ciro." He twists his head. "Sydney stays."

He smiles. "It's about time, brother."

In the back of my mind, I was plagued with contemplation. I needed to know who in my circle wanted my wife dead. The way Blair acted comes to mind, but she didn't think she was alive until after the race. Maybe she was waiting because her father and the judges suspected Pyralis was, in fact, Lillith.

We dock the boat, and I help Lillith and Niro off, staying close behind them.

"Can we visit Jimmy's mom?" Niro says in a sweet little voice.

His eyes are huge like saucers, waiting for his mother to reply. He's a good-looking kid. Agnes was sad to see him leave. She gushes over him every chance she gets. She reminded me of my mother and how proud my parents would be to see me married to Lillith and Niro.

Lillith searches for me through the guys, already getting things off the boat. "I'm sorry. He made a little friend–"

"It's alright. We can visit on the way back home. We have a couple of things to finish first. There is a large shipment I'm sure you would want to look into," I say, giving her a wink.

Food. Lots of food. Supplies. I managed to get the grid up and running. Ciro and I put our pride aside and worked tirelessly for three nights since we returned from the fundraiser. I wanted to do right and make my wife proud.

We have to race so that it doesn't draw attention to us if we both pull out. Bets are on, and people want a show. She has to lose, but the winning pot will be distributed among the people. If she wins, there will be a target on her back bigger than her current one because of her father.

"I can't believe you're doing this to me! To us!" Blair cries, storming down the dock and tugging Sarah along.

"You did it to yourself. Get lost," Ciro says triumphantly. "Take your little sidekick with you and go torture another asshole."

The clouds are thick in the air. A heaviness settles in my chest, and it's because I know this is the end of it all. The racing, my time spent as Kill, has morphed into my time needing to be consumed as Mr. Cross. Husband of Lillith Cross and father to Niro Cross. Running an underground black market after I killed her father. But I would never tell her that.

If I did, she would stop me. My wife does not have an immoral bone in her body, but I do. Not when it came to her and our son and someone wanting to harm them. She would overlook the danger her father put her to spare his life, but I won't. I couldn't.

If he stayed alive, she would always have to worry, and I

would spend every waking moment looking over my shoulder, wondering who or when they would try to kill her.

I was going back on my agreement with Mr. Sinclair because I fell in love with his daughter and my son. I wouldn't change that feeling for the world. It was the first time I knew what my parents felt for each other. I understood what love meant. What it felt like deep in your soul. The good kind. The kind my wife read about in her beautiful books. The ones her father warned me about when he mentioned Lillith and her stupid books. I read beautiful pages of different lives in the years she was gone. The characters have other desires and temperaments but want the same thing. To fall in love. I couldn't forget the sex scenes, either.

"What are you doing?" Lillith asks when I walk up behind her and kiss her neck.

"I'm kissing my wife." I press my lips to her soft skin. "He's asleep in the next room. I've been dying to be inside you all day." I sense her smile. The raised goose bumps on her skin give it away while I pull her suit over her shoulder and down her body. "I want to fuck you, Mrs. Cross."

She turns around, her eyes caressing my face while she pulls her suit off the rest of the way until she's naked. The music plays in a low thud in the background, coming from the main room of the Cocoon. The glow from the lights coming from the white bed in the bedroom illuminates her skin and tight pink nipples on her upthrust breasts.

"How bad?"

I pull my shirt over my head, tossing it aside. "Bad."

She drops to her knees and pulls me out, teasing the tip of my cock with her tongue. She glances up. "Fuck, you're gorgeous."

Her lips curve in a salacious smile. "And you're big..." Her velvety tongue licks the tip. "Hot." She takes me inside her wet mouth, and my eyes roll back in my skull. Arousal shoots to the tip of my cock, swelling inside her mouth.

I groan, sliding my fingers into her hair and gripping it hard. She takes me deep, and I feel the back of her throat. Saliva drips down her chin. "Every hole in your body feels so good and wet, Lillith. I want to burn inside you."

She moans, throating me in a rhythm; I see her nostrils flare when she takes me in her throat, moving faster. Her hands grip my hips. Her short nails dig into my skin, leaving half-moon marks. I fuck her mouth, watching her eyes fill with tears like a kaleidoscope of aquamarine shades.

I focus on my wife, my latest prosthetic eye recording how beautiful she looks.

"My eye records now."

She looks up and pulls me out of her mouth, getting to her feet. "Everything?"

I nod. "Like right now. I wanted you to know and the other times too."

"You've been getting off on us?"

I nod again, boldly. She presses her breasts against me, grasping my wet cock, rubbing the tip on her slit. "And now?" she asks softly.

I pick her up, grabbing her by her thighs and tossing her on the bed, giving her a predatory look.

"Now, I'm going to fuck you, and later, you're going to see what I see when I'm inside you, making you mine."

I slam inside her in one hard thrust, hearing her audible gasp. "Yes!"

"Hold on."

I place her legs over my shoulders, spreading her legs as far she can go while grinding in her cunt." Mmm...Kill."

"Bad girl," I growl, pounding into her in a series of thrusts. Her nails dig into my shoulders, spurring the animal inside me to go harder and faster. I've made love to her since she returned, but this....this is different. I wanted to own her body and soul. I had her love, but I wanted more. I wanted her mind and her dreams. The scent of her skin mingling with mine after a shower or when she sweats.

I want all her children to be mine and only mine, and when I die, I want to make sure it was with her when her time came, and only because a higher and unknown force demanded it. There was no way I was leaving the earth without her. Everywhere she was, I wanted to be, and where I was, she would be there. I knew firsthand what life was like without her and Niro; I almost didn't survive it.

This love—our love was ours, and I would burn in her embrace in this life and the next because we were meant to be.

"Ahh, I'm coming!" Her sweet cries filled my ears, making sure I see the rapture on her face when I spill inside her.

"I love you, Lillith Cross." I kiss her forehead. "Forever," I rasp.

"THIS IS THE GRID?" she asks, looking at the screen in one of the rooms we have set up in the Cocoon. The hideout. "How will it help people find shelter? A place to sleep?" She looks up.

"Here, Lillith," Ciro replies. "Underground."

She looks around and smiles. "This was the purpose of creating this place."

I smile. "Yeah, a city. Underground. Undetected." I rest my chin over her head while she looks at the grid where people can share resources they acquire for things they need. Basic cost for medicine, food, and supplies. Like a peer-to-peer network.

"How does it work?"

"In the old days, they would barter for resources. What one person has, the other needs, and so they agree, but they can't overinflate, or we cancel them."

"You mean you kick them off the grid."

"Exactly, and you know people have been starving for so long that no one will do it. They will follow the rules, or they get kicked out. Erased. Even if someone ratted us out—"

"No one would vouch for them, and they would disappear for participating in illegal activity by the Utheans."

"Exactly," I say softly.

"What about the race?" she asks.

"We race, but you lose, Pyralis," I say, using her race handle. "Don't get any funny ideas."

She steps away and turns, looking between Ciro and me. "What if I did?"

"I would have to kill everyone," I deadpan. I pull a strand of hair out of her gorgeous face. "You won't win because you care about the people as much as we do."

When Lillith leaves to tend to Niro, Ciro glances up from the screen. "It's that troll."

My eyes dart to the screen. "Her little ex-boyfriend."

Ciro nods. I smile, but it doesn't reach my eyes. Ciro swallows thickly.

"He knew where she was the whole time. He always kept a safe distance."

I push my mask off my face. "Where is he?"

Ciro pulls up the map of the mainland on the holographic screen. "He is... here." He points at the dot flashing like a beacon.

"Let's go." I pull my gun from the holster on my back.

"What are you going to tell her?"

"That I have to go somewhere with you."

"Tell her, Kill." He pauses. "I see that look in your eye."

I pull my mask over my face. "I'm going to kill him. It doesn't matter if she wants me to or not. He's a threat and a fucking traitor."

"I get it." He places a hand on my shoulder. "But tell her."

"Tell me what?" I close my eyes when I hear her voice. Ciro moves to get Niro.

"Come on, I have something to show you." Niro smiles with fondness at Ciro. Jealousy creeps up, but I push it down. I have nothing to be jealous about, and Ciro is right. I should be honest with Lillith.

"It's that little troll," I say when Ciro leaves the area with Niro.

"You mean Ethan?" She glances at the gun with a worried expression. "What's going on, Killian?"

"He's been playing you. It's him, Lillith," I say savagely. "The whole time."

She looks away, but I don't miss the pain flickering in her eyes at the betrayal.

"What are you going to do?" she asks, wavering on the brink of tears.

"What I have to, Lillith. I wasn't going to tell you, but you need to understand. They won't stop until they take you from me. You were never supposed to survive this long."

"Does it ever stop?"

"I know it hurts that he betrayed you–"

"I'm worried about you going out there. I couldn't care less if he did. I care...about you."

I push my mask off and pull her in my arms. "I love you." I hold her tight. "But I have to kill him...and your father." She nods, and tears spill down her cheeks.

"I understand."

"It's okay, Lillith. Ciro and I have to go now. But you need to stay here with Niro. It's safe here. If anything happens to me, and I don't come back, you take the car back to the boat, and you go home. The barcode tattooed on my skin is proof of me leaving everything to you if something happens to me. It's a blueprint...of everything. Our family's legacy."

She smiles. "You're my family."

"I am, and so is our beautiful son, Lillith. You have done an excellent job with him. I thought you should know that."

She has, and I wanted to tell her in case something happened to me because she is everything to me.

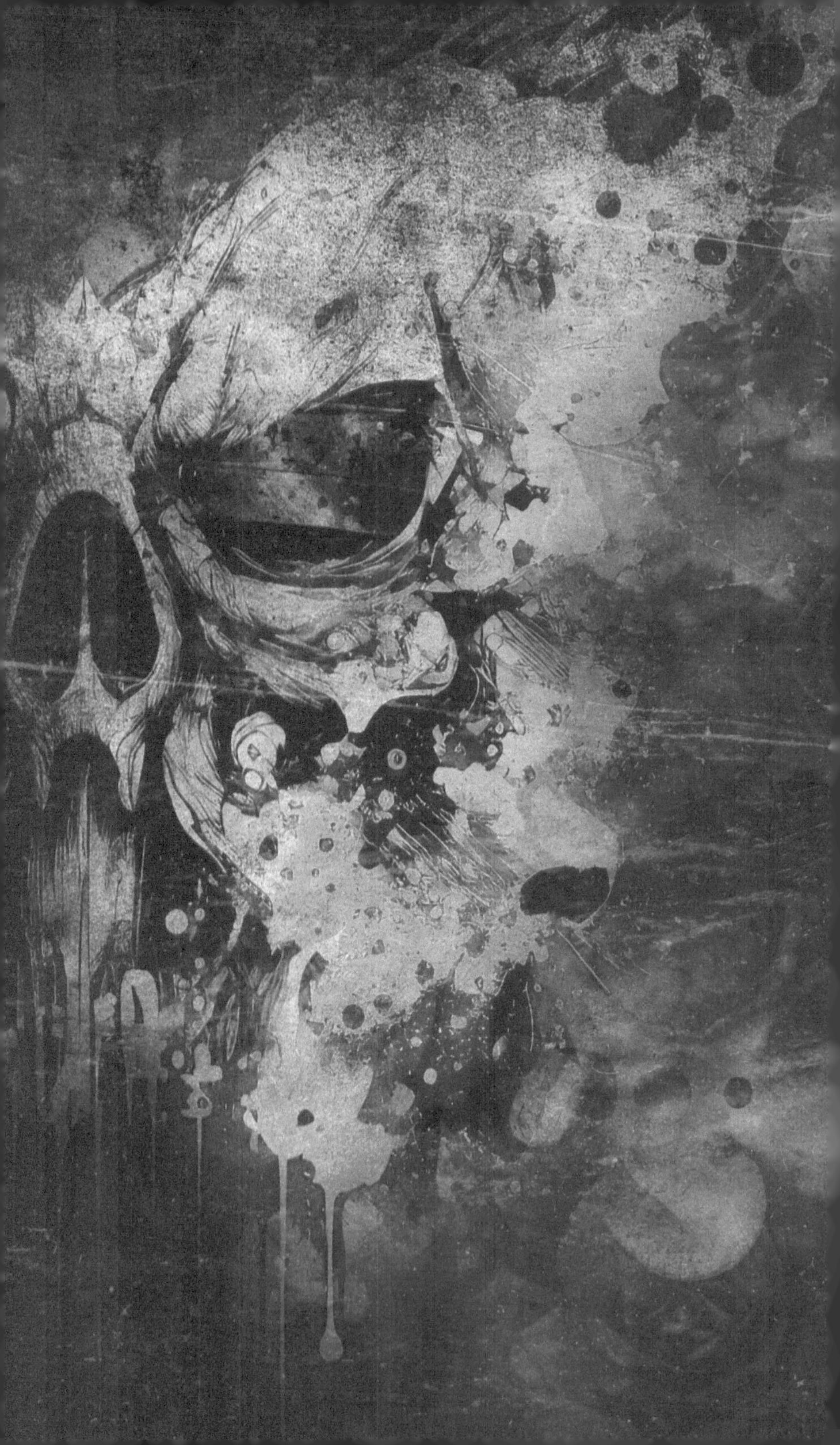

# 47

## KILLIAN

"Is this it?" I ask Ciro.

He checks the map and scans the area. "Yeah."

Pollution in high-area air creates a constant gray cloud that blots out the light and gives the neighborhood a gloomy feel. Buildings surround the streets, but they are in a terrible state of disrepair, with broken windows and decaying facades. Their formerly vivid hues are dulled to a consistent, dreary palette of grays and browns. The walls are covered with graffiti and other visible indications of disintegration, creating an atmosphere of desolation and disrepair. FUCK THE UTHEAN THE CITY OF GOD AIN'T SHIT is written in huge letters across the buildings.

Hardly working rusty automobiles litter the streets, adding to the history of the hazardous air quality that cast thick clouds once emitting poisonous emissions. The roads are riddled with potholes and fissures, making travel dangerous for pedestrians. The remaining lamps flutter on and off, providing dim, unreliable pools of light that do nothing to banish the darkness.

Even with the few remaining residents, you can't help but feel a palpable air of despair. They shuffle about looking discouraged, their ragtag wardrobes reflecting the difficulty of making ends meet. Residents' relationships are tense due to the prevalence of theft and the need to protect their few resources from the hands of the desperate.

"It's giving me the location of this building on the right."

We both checked the weapons we brought with us. My latest creation. I pull out the smooth, obsidian-black weapon with elaborate, throbbing red veins carved onto its surface. It gives out a deep hum that makes people nervous just by listening. It uses a mix of cutting-edge bioengineering and brain manipulation tech to function. All of which I created.

Dark energy is a terrible force that seeks out and destroys the brain circuits of living things in a concentrated burst when the gun is triggered. Upon contact, the energy penetrates the victim's nervous system, releasing agony that reverberates throughout their whole being, from the skin deep into their soul. This weapon causes the victim to experience terrifying hallucinations by drawing on their primal anxieties, regrets, and traumas. The sufferer cannot discriminate between the actual world and their warped views as the eerie illusions blend perfectly with reality.

Altering the weapon to a different mode may mentally and physically harm its target. Paralysis, convulsions, and extreme nausea are only some physical symptoms brought on by the energy's disruption of cellular structures. The weapon is intended to cause psychological and physiological trauma that continues to manifest itself long after the first assault has ended.

"Have you tried this on anyone?"

"Nicholas Hawke."

"That was you?" Ciro asks incredulously.

Everyone heard of Hawke Industries CEO's decapitated body being found on the balcony. No one knew how it happened. The only technology capable of doing something like that is a Uthean patrolling the area and finding an imminent threat.

"He threatened Lillith and eye fucked her."

"Good." He looks at the weapon in his hand. "So it works."

"Apparently, it does."

"She was right?"

I frown. "Who?"

"The fortune teller and her prophecy."

I lean back and turn my head toward Ciro. "You believe it."

"I do. I also believed her when she said you two were meant to be." He looks out the windshield, lost in thought. "You're the savior of the people. You will save millions, and Lillith"—he swallows— "is...everything."

"She cares about you, and I want to thank you for caring for her and Niro."

He glances at me. "Your name fell from her lips when she gave birth to Niro. I held her hand, but it was your name she called out for when she pushed."

I open the door. "And it's her name that I'll kill for." I step out. "Let's get this motherfucker."

We walk up to a building with a side door. It's dark, but Ciro pulls the door open, and we enter a dark hallway on the first floor with doors to old apartments. He looks at the map and nods toward a door with a picture of a red rabbit. I check my gun, ensuring it's on and ready to go.

"Here."

I nod. "Ready?"

"One, two."

"Three."

I kick the door open. The door flies open, hitting the wall.

Ciro goes in first, and we come up to a door, and I can't believe my eyes. Ethan is fucking Blair against the wall. Her eyes go wide when she spots us.

"Honey, I'm home," I sing-song.

"It's not what you think!" Ethan cries. I shoot, and his head inflates and implodes.

The little troll thinks I give a shit.

Blair crouches naked on the dirty floor while Ciro aims his gun at her head.

"I-I'm sorry, Kill. It meant nothing," she stammers. Her arms and legs are shaking. I turn my head, waiting for her to look up, but she's cowering. Ciro glances at me briefly, waiting for a signal.

I widen my stance, knowing this can go only one way. "Look at me, Blair." She looks at me with her tear-streaked face and mascara running down her chin. Terrified.

"What did you see in her, huh?" she asks grudgingly. "What was I supposed to do when she took you away from me!"

They say jealousy is a bitch, and it can make you do crazy things. I believe it now. The way I blew the little fucker's head off. The way Blair betrayed me. Jealousy is like a cancer, and there is only one cure. The hum of the gun drums light up, and then her head implodes when the laser goes off.

"Fuck, Kill. You blew her head off!"

I stare at her twitching corpse on the ground. Blood bubbling on the floor. Brain matter splattered all over the dirty walls like paint.

"Let's go."

Ciro keeps looking back, crossing through the tiny apartment. There is disbelief in his eyes when he turns to leave the hallway. "You killed her."

"Yeah, she wants my wife dead. Now she doesn't have to worry about my son asking me so many questions."

When we reach the exit of the building, Utheans search for the car with their scanners shining a light over it. "Fuck. Can you erase the feed of their scanners?"

"No signal."

"Shit."

I peered through the hole to see how many. "They probably sensed the guns going off."

"Yeah."

"We can't shoot them. More would come, and it's just the two of us."

"No shit. We have to come up with something."

"They're tracing the car. How the fuck are we going to get back to the Cocoon?"

"I'm not. You are."

"Where are you going?"

I check out the location, and I'm two miles from the docks. If the Utheans run a trace on the car and find me here, they will know I killed Ethan and Blair. It will get back to me. The good thing is that Ciro is the only one who knows about the grid. I couldn't trust anyone but him.

"I'm going to the boat. I need to get back to my house. Bring my wife and son back home. I will create a diversion."

"How would I get to the Cocoon?"

"You have a car there. You can bring her back on the second boat to the island."

I hate trusting him with my family's life, but she's dead if they trace me here. They will kill me or put a bounty on my head as an enemy of the state. One soldier can't kill an army by himself.

I pull my mask off my face and look Ciro in the eyes. "I'm

trusting you with everything I've got. Bring my wife and son home."

He nods. "I will." He pushes my mask down over my face. "Go."

The Utheans can detect the weapons when they go off, so I run in the opposite direction, looking for a rear exit. I find it on the third turn. I run out and fire the weapon to an open field of debris. I hear the sound of their aircraft, giving Ciro the all clear to get in the car and get my family.

I run back inside the building toward the other exit and run the two miles to the docks.

# 48



Hearing footsteps outside the bedroom door, I move slowly, trying not to wake Niro. I watch the door being pushed open, thinking it's Killian. Ciro rushes in, and I know something is wrong.

"Where's Killian?" I rush out.

"He went back. Utheans were patrolling the car. He created a diversion, and I was able to come back."

"How is he getting to the docks?"

Ciro gives me a grim look. "On foot."

Sarah rushes into the room, terrified. "Where's Blair?"

Ciro slides his gaze to Sarah. "Why do you want to know? Where did she go, Sarah? Why are you so worried about Blair?"

I see the terrified look cross her face as she backs out of the room. Something is off.

Ciro tosses the keys to me and draws a weapon from the back of his pants, aiming it at her head. "Get Niro and wait for me in the car, Lillith."

"You don't understand. I wasn't part of it, Ciro. You have to believe me. What did you do to her?" she cries. I look at Ciro and Sarah, trying to pick up a sleepy Niro in my arms, trying to figure out the same thing. What does Blair have anything to do with Ethan? What is she talking about?

Ciro shakes his head. "I can't believe you would do it. Why?"

Sarah looks at me and responds begrudgingly, "Because she is the reason for all of it." Her top lip curls. "All of you salivate like dogs when she's around. She has everything, while we get the scraps."

"Where's Blair?" I ask Ciro, but I have an idea.

"She's dead. Killian blew her fucking head off after we caught her fucking Ethan. They're traitors, Lillith. They want to serve you to the judges on a platter. They want to destroy us."

"Shoot her," I say quietly, leaving the room.

"You bitch!" A humming sound assaults my ears, and then a thud and silence. I run toward the car with a drowsy Niro in my arms.

My feet are shaking when I reach the black car, fumbling for the right key to unlock the door in my hand.

Sweat drips down my back when I finally get Niro inside the back seat. I want to go home.

Ciro walks to the driver's side, and I look up. "Get in, let's get out of here."

When we reach the docks, the waves are the only sound besides the humming of the powerful gas engine. The sky is pitch black, and the smell has me crinkling my nose. It smells like rotted fish and the ocean.

Ciro opens the door and jumps out. "Come on."

When we get safely on the boat, and it pulls out to sea toward the island, I glance at Ciro. "What happened?"

"You heard Sarah, and I did what Kill would have done."

"Blair—"

"Is dead."

"Kill—"

"Yes, Lillith. Ethan and Blair were a threat. They were all in on it. It was like they were waiting for you to appear. Since Kill didn't tell anyone on the island about you supposedly dying when you jumped off, they assumed he had you hidden somewhere. It is the only thing that would make sense. Then Ethan conveniently showed up and put the pieces together."

"Have you heard from Killian?" I ask.

I need to know he's safe. I watch Ciro turn to the screen, trying to call him, but it keeps saying no signal.

"I can't get through," he says frustratingly.

Fear claws my insides. I check on Niro, and he's sound asleep. The boat cuts through the dark waters of the ocean. Looking at the screen, I watch the speed and glance at Ciro.

"I don't want to increase the speed and drain the power just in case. We have enough but didn't have time to charge the boats, and sunlight is hours away."

I nod. He's right, and it makes perfect sense. All we can do is wait until we can get there.

"It's alright, Lillith. He's alright. Kill...he loves you too much to die. He wanted to make sure he had an alibi."

I was afraid of that, but I don't trust my father. He's manipulative. He doesn't want anyone to know he's broke. My father would kill anyone to save himself.

When we reach the dock on the island, it's dark. You can't see the lights that usually line the docks, which tells me something is wrong.

"Why is it so dark?" I ask, looking at Ciro holding a sleeping Niro.

"I don't know."

I move to take Niro, and something hard pushes against my

head, causing me to freeze. "I wouldn't do that if I were you." A cold chill runs down my arm, snaking itself in my chest.

"Let her and the child go," Ciro demands, moving forward, but the metal weapon digs into the side of my head.

"At first, when I didn't see him parading around with his new wife, I figured she already folded and gave him a child, so he killed her, but when I found out she is indeed Pyralis"—he sucks his teeth—"that made it more interesting."

"Father, stop it. Where's Killian?"

"I'm afraid your time has run out, Lillith. Your husband is a bit indisposed at the moment. You see, I came to finish the job." He pushes the gun into my skin, and a searing pain explodes in my skull, causing me to gasp.

"Let them go," Ciro demands, stepping forward.

"I wouldn't do that if I were you. I'll blow her head off."

"What do you want?" I ask.

He's here for something, and it isn't a family reunion.

"I want the technology. The blueprint of all of his technological designs. It will make me rich. Very rich. It's about time the world is introduced to what he's created and controls. Not some stupid kid so in love that he is willing to die for her. What a waste of talent."

I close my eyes. The barcode. Killian said it's a blueprint. At first, I thought he meant his estate. His parents' accounts are like an inheritance, but it's much more than that. That is what they were after when my father killed his parents. They wanted the blueprint, but it's on Killian's body. His eye. The barcode is the key. He's the key to everything.

"You won't get away with it. If you kill me, you get nothing."

"I get a grandson."

My eyes widen in terror. "Leave my son out of it."

"Why, Lillith...? He's my grandson."

Ciro glares at my father. "Where's Killian?"

"I'll give you what you want, but you must take me to Killian first. If something happens to him... to any of us, you get nothing," I say, trying to muster sternness.

"That works." My father sniggers. "It's too easy."

He shoves me toward the house, and I fumble, trying to find my footing. I look back, making sure Ciro holds Niro tight. He nods silently, telling me he has Niro. I know Ciro would die protecting him.

When we enter the house, it's dark with a solemn presence. Is Agnes alright? I know the rest of the staff aren't here at night, but Agnes lives here.

"His office," my father says with the weapon aimed at my head. I take the next left, staring fiercely down the hallway to the door that leads to Killian's office.

When we reached the room, I begin to breathe raggedly. Killian clutches his arm because my father shot his arm almost clear off. Agnes lies on the floor. I don't see anything wrong with her, but I figured she was hit trying to help Killian and got knocked out.

"Killian!" I cry out.

Ciro runs into the room, and I shake my head frantically. "Go!" I mouth to Ciro, trying to tell him to take Niro.

His eyes widen, telling me he isn't leaving me, but my eyes plead with him to take my son to safety. When my father steps farther into the room, Ciro steps back, and I slam my hand on the button to shut the door with us in it.

My father swings the weapon, hitting me across the face. "You bitch!" Pain radiates across my face like I was hit with a metal beam.

"I'm going to k-kill...you," Killian gasps, clutching his arm, trying to stop the bleeding. His body is doubled over. His mask is half off his face.

"I doubt that," my father mocks. "I think you would need two arms, and you currently have one and a half."

"You bastard," I seethe. Angry tears slide down my cheeks.

"Funny how you're defending a man who agreed to kill you after you gave him a son. The way you defend him is touching. I thought you would be repulsed, but you're just like your weak whore of a mother. Cares too much. It gets you killed. I told her to get rid of you when the doctors told her she was risking her life, but she wouldn't have it. Then, at the fundraiser, the most eligible and good-looking man on the island had eyes only for you. Too bad I had ill plans for him and his parents, but like cockroaches, they survived. Even through a nuclear blast. A war. Missing body parts. They manage to survive, even in filth." My father smiles and chuckles victoriously. "How sweet it was when he fell for the bait, using you. I never thought you would love a man with a face like that. You were so stuck up and full of yourself, but I knew how to get to you. I had Ethan pop your little cherry and watch your every move before I gave you away to the one they call the moth." He looks at Killian. "You didn't think I would give her to you a virgin, did you? I told your father, Cross, that I would destroy everything he loved for not giving me what I wanted. When you looked at her that day, you followed her like a lovesick puppy; I knew I had a plan B if you weren't in the car with your parents. If you survived, I knew how to destroy you."

Control.

My father wanted the technology to control the island and the judges. He knew Killian's parents were helping the people on the mainland. My father wanted to play God.

"You think"—Killian gasps for air—"you can just get what you want by killing me. Killing Lillith." Killian laughs, blood dripping down his chin. He smiles, his teeth full of blood. "If I die, you get nothing. If she dies, you get nothing." Killian taps his temple. "It's in here, and you just fucked up your only chance to get it." Killian spits blood on the glass desk.

My tears slide down my cheeks. I turn my head and pin my father with a lethal glare. "He's dying, so you might as well kill me."

"What about your son?" My bottom lip trembles, knowing I have my trust in Ciro and hope Killian will survive. "I'm not like you. I die for the ones I love."

I hear a click and then a humming sound behind me. When I glance up at my father, who was supposed to love me since the day I was born, his eyes widen in panic. My heart beats a million miles a minute. I see his eyes pop out of his head sideways, splattering all over me.

I scream when his decapitated head falls forward. I step back, watching his body twitch.

"Lillith!" Ciro's voice booms through the door. "Lillith!" he screams.

I look at Killian, the weapon in his hand falling from his fingers, and he falls over the desk.

I push the button. The door whooshes open, and Ciro runs in, looking me over to make sure I'm okay.

"I'm fine." I run over to Killian.

"Get the fucking doctor, Ciro. Dr. Archer," Killian murmurs. "He knows what to do."

I press my lips over Killian's. "I love you. Please don't leave me. Please!" Tears run rapidly down my face. My fingers shake when I try to apply pressure, wrapping a tourniquet over his upper arm.

"I love you, Lillith. Since...I first saw you." His eyes close. My vision blurs, going in and out.

"Ciro," I gasp, trying to keep my eyes open. "Help him." I see the floor become the ceiling. "Help..." Everything goes black.

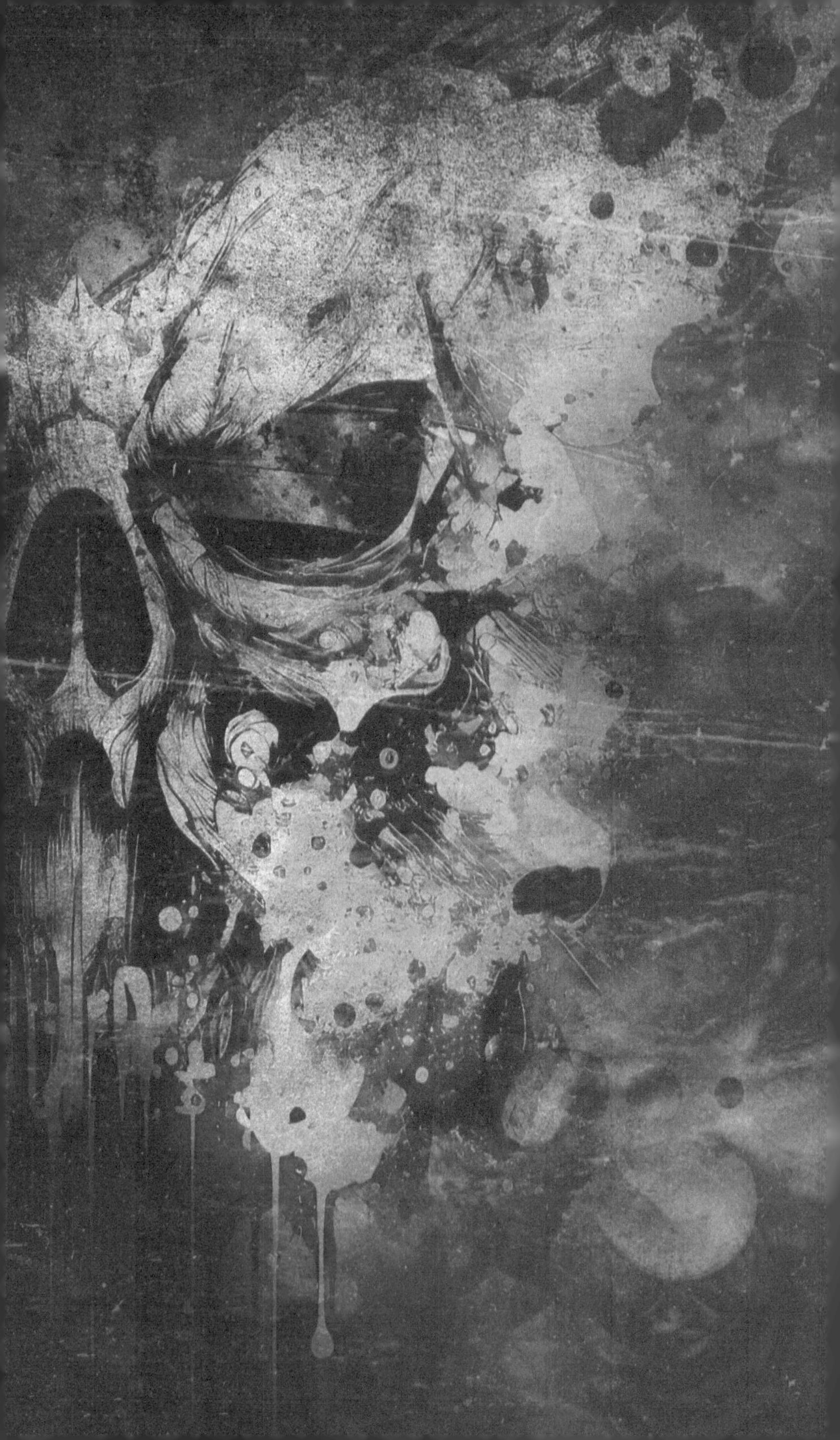

"You can't race, Pyralis."

"Why not?" she asks with a mask over her face that reads FLAME.

I grin, pulling her to my side. "Because you're pregnant, Mrs. Cross, and you can't race."

She tilts her head, and I feel her gaze burn through my mask. "Then you better win."

"Is Dad a Uthean, now? Jimmy keeps asking." Niro asks in his little voice.

I lean down and grin. "No, I just have cool parts."

I designed a robotic arm after Lillith's father blew mine off. I sent his decapitated body to the judges. Because his attempt was an act of terrorism on the island, we got off, but they didn't know about the grid. They don't know exactly what happened, but we do. The border between humans and machines becomes blurred as technology progresses. In this harsh world, the merger of man and technology symbolizes a monument to the fight for existence and the price paid for power. Still, my price was love, and I would do it again.

Because without love, there's nothing. No purpose for humanity to exist. Which leaves the burning question, what are we fighting for if it's not love?

I look up at the glass box before heading to the Cocoon, the sound of the crowd going wild since Pyralis forfeited her race. The bets were up. Ciro nods across the track, looking at the numbers flicking higher and higher. The people would be proud. The rich think they are betting against each other for greed, watching the people scream. I'll keep winning. I'll keep protecting my family and the people.

In the wake of the collapse on the surface, subterranean settlements arose, and these distribution sites are indicated by dimly lit chambers placed at key locations. As the drones I control enter the rooms, the lights flicker on, bathing everything in a warm glow and throwing ghostly shadows on the walls. Locals congregate, each holding an ID chip that will allow them to get their allotted food supply.

Mechanical beeps and rumbles announce the drones' arrival at each distribution center. The much-needed supplies are hidden behind hydraulic doors that swing open to expose storage chambers. The ration container glides open with a hiss as residents move forward and scan their identity chips against a tiny panel. As those in the section get their food and water, a source of sustenance in an otherwise dark and uncertain world, a faint, antiseptic aroma permeates the space. Still, there is only one person I came to see. Walking toward my wing, I push open the door and frown.

"Where is she?" I ask Agnes when I see her with Niro on the bed, reading him a story. After suffering a concussion that night, she acted like nothing happened. She goes everywhere Niro goes now.

She smiles. "She's waiting for you. Your office, I think," she says, giving me a wink.

Curious. I waste no time barging into the main area, expecting Ciro but finding my sexy wife in nothing but a thong and a black mask that reads FUCK ME in dripping red acrylic paint.

"I think you're having too much fun."

"I think I want to get fucked...hard," she says in a sultry voice, bending over, showing me how dripping wet she is for me.

Shutting the door, I pull my cock out and fist it in my hand. "Here?"

She twists her head. "Everywhere."

She slides her fingers over the smooth metal that makes my fingers when I place them on the desk.

"I think you like this a little too much."

"I do." She wiggles her ass over my cock, making the bead pooling at the tip drip on the floor. "I think you're fucking hot."

I smile. "Oh yeah?"

"Is that why you're wearing a mask?"

She nods. "You wear one all the time."

I pull my mask off and grin. "How about now?"

"Perfect."

"You're not going to take yours off?"

She shakes her head slowly, stretching her hands out in front of her like a cat. "No, I want to be a bad girl. Fuck me, Kill."

I smack her ass, leaving a red mark on her skin. "What did I say about calling me Kill?"

# BONUS SCENE

## LILLITH

Two Years Later

"He's asleep," Killian says, shutting the bedroom door.

The bedroom his mother decorated is now where we read and make love most of the time.

Looking at the ceiling, I lean back on my elbows and arch to get a good stretch. "I thought he would never fall asleep. He doesn't want to miss seeing his little sister be born."

Ciro recorded the day I delivered Niro and gave the footage to Killian. Out of respect, he didn't film the birth in detail. I remember that he kept a respectable distance. They are in a better place now.

The bed dips, and when I relax, Killian is between my legs, pushing them open. "I read to him for forty-five minutes until he fell asleep. He's a tough one when he wants something."

I sigh. "Kind of like his father," I tease.

"Did I tell you how beautiful you look pregnant with our daughter?"

I smile. "All the time." He places tender kisses on my stomach, his metal fingers tugging the negligée. "I don't look beautiful. I'm carrying a beautiful human. There's a difference."

I look like a whale at sea, but he has never made me feel anything less beautiful. He only leaves my side if it is to tend to Niro. He's amazing with him. He takes him swimming in our indoor swimming pool. He teaches him how to fix droids and build new ones for kids on the mainland. He shows him how to be a good person. Teach him values, love, and, most of all, to care for everyone. To not judge based on a person's looks or where they come from.

"Oh yeah?" He places a kiss on my lower belly. My nipples respond, aroused under the translucent lace.

His tongue peeks out, licking my stomach.

"Killian...What are you doing?" I ask breathlessly.

I'm soaking wet.

He looks up, and his eye shifts. "I'm going to show you how beautiful you are. The doctor said sex is good for you since there are no complications."

He holds himself above me and licks my nipple. I might explode from the intense pressure. I'm so sensitive, and he knows it. We have been going at it like a bunch of rabbits.

"It's not like I could get pregnant twice."

His eye shifts again, and I know he's recording us. "I want more."

"More what?" I ask playfully.

"Babies. I want you to have all my babies."

"You want a clan."

"I want to fill this house with memories of my wife and our children."

"Let's see how you feel after we have our daughter and you can't sleep. Like ever. She will wake up every three hours to feed, and then when she is older and likes a boy,

"He swipes his finger between my thighs, brings it to his

mouth, and sucks. "Mm...pregnant pussy," he groans. "My favorite."

That is so hot.

He kneels between my legs. He pulls himself out, stroking the tip of his hard cock between my thighs. I can hear how wet I am with each stroke.

"Killian," I cry out.

"Open your legs for me, gorgeous. I want to see what I live for—what I would die for." I gasp when he slides inside. "Hold your thighs, baby." I'm spread open. His gaze holds mine when I clutch my thighs. He holds himself up with his hand on the bed, pushing slowly the rest of the way. "I told you you were going to be full of me. Part of me... inside you... He grinds his hips. "Always."

'I love you, Killian."

"I love you more. Every moment of every day. You're my wife, always and forever."

# ABOUT THE AUTHOR

Carmen Rosales is an emerging Latinx author of Steamy, and Dark Romance. She loves spending time with her family. When she is not writing, she is reading. She is an Army veteran and is currently completing her Doctorate Degree in Business and has the love and support of her husband and five children. She also writes under Delilah Croww for her DARK romance horror stories with really dark themes.

Join her VIP list- carmenrosales.com and delilacroww.com

She loves to see a review and interact with her readers.
    Scan the QR code to follow her on Social Media and sign up for her Newsletter: